PONY GIRLS

Books by Richard Hoyt

Cool Runnings
The Dragon Portfolio
Fish Story
Head of State
The Manna Enzyme
Pony Girls
Old Soldiers Sometimes Lie
Siege
Siskiyou
Trotsky's Run
Vivienne
The Weatherman's Daughters

PONY GIRLS

A John Denson Mystery

Richard Hoyt

A TOM DOHERTY ASSOCIATES BOOK
NEW YORK

PONY GIRLS

Copyright © 2004 by Richard Hoyt

This book is printed on acid-free paper.

A Forge Book
Published by Tom Doherty Associates, LLC
175 Fifth Avenue
New York, NY 10010

www.tor.com

Forge® is a registered trademark of Tom Doherty Associates, LLC.

Library of Congress Cataloging-in-Publication Data

Hoyt, Richard, 1941-
    Pony girls : a John Denson mystery / Richard Hoyt.— 1st ed.
      p. cm.
    "A Tom Doherty Associates book."
    ISBN 0-765-30616-6 (acid-free paper)
    EAN 978-0765-30616-6
    1. Denson, John (Fictitious character)—Fiction. 2. Private investigators—Washington (State)—Fiction. 3. Horses—Crimes against—Fiction. 4. Indians of North America—Fiction. 5. Washington (State)—Fiction. 6. Shamanism—Fiction. I. Title.

PS3558.O975P66 2004
813'.54—dc22

2003071105

First Edition: May 2004

Printed in the United States of America

0 9 8 7 6 5 4 3 2 1

For my friend, Avi Feuer, and
his sons, Ari and Boaz

"Chantilly lace, a pretty face, a pony tail a-hanging down, makes the world go round, round, round."

—The Big Bopper

PONY GIRLS

1 · *In the fog*

A surreal fog had settled over the northern Oregon coast on the morning of the best clam tide in a decade. Receding far to the west, the retreating tide revealed a vast stretch of wet sand, virgin territory for clam diggers. The gods endowed with the ability to deliver such bounties as great clam tides and grand weather had on this occasion, perversely, given us a far-out fog. You might find and dig clams in abundance this morning, but you wouldn't see oncoming traffic, the center line, or the shoulder of Highway 101. Such a fog! Wet and white, cold as a corpse's kiss.

I drove my Volkswagen microbus south past the gas station and convenience store that called itself Chokecherry Bend. Concentrating on the white fog line, I stared, transfixed, at the side of the winding coastal highway. Beside me, Annie Dancer also strained to see the line.

Never mind that the State of Oregon had placed fancy guard-rails on the curves that dropped straight down into the Pacific Ocean; riding on the edge of a precipice in the densest fog imaginable was an unnerving experience.

Suddenly, two dim lights dead ahead.

"Watch it!" Annie cried, alarmed.

I moved to the edge of the road as another doughty traveler, driving a Suzuki SUV, passed in the other direction. I said, "I remember a fog like this about ten years ago. Willie and I were—"

"Pay attention!"

Another pair of headlights.

Annie said, "If you had any brains, you'd pull over to the side of the road and wait until this burns off."

"Right. And miss the best clam tide in ten years."

"The clams can wait. I want to enjoy my cup of coffee to-morrow morning."

"I am John Denson, intrepid moron. No veteran driver of a VW bus is more skilled than me. Nobody ever accused me of having brains or of being sensible. That's offensive!"

"Concentrate," she said.

There was the turnoff leading downhill. Yes! Although I had been down the road many times, how I had seen it in the fog was beyond me. It was a narrow gravel road carved from a cliff overlooking the beach that was our favorite place to dig clams. The road down the face of the cliff was ordinarily too much for tourists. Clam diggers drove from Portland on Highway 26 to Highway 101, an important red line on their road maps, to take advantage of the best tides.

The problem with the red-line highways, as opposed to the thinner black-line roads, was the annoying number of lumber-ing "recreational vehicles," driven mostly by retirees who felt it was a perquisite of age to clog up the highways if they damn well pleased. Saving for their future like everyone said they should, they had yielded their lives to the drudge of nine-to-five. They had been obedient and patient, the necessary drones of the consumer economy. Now, joints aching from arthritis and bowels unresponsive to mere prunes, it was their turn to cram a little fun into what remained of their lives. Maybe they didn't hump a whole bunch anymore, but they could afford the payments on an RV. The rest of us could stuff our complaining and be patient.

The nameless beach was narrow and rocky except at extreme low tides. Most people balked at the idea of driving a vehicle down a narrow road chiseled from the side of a precipice by gleeful engineers. To the left, rock. To the right, nothing. An unnerving experience. The narrowness of the beach, the rocks, and the spooky drive down the side of a cliff made most people avoid the place.

The beach was flanked by barnacle-covered promontories of solid rock that took a hard pounding from the surf at high tide, sending gauzy sheets of salty spray high into the air. In our many clamming trips to this beach, we had yet to meet another digger, which is why we liked it.

Having successfully negotiated the road to the bottom of the cliff, I parked my bus. Annie and I piled out.

"Call me John Sees the Fog," I said.

"Right," Annie said dryly.

I slid open the side doors of the bus, and we eagerly retrieved our plastic buckets and clam shovels. This was the southern edge of razor clam range on the Oregon coast, and we were hopeful of scoring our limit of the delicious, long clams. There were other good clams as well, but the fun was going home with razor clams to sauté in Tillamook butter, to hell with the cholesterol. Well, that and the pungent-smelling wild onion that was akin to garlic but not quite.

Bundled against the chill morning wind sweeping in from the ocean, wearing gloves and stocking caps to keep our ears warm, we set out through the fog in the direction of the distant surf that was a muted roar to the west.

Annie suddenly stopped. "Hear that?"

"I didn't hear anything," I said.

"Shush, listen," she said.

Then I heard it, barely discernible, a kind of high-pitched, fearful squealing, a desperate crying out. And not just from one beast, from many. It very nearly gave me goose bumps.

Eeeeeeoooooooeeeeee.

We both began walking rapidly in the direction of the squealing.

"Spooky," Annie said.

In ever-quickening, urgent strides, all but running, clam gear rattling in our plastic buckets, we plunged into the enveloping fog, heading north where the beach ended at the base of a peninsula of solid rock. We could see nothing. But the farther we progressed toward the distant roar of the surf, the louder the squealing, which was coming from multiple sources.

"What are they?" she asked.

"We'll find out soon enough," I said.

As we drew near the source of the crying out, the air was filled with the squealing.

A pathetic chorus of *eeeeeeoooooooeeeeee* it was.

Louder it got, louder still.

EEEEEEOOOOOOOEEEEEE.

The agony of the chorus of lamentation was startling. Then we were there, at the barnacle-encrusted base of the promontory. The crying out, loud and insistent, was all around us.

I stepped on something. It moved. I jumped back as if I'd stepped on a snake. "Jesus!" At the same time, I saw the forms looming all around me.

"Beached whales!" Annie said.

I had stepped on the edge of a flipper. I bumped into the whale's underbelly.

"My God. What do we do?" Annie asked.

I said, "No reason to be afraid of them. They'll all die if they don't get back in the water. They're mammals and can breathe, but their bodies are used to being supported by the water. Here on the beach, they're being crushed by gravity."

"What happened to them?" she asked. "How on earth did they manage to beach themselves with an entire ocean out there?"

"Maybe they got mixed up in this fog, confused," I said. "Something."

"Mixed up? Confused? You want to tell me how that happened?"

"Happened to the captain of the *Exxon Valdez*," I said.

Annie said, "The *Exxon Valdez* was an oil tanker. How could this many whales possibly run aground all at once? What's the connection?"

I said, "The connection is that they somehow failed to follow elementary rules of navigation. The captain of the *Exxon Valdez* had the proper chart, but didn't pay attention to it. A whale has an internal chart. Nobody understands how they could possibly beach themselves. But this isn't the first time they've run aground. It's happened on the Oregon coast three or four times that I can remember."

"It has?"

I said, "Forty-seven whales once beached themselves on the coast of Massachusetts. Or maybe it was thirty-seven. Something awful. Let's see if we can find out how many there are in this disaster. The adults are too heavy to move, but if there are babies, maybe we can wrestle or drag them into the water."

I felt my way along the flank of the whale next to me until I came to its head. The whale, likely feeling my hand, was silent. Then I came upon a large, mournful eye. The whale was watching me. It cried out silently, seeking my help. Beseeching. Pleading. *I see you standing there, two-legged animal. Help me. Do something.* Stupidly, as if the whale could understand English, I said, "We'll do everything we can, pal. Hang tough."

Such was the crude dialogue between us mammalian cousins.

I used my cell phone to call 911. A woman answered. I told her what Annie and I had found.

"What? Say again, please."

"Stranded whales. Dozens of them. It's awful. We need help getting them back into the water." I gave her the directions to the beach.

"Stay put. Do what you can for them. I'll alert the fire departments at Seaside and Tillamook. Seaside has a chopper."

"Got it," I said. I hung up and took a deep breath.

I couldn't stand to remain in front of that whale's hopeful eye. I moved on. How many whales were there? Scores at a minimum. It was impossible to get an accurate count. Annie and I moved among their distraught forms. Even if we did find babies, it would be hard to do anything for them when we couldn't see.

After hiding the full extent of the hideous disaster from us, the fog suddenly thinned like a curtain lifted by a heavenly puppeteer, revealing the stricken whales under a warming morning sun. As it did, the squealing began to lessen in intensity. Were the whales wearing out? Or, able to see for themselves the full extent of their predicament, were they becoming resigned to their fate, quickly losing their resolve?

Slowly, Annie and I were able to make out the full extent of the disaster. A herd of forty-one sperm whales had somehow managed to run aground at this narrow beach at high tide, and now, with the water far beyond their reach, they were doomed to die. Of these, six were babies, their bodies small enough that they were better able to withstand the crushing gravity.

One of the whales, by far the largest, a hoary old bull, most likely the leader, was also the farthest inland. It was apparently this misguided old bull, whose skills as a leader had likely waned, who had led the ill-fated turn toward the beach.

We could try to get the babies back in the water, but to what fate? A baby whale, like a human, was slow to mature and needed the protection of its mother in order to survive. Still, we had to try. We humans and whales were in the same fix. All life was transitory. Whether it was man helping man or man helping whale, the difference was not critical. Better that the whales die in the water, a natural place for a whale to meet its end, than to smother, stranded on a rocky beach, surely a pathetic end. Turned around, better for a human to be buried in Mother Earth than to float around in the water, food for seagulls and passing fish.

2 · A question of corpses!

I sprinted to my bus and drove it to the stricken whales. Annie and I did a lot of camping when we went fishing or collecting mushrooms and edible wild plants, so I always carried rope in the back. For a driver of a thirty-five-year-old vehicle with an air-cooled engine, rope was as necessary as a spare tire. More than once, with my fan belt gone south, I had to have my ancient vehicle towed ignominiously to a gas station.

"Triage!" I yelled. "We start with those whales most likely to survive."

"The ones we can get to the water the quickest," Annie said.

I agreed. "Smallest first. Makes sense."

The smallest of the calf whales, which weighed maybe a hundred and fifty pounds, was a candidate for my bus. We fashioned a kind of rope sling that we slipped under the calf. On the count of three, with a collective grunt, we slung the little whale into my bus. With Annie in the back comforting the calf, I popped the clutch and buzzed to the distant, receding surf, where we wrestled the whale into the water.

It squealed weakly, wallowing pathetically in the cold Pacific water that was its rightful place. But it was alone and without its mother. Not knowing whether it would live or die, we turned our backs on the infant, hoping it would stay put, and returned to the stranded group to try to save another.

We were able to grunt the next smallest whale into the bus. We got it to the water where it joined its cousin, but the next largest whale was clearly too much. We quickly looped a rope around the tail of this whale. Idling the bus in low gear, we started dragging it to the distant, still receding surf. The whale squealed in agony from the pain of being dragged over the rocks and gravel.

We finally made it to the water, but the whale looked like it was about to croak from the punishment it had taken. Its underside was cut and bruised, and the poor thing was gasping for breath. The three whales in the water were not dumb. They understood intuitively what we were trying to do. Watching us with hopeful, grateful eyes, they waited for us to retrieve more of their group. They needed at least one adult whale in order to survive.

We were hardly more than fifty miles north of Newport, where the story of Keiko, the baby whale, had unfolded. Keiko had been part of a popular tourist attraction in a huge aquarium in Newport and was part of a Hollywood movie before infuriated whale lovers cried foul. An aroused public opinion, feeling sympathy for their fellow mammal, succeeded in getting Keiko flown to a pen in an inlet in Iceland where marine biologists gave her lessons on how to survive in the open ocean. The final tab to save that single leviathan was said to exceed the gross national product of Zambia.

Nobody on the Oregon coast wanted a repeat of Keiko.

As we drove back to the larger group, I remembered the earlier instances in which whales had beached themselves on the Oregon coast. In the end, the sick question was what to do with the corpses? Should they be left in place to rot, stench rising by the hour, food for passing seagulls? The economy of the Oregon coast depended on tourism, and the locals wanted to keep their beaches neat and tidy. Their best allies were the gluttonous, winged rats that patrolled the profitable strip of sand.

I remembered two earlier solutions to the question of how to dispose of the dead whales. In the first, local authorities doused the corpses with kerosene and cremated them. Their blubber blazed for days. The grotesque pyre made good television, but caused traffic jams by curious day-trippers from Portland. The day-trippers were mostly cheapskates bringing their own sand-wiches and potato salad in plastic coolers. While day-trippers did spend some money in local establishments, buying Coca-Cola and corn chips, they mainly got in the way of more prof-itable vacationers and weekenders who filled the local hotels and motels for fun on the beach.

Both the tube people and the coastal authorities far preferred the second, more imaginative, if sick solution. With cameras recording the action from various hip angles, enterprising au-thorities poked explosive charges down the throats of the dead whales. Then they retreated to a safe distance and detonated the charges with a remote, hurling huge chunks of blubber and en-trails high into the sky. Heads up, everybody! Later, the high tide swept the remains out into the sea for fish food and the beaked flying rats. Just like that, the beach was clean. Neat!

The detonating of dead whales was an amusing spectacle for those with the imagination of an eight-year-old. You should have seen those whales blow! Hoo-wee! A story to tell the grandkids. Unfortunately, exploding blubber offended the sen-sibilities of whale buffs.

As we got back to the weakening adult whales, a helicopter from the Seaside fire department arrived, followed closely by a chopper from a television station. The Seaside chopper landed less than ten yards from our bus. We were lucky it didn't land on top.

It was amazing that the fire department helicopter got there first. The word of forty-one beached whales by now having been relayed to Portland, there was likely a squadron of television choppers on their way full speed, the reporters and photographers eager to capture dramatic images of dying whales to thrill and entertain viewers eating supper.

The helicopters were clearly not able to lift an adult whale in a sling, so there wasn't much the firefighters could do but wait for drivers summoned from construction firms to arrive with flatbed trucks and forklifts. The thinking was that somehow, with a little luck, they could get a vigorous adult female to guide and protect the three babies that waited in water just deep enough to keep them buoyant.

There was no way to comfort the stricken whales. One by one, they expired, with excited television cameramen moving among them getting close-up shots of the stricken leviathans. Dying whales! Yowza! Hot damn! Stay tuned!

3 · *Erika von Bayer*

Unable to stomach the sick spectacle, Annie and I sat disconsolately on the far side of our bus with our backs to the awful scene. It was either that or rush the cameramen with driftwood bats and face felony assault charges.

A young female firefighter with a radio transceiver at her ear and a high-powered lantern in her hand ran right in front of us on her way to the Seaside helicopter. She plopped onto the sand, leaning against the struts supporting the landing rails. She said, "Did I run past two people leaning against a VW bus?"

"Yep," I said. Close as she was, I could hardly see her.

"Isn't this fog something? Name's Melanie. I'm with the Seaside Fire Department."

We introduced ourselves.

"Now I see you," Melanie said. "Lucky I didn't trip over your feet in this murk. After we almost landed on your bus, the captain decided we have to make sure incoming choppers don't pile on top of one another. Somebody could get hurt and helicopters are expensive and all that. We have to think about the taxpayers. So who do you think gets to help save the lives of whales and who gets to sit and talk down incoming choppers?"

"Why, you do! Goes without saying," Annie said.

"I'm the newest member of the force, a rookie. I suppose that could also explain it. You're the ones who found the whales, aren't you?"

"Unfortunately," I said.

Melanie said, "If you people hang around here long enough, maybe Erika von Bayer will show up. They say she's back in Portland for a visit. With forty-one beached whales, the Zone has likely got her in the air already."

Her voice dripping with sarcasm, Annie said, "Beached whales and Erika von Bayer on the same day? Wow!"

Melanie said, "Hear that? Incoming choppers." She waggled a beam of light upward into the fog as she talked to the pilot on the transceiver, guiding him away from my bus and the other helicopters.

Then the sightseers began arriving. They had heard about the tragedy on the radio and were eager to get in the way. Alas, the Oregon State Police, who were just no damn fun, blocked off the road leading to the beach, allowing only police, firefighters, and journalists to proceed.

The firefighters from Seaside and Tillamook cordoned off the immature whales in the water with a fence of human pickets, an insufficient solution once the tide started coming in. There wasn't a whole lot they could do except wait for a superior to make a decision, hence take the ultimate blame for failing to save the whales' lives. The responsibility was quickly bucked up the line, each subordinate hoping fervently that the whales lived long enough for the governor to take the blame. If the governor, who lived in Salem, acted swiftly and was lucky, perhaps he could foist off the responsibility onto the secretary of the interior. In all, it was a kind of blame race.

The firefighters took turns in the frigid temperature of the North Pacific. A half hour in the water without a wet suit was croak time. When the masculine baggage of the male firefighters had shrunk to the size of little smokies and green peas, they were replaced so they could warm up. The two female firefighters in the shifts were anatomically less vulnerable in that respect, but no less susceptible to hypothermia. They took their turns in the cold water along with the men. Being women, they were especially distraught at the doomed babies and held their places in the water with extra determination. They stood side by side with their male colleagues, bent over with feet wide and rumps poked out for better balance. But their eyes were especially sad at the sight of the frightened, doomed baby whales. The male firefighters pretended to be equally distraught, but theirs was largely bogus emotion and everybody knew it.

The firefighters' heroic effort to save the little whales was faithfully taped by the television cameramen who formed a semicircle around the action, Sonys whirring.

As the tide started to return, it became clear what would eventually happen. The surf at that isolated beach was channeled between the two rocky promontories. The energy was concentrated. The surf was consequently huge. It was so mammoth, in fact, that the state had built a turnout on the highway above so tourists could watch the awesome swells rise from the sea and the grand breakers, trailing sheets of spray, race between the flanking rocks.

Eventually the most determined and sympathetic firefighter would be unable to stay in place. All told, the unfolding tragedy was a kind of bad luck lottery. Someone, the fire chief, the governor, or the secretary of the interior, would be publicly forced to explain why it was he had failed to save the lives of the whales.

With the exception of the huge bull that had apparently led the others onto the beach, the mature whales plus the remaining three babies were dead by the time the first flatbed truck arrived. The three infants in the water were left alone. They too would likely never make it. How were they to find more of their kind in that vast expanse of water that was the Pacific Ocean? Which way were they to go? Southwest? West? Northwest?

Would some outgoing tide wash the dead whales out to sea? The answer, unfortunately, was no. The dead whales were far too large to be affected by a little foam. Nobody could dodge the question of what to do about the corpses. Burn 'em or blow 'em up?

Eventually Annie and I could take it no longer. With the tide coming in, the sun shining brightly, and the determined firefighters being pounded with ever growing breakers, we went to the ocean and waved good-bye to the baby whales, wishing them luck.

There was much commotion among the journalists still leaping from helicopters that continued to land on the beach. Melanie had been right in her prediction. Zone One Worldwide was not about to let Erika von Bayer pass on the whale story.

There, among her colleagues, her blonde hair blowing in the wind that had kicked up, sending the thinning fog inland, was Erika, the KATU-TV reporter hit the big time. To Portland area viewers and her former colleagues, Erika was an "I knew her when" journalist.

Erika was far more than another pretty face who could ride a horse. Quicker than she could saddle Don Conquistador, she had gone from the University of Oregon to KATU-TV in Portland and on to become the new *deus ex television monitor* for Zone One Worldwide. Out there, on the scene, she became an adventuress in the manner of CNN's Christianne Amanpour, the storied veteran with the snobby Southern English accent.

Erika had a rich voice, presence, and a serious, responsible way about her that attracted viewers. She seemed genuinely to be doing her best to avoid sensational half-truths and get a story right. And despite her youth and relative inexperience, she was both believable and respected.

CNN's producers tried to pretend that despite Erika's growing ratings, she was a pathetic imitation of Amanpour. Never mind that her German father had been accused of killing his European competitors' jumping horses before somebody detonated his car, the Zone's producers understood that a large part of Erika's attraction was the incongruous combination of a cowgirl with a sexy German accent.

At least once a year, Zone One spirited its exotic cowgirl reporter off to do a rodeo story and run the barrels to show the folks that she knew how to ride. She taught Don Conquistador to do tricks, which she occasionally displayed at the National Wild Horse and Burro Championships in Reno, Nevada.

As Erika strode across the sand to the dead whales, everybody secretly watched her, later to tell their friends that they had seen Erika von Bayer up close.

There was nothing Annie and I could do but get in the way of the cops and firefighters stuck with the corpses of thirty-seven dead whales and one more, the old bull in the lead, about to die. We could not abide witnessing the videotaping of a tragedy turned into international spectacle. Inevitably, Erika von Bayer and the other reporters—wanting to report every delicious detail of how we had stumbled onto the tragedy—would seek us out, thrusting microphones into our faces.

Without looking back, feeling low-down in the extreme, maximum bummed, we climbed wearily back into my bus and drove back up the side of the cliff to Highway 101.

4 · Good-bye old friend

That night Annie and I were in our cabin having elderberry wine and fried Indian bread and huckleberry jam. We had vowed we wouldn't, but in the end we turned on the box and along with everybody else on the planet watched the blazing corpses of the dead whales on the beach. A firm from Japan had offered to solve the problem by butchering the whales, offering to donate many millions of yen to Oregon schools, but the anti-whaling forces howled in protest. How were they supposed to keep the prowhaling forces at bay if greedy public officials in Oregon agreed to sell them whale meat? No, no, no, a thousand times no. Try that and the antiwhaling lobby would organize a national boycott of all things associated with the State of Oregon.

I say we watched the box. That's not all of it. Apparently curious about the local girl turned star, same as everybody else, we watched Zone One. We had seen Erika von Bayer on the beach. Now we wanted to see what she looked like reporting to us on television.

Erika was good, I'll give her that. As she reported on the bid by the Japanese to buy and butcher the whales, and the final decision to burn the bodies, her face mirrored, with apparent sincerity, the tragedy of what had happened.

With a ghastly panorama of dead whales behind her, she said, "These magnificent leviathans of the sea have a special place in the human imagination. Earlier today, I said good-bye to the last of the whales as it lay dying on the beach. A zoologist arrived here from Oregon State University tells me this whale, the largest, is a bull and most likely the leader."

The camera followed Erika. She stopped by the large, baleful eye of the remaining live whale, the old bull. Her face solemn, she said, "Here I stand with this nameless whale. He is, they tell me, minutes from death. His breathing is labored. He waits. If he was the leader, as biologists tell us is most likely, *he* was responsible. And yet this. Grounded. Dying. If he could talk, we would ask him how he made this terrible mistake. Whatever was he thinking? What are we to make of this awful tragedy?"

Behind Erika a small, curious-looking woman of indeterminate age, but with a wicked, if not downright wild body, leaned against the huge whale, embracing it. She was clearly posturing, bent on milking all the attention she could get. *Focus on me, camera. Let the world see what a loving, caring person I am. I love whales so very much. See, I am giving this yucky old bull a good-bye hug.*

As part of its traveling gear, television news crew needed one of those storied hooks like stage managers had in vaudeville so they could unceremoniously yank posing idiots like her out of the picture.

Erika gave the huge bull a pat. "Good-bye, old friend. Good traveling." Then she stepped to one side so she could address the camera with both the dying bull and the blazing whales in the background.

The weird woman hugging the whale shifted as well so she could remain in the picture.

Erika said, "Tonight we watch, saddened, stunned, as the flames consume the bodies of thirty-six sperm whales on this isolated Oregon beach. The bull behind me, who apparently led the others to their end, will soon be dead as well. Three baby whales are out there in the cold waters of the Pacific looking for adults of their kind. The outlook for their survival, zoologists tell us, is not good. We watch. Collectively, we weep. Whales or humans, this is a sad, no-good, lousy day for us all. This is Erika von Bayer on the death beach."

5 · The flow of the River Mustang

Two months later, there was a rash of unexplained deaths of prime Spanish mustang stallions in Oregon and five other western states. While authorities in those states were investigating the possibility of foul play, there was no confirmation that the deaths were anything more than a run of bad luck. Since the killer, if there was one, crossed the borders of several western states in pursuit of his equine victims, the FBI was called in.

The small firm of Denson, Dancer, and Sees the Night also got in on the action. An informal group of concerned horse lovers, Native Americans, and environmentalists, collectively calling themselves the Ad Hoc Committee to Save the Spanish Mustang, hired us to investigate the deaths.

Willie Sees the Night went to southeastern Oregon to investigate a mysterious helicopter that had been seen flying in the area where the Bureau of Land Management monitored and managed herds of wild horses.

Annie and I were playing chess in our cabin in Whorehouse Meadow when Willie called. "A chore for you, Dumsht. I want you to go to place called Ames and Bounds in Sheridan, and talk to a veterinarian named Dr. Sylvia Bonner. She and a woman partner owns the place. We're told that over the last year, Bonner took sperm from a number of the stallions that are now dead. If she gives a damn about horses, she'll talk to you."

"Talk to me on what pretense."

"Tell her the committee is thinking of starting a sperm bank of semen from stallions with classic conformation, and it needs to learn about artificial insemination. We want to know how the sperm is frozen and shipped and how long will it last. That kind of thing. See if she volunteers anything."

"I can do that."

He paused. "And one more thing. We don't have any reason to believe she has done anything wrong, but you should pay attention to her reaction. Liars' eyes and the rest of it."

Ames and Bounds had its laboratories, barns, and horse pastures on a ranch near Sheridan, Oregon, about twenty miles west of Portland. I parked my bus in the circular, gravel parking lot in front of the main office and went inside.

Wearing a white lab smock, Dr. Sylvia Bonner was waiting for me in her reception room. She was a studious-looking woman in her early forties with short brown hair cut in bangs just above her eyeglasses. She was not unfriendly, but she was not warm either.

After introductions, Bonner ushered me into her spacious office. Her desk was covered with photographs of horses. A large picture window overlooked a beautiful green pasture upon which roamed a half dozen beautiful mares. They were not thoroughbred racing horses. They were Spanish mustangs—Appaloosas, pintos, buckskins, palominos—mixed in with some quarter horses. A quarter horse, bred for quick spurts of speed and for agility in stopping and starting, was the horse of choice for cutting cattle, roping, and other ranch work.

Bonner poured us cups of coffee from a silver urn on a coffee table in front of her desk and we each took a seat. "So then, the Ad Hoc Committee to Save the Spanish Mustang wants a primer on the artificial insemination of horses?"

"Correct. How long as it been around? How does it work? The basics."

She was wary, although she did her best to mask it. "Anything I can do to help. Cyropreservation was first used with a bull in 1949 and with a stallion in 1957. We reduce the metabolism of the sperm cells to the lowest temperature they can survive without losing their ability to fertilize an egg. They have to withstand the drop in temperature, ice crystal damage, and dehydration."

I said, "Sounds complicated. In practice how does it work?"

"We use an artificial vagina to collect the sperm into a filtered receptacle warmed to thirty-seven degrees Celsius. The filter eliminates gel fraction, a product of seminal vesicle, an accessory sex gland. We check to see if the sperm are normal, strong swimmers after which we extend it with skim milk and glucose and spin it in a centrifuge."

"Spin it?"

She said, "To separate the spermatozoa from the seminal plasma. We extend it again with sugar, egg yolk, milk, glycerol, electrolytes, and antibiotics. Several systems are used to freeze it. Which one do you want?"

"The one you used in the stallions that were killed."

She refilled both our cups of coffee, using the break to weigh her answer. She said, "I use the standard vapor technique. I place the extended semen in five-milliliter plastic straws with bar codes on the side identifying the stallion and the date I took the semen. I seal the straws with a powder that solidifies when it comes into contact with the semen. I cool the straws to minus one hundred sixty degrees Celsius in a Styrofoam box containing liquid nitrogen vapor. Then I take them to minus one hundred ninety-six degrees Celsius in liquid nitrogen. I transport the straws in an insulated container to keep the temperature constant. And there you have it."

"And when you thaw the sperm?"

"I thaw in water at a fixed rate."

"And the drawbacks?"

"Only twenty to thirty percent of stallions produce sperm that freezes well. Another forty percent will yield semen that freezes okay. And you can almost forget the remaining thirty percent. A stallion's owner has to know which extender works best for his stud's sperm."

I looked out of the window at a palomino mare galloping across a field. "Other problems?"

"Fresh semen delivers higher conception rates. Frozen semen doesn't last long after it's thawed, so we need to know the exact time a mare is ovulating." She glanced out of the window. "We're checking that mare out there every eight hours with ultrasound to determine the exact time of her ovulation. If we have to, we'll induce ovulation with hormones. We can have conception rates of sixty to sixty-five percent with frozen semen correctly used."

Bonner had not pursued the subject of the dead horses. Why? Watching her eyes, I said, "Tell me what you think of these prize mustang stallions going down? A run of bad luck, do you think, or possible foul play?"

Bonner turned, gesturing at the photographs of the horses on the walls. "The drawings of horses in the prehistoric caves in France and Spain were tarpans, domesticated by Scythian nomads about 3,000 B.C. The last wild tarpan died in Russia in 1876, but two German zoologists did their best to genetically re-create the original using the so-called Polish Primitive Horse. There are now about one hundred tarpans worldwide, including several owned by individuals in the United States."

"And their origins more recently?"

"The horse we call the Spanish mustang or Spanish Barb is descended from the Andalusians and the Jennets brought here by Christopher Columbus on his second voyage. The Andalusians and the Jennets were descended from the North African Barb, brought to Spain by the Moorish invaders in 711. Interesting that horses bred by Berber nomads in North Africa turned the sedentary Plains Indians of North America into nomads themselves."

I said, "The history is interesting, but you didn't answer my question about the dead stallions."

Bonner grimaced. "Bad luck, I assume. The FBI is investigating the deaths. I take it we'll soon find out one way or another."

"What you're really saying is that you suspect foul play, but don't want to say so."

"I—" She closed her mouth. Then she said, "Mr. Denson, all equine semen is a kind of biological river that flows from sire to dam into the vessel of a foal on and on through generations and millennia. The Spanish mustang sperm is a New World branch that flowed ultimately from the loins of the horses drawn by Cro-Magnon artists on the walls of caves in Spain and southern France hundreds of thousands of years ago. The artists recorded their image alongside the bison they would ultimately pursue on the Great Plains of North America, one of those improbable coincidences that gives one pause. It would be a tragedy of unspeakable proportions if, out of greed, malice, spite, or stupidity, the flow of the river of mustangs should run dry in the American West." She glanced at her watch, a sign that I was overstaying my welcome.

When I stood to go, she was clearly relieved.

I paused at the door. "It strikes me that with that many prize stallions dead in so short a period of time, something is happening that is not good."

Sylvia Bonner looked grim.

6 · Mustangs down

Annie and I were waiting in line at Baby Dave's convenience store beside the Elk Creek Exxon Station, when Baby, a six-foot-eight-inch, bearded giant—a one-time defensive tackle for the Oregon Ducks—told us the big news on the tube was that the FBI had concluded that some blockhead had, during the previous six weeks, killed twenty-two prime Spanish mustang stallions in six western states.

Baby scanned our oatmeal. "Seven down on Oregon ranches. Six in Montana. Four each in Nevada and Utah. Three in Idaho. Two in Washington. These stallions were supposed to be the best of the best, champions and all that. When the ranchers learned that other breeders were losing stallions, and it dawned on them what was happening, the killer quit. He was done. The story is everywhere, on CNN, CNBC, the Zone, all of 'em." Knowing we would be interested, he picked up the remote.

"Try the Zone," I said.

Baby turned and popped on the television set on a shelf above the glass cigarette case.

The Zone's Portland stringer, KATU's Dovie Rodriguez,

Erika von Bayer's former colleague, was interviewing a round-faced man with jet black hair.

"That would be Sheb Gooddall, the local FBI honcho," Baby said.

Gooddall had one of those heavy beards on a pale complexion that gave him a permanent five o'clock shadow. Looking grim, he said, "What we've got here are twenty-two stallions dead under varying circumstances. A mysterious broken leg. Unexplained convulsions. A sudden violent fever. An apparent heart attack. Under the circumstances, this is an astonishing number. The owners, who trade horses and stud services with one another, began asking themselves whether this was just a run of rotten luck. That's why we were called in."

"And you found what?"

"We exhumed the horses and found that the fevers and convulsions were all induced by one form of poison or another. The leg fractures were not consistent with any known form of equine accident."

"You're saying the horses were murdered," Dovie said.

Gooddall sighed. "Murder? Not legally. The term 'murder' is reserved for a homicide, the killing of a human being. The killing of a horse is an outrage, but legally not murder."

Dovie blinked. "Not murder?"

"No, but I assure you that the FBI will put all available resources into finding whoever did this. We are giving it the same attention as we would a murder."

"And what have you found so far?" Dovie asked.

"We've learned that for the last year an anonymous individual hired an Oregon veterinarian to buy and collect nearly all the semen the stallions could produce, sending the frozen sperm in professional shipping containers to commercial drop boxes in Seattle and San Francisco."

"An anonymous client? Is this semen valuable?"

"If the dead stallions had been champion thoroughbreds, the value of the frozen sperm would theoretically grow by the day. But we're not talking about thoroughbreds here. We're not dealing with Arab sheiks or Kentucky colonels. Breeders of Spanish mustangs love horses and history. These mustangs are friendly, durable, aesthetically beautiful horses with a special place in the lore of the American West and in the lives of the Plains Indians. The sperm would bring from five hundred to a thousand dollars a dose, so profit doesn't appear to be the motive."

"And how long will the sperm last?"

Gooddall said, "Properly stored, we're told it will last indefinitely."

Then it was on to a commercial, and Baby turned off the set.

7 · Murder in Baden Baden

Erika von Bayer's father had been accused of killing jumping horses in Europe. Coincidences did happen, it was true. But horse killing coincidences had to be rare. When we got back to our cabin on Whorehouse Meadow, Annie used her computer to download articles from the on-line editions of the *International Herald Tribune*, the *Daily Telegraph* in London, the *Times of London*, and the *New York Times*. For the fun of it, she compared those articles to stories about Kurt Herzog von Bayer's wife and daughter that had been published in the *Oregonian*.

Erika's mother, Marya, told an *Oregonian* reporter that, after having been accused of killing the mounts of his competitors in jumping competition, her husband had been killed in a car accident. The European papers reported that the German police suspected that it was Marya herself who hired her husband's former stable hand to kill the jumping horses, after which she murdered both the stable hand and her husband.

Annie wrote a summary of the controversy to help us see possible connections between the European horse killings and the mustang stallions killed in the Pacific Northwest:

Marya von Bayer is the sole offspring of Thompson Sturgis, founder of BioSource, a Portland area company that did pioneer work in gene research following the early publications on DNA by James Watson, Francis Crick, and their colleagues in the 1960s. Marya was no beauty. By the late 1970s, BioSource, in the hunt for profitable cancer antidotes, was conducting early research into gene manipulation. A visiting German geneticist with an obsessive interest in the subject was not so stupid as to understand the benefits of courting Thompson Sturgis's daughter, Marya, then in her late twenties.

The handsome Kurt Herzog von Bayer—in the English style, Duke Kurt von Bayer—was an adjunct research professor of biology at a university in Baden Baden, the site of an internationally famous spa near the Black Forest in southern Germany. Skilled in the lab, Herr Doktor Kurt Herzog von Bayer and his mother, Gretchen Herzogin von Bayer, were among the most successful breeders of Hanoverian jumping horses in Europe. Kurt was equally adept at riding jumping horses. That and jumping women.

Marya, thrilled at having attracted the attention of a duke, married Kurt and moved to Baden Baden. Alas, when the honeymoon was over, Kurt Herzog von Bayer dropped the Herzog, much to the annoyance of his family, especially his mother, who was proud of the title. He declined even to call himself Herr Doktor Kurt Bayer. He was plain old Kurt von Bayer who ran around in sloppy Adidas running shoes when he wasn't wearing his fancy riding outfits. He divided his time between BioSource's new German lab in Baden Baden and riding the jumping horses that he and his mother bred at their stable.

The sole issue of the marriage, Erika attended an international high school in Germany and later enrolled in the School of Journalism at the University of Oregon. While a student at Oregon, Erika rode her mustang gelding, Don Conquistador, a handsome pinto, to numerous barrel-racing titles on the Northwest rodeo circuit.

The German police suspected that Kurt hired his former sta-ble hand, Hans Juergen, to kill his competitors' jumping horses, after which he murdered Juergen. As the inquiry began, Kurt was murdered by a bomb placed in his vehicle.

Had Kurt been murdered in retaliation for having killed the horses? The horse killer was never identified, nor was Juergen's murder resolved. Suggestions arose that the pathologically jeal-ous Marya, furious over her husband's notorious philandering, had framed her husband for both the horse killings and mur-der. Did she then murder her husband?

A preliminary investigation failed to find enough to keep Marya in Germany. Having radically transformed her appear-ance through plastic surgery, she moved back to Oregon and built a modernist house in Portland's west hills. She also bought the largest wild horse ranch in the state, just northeast of Salem, renaming it the Marya von Bayer Stables. Marya's fore-man and his assistants bred mustangs with lineage traced to the Kiger and Riddle Mountain herds of wild horses in Oregon, the Sulphur herd in Utah, and the Pryor Mountain herd in Montana—arguably the most pure breed of Spanish mustang found in the wild. The Marya von Bayer Stables used the Inter-net to sell both horses and semen from its champion stallions.

To the coincidence of horse killing in Europe and the United States, Annie and I added a second intersection of circum-stance: Along with his mother, Kurt had been a breeder of Hanoverian horses; after moving to Oregon, Marya became a breeder of Spanish mustangs. One coincidence was a company. Two was a whole lot more than a crowd.

Rereading Annie's summary, I said, "When Marya took off for the United States, she made herself unavailable for further interrogations and forced the German police to come up with enough proof to file for extradition. Hard to do in a murder case."

"Frustrating for the German police and Kurt's family. What do we do next?"

I thought about that for a moment. "With the FBI's conclusion that the mustang stallions were deliberately killed, the full story of what happened in Europe will come out."

"Putting Marya on the short list of suspects."

"It's inevitable. Marya maintains a home in Portland in addition to her stable. Put yourself in Erika's shoes. You're a journalist. Your mother has been accused of killing horses and of murdering your father. You love horses. You ride your mustang Don Conquistador in competition. What would you want most of all?"

Annie looked incredulous. "Put the horses aside. I love my father. I wouldn't care if the murderer was my mother. I'd want the truth, the whole truth and nothing but."

"I agree. What do you say we send the beautiful Ms. von Bayer an e-mail at her Zone One address. 'Hey, remember us. We're the private investigators who found the dead whales. We're now investigating the killing of the mustang stallions. If you ever come to Oregon to visit your mother, we'd like to talk to you. Perhaps we can share information and get at the truth. Blah blah blah. And et cetera.' She probably won't reply, but what the hell."

Annie wrote a note and beamed it off to Erika at Zone One. Annie and I then punched on the box to see what else we could learn about the developing horse killing story. It was ad time. We tapped the mute button and set about cooking some popcorn that we had grown ourselves.

When the popcorn was ready, we opened bottles of our homemade Oddball Ale and settled in on my Goodwill Industries couch, leaning against one another. Annie was marginally bony but warm and soft and reassuring at the same time.

We abandoned the commercial channels and tried Oregon public television, tuning in just in time to hear a primer on wild horses, of generous PBS length, by Gerald Riggin, who monitored Oregon's wild horse herds for the Bureau of Land Management.

8 · Of Kiger and Riddle

A rugged, but slightly built, intense man in his midforties wearing thick eyeglasses, Gerald Riggin was in a studio in Burns. The familiar Edgar Barnhouse, an older, thoughtful PBS figure, interviewed him from a studio in Portland.

Riggin said, "The mustangs of the Kiger Habitat Management Area and the Riddle Mountain Habitat Management area are believed to be genetically identical to the Spanish Barb brought to the New World by the Conquistadors in the seventeenth century. They're also similar to the feral horses found in the Sulfur herd of Utah's Cedar Mountain Herd Management Area and in Montana's Pryor Mountain National Wild Horse Range."

The camera cut to Barnhouse, who said, "Just how many wild horses are we talking about here?"

Riggin said, "The BLM maintains a herd of fifty-one to eighty-two mustangs in the thirty-seven-thousand-acre Kiger habitat. We manage from thirty-three to fifty-six head in twenty-eight thousand acres around Riddle Mountain. These two herds increase at a rate of about twenty percent a year. When there are more horses than the habitats can support—usually once every four years—we round up the excess mustangs and make them available for adoption by the public at our wild horse corrals in Burns."

Offscreen, Barnhouse asked, "What can you tell us about the stallions that were killed?"

"The dead stallions were all descended from mustangs with origins in the Kiger and Riddle Mountain herd, the Pryor Mountain herd in Montana, and the Sulphur Herd in Utah's Needle Mountains. Breeders in several western states have been producing mustangs that geneticists believe are nearly identical to the original Spanish Barb. We encourage this. If, despite our best efforts, an unaccountable disease or winter storm decimates the wild herds, the bloodlines of these unusual horses will be maintained."

Barnhouse went on-screen. "And what can you tell us about the business of breeding?"

Back to Riggin. "I'm a bureaucrat, not a rancher, but I do know that when a foal is born, the breeder ordinarily records both sire and dam in the Spanish Mustang Registry, founded by Robert I. Bislawn in 1957. To prevent inbreeding among their mustangs, breeders within trailering distance swap the services of their studs. When the distances are too great, as they often were out west, they resort to frozen sperm and artificial insemination."

I noted that Riggin had not mentioned the presence of an unknown helicopter cruising the area of the Riddle Mountain herd. The Bureau of Land Management used helicopters to round up wild horses in its 200-mile-long Burns District—including both the Kiger and Riddle Mountain horses—but this chopper was not theirs.

Cut to Barnhouse. "Well, there you have it, the story of Oregon's Spanish mustangs by the BLM's Gerald Riggin."

Which was when the phone rang.

———

Annie answered the call, listening to whoever was on the other end. Then she caught my eyes. To her caller she said, "Say again. That would be Zone One Worldwide?"

She listened again, then said, "Give me a moment, please." She put her hand over the receiver.

"This is Erika von Bayer's assistant. She says Ms. von Bayer has read our e-mail and is interested in talking to us."

"Say what?" I said.

"She says she remembers us from the whale story. She wanted to interview us but we had disappeared. She's in Portland right now."

"Make an appointment," I said. "We're all partners."

Annie removed her hand from the receiver. "John Denson will be pleased to talk to Ms. von Bayer." She handed me the receiver.

Annoyed, I gave Annie a look.

She said, "Oh, come on, Mr. Senior Partner. It won't hurt you."

On the other end, the famous voice of Erika von Bayer said, "Mr. Denson?"

She sounded sexy as hell. I said, "Yes, ma'am. I'm pleased that you called. To be honest, we really didn't expect an answer to our e-mail. And so quickly!"

"I'm looking at a report my producer's assistant quickly assembled from an Internet check. Let me see if he got it straight. You're a former newspaper reporter. Ms. Dancer was an FBI agent. Mr. Sees the Night is the human form of coyote."

"That's right, ma'am. He claims to be a sorcerer. He either does or does not run around at night howling at the moon. He's now somewhere on the BLM mustang range south of Burns checking out a mysterious helicopter that's been seen flying in the area of the wild herds. Whether or not the helicopter has anything to do with the stallion killings, we have no idea."

She said, "I take it you know about the horse-killing

controversy in Europe that preceded my father's death and the allegations about my mother."

"We read stories in the files of the on-line editions of European newspapers."

"My mother is not beloved by the other breeders, who resent her using her fortune to buy the best available mustangs no matter what the price. I find it impossible to believe she has anything to do with killing horses—in Europe or the United States. I want her name cleared of suspicion."

"I see."

"I have a professional interest as well. Any television network that cracks the mystery will receive a profitable spike in Neilsen ratings. I propose a swap. I'll help you any way possible in return for your pledge to pass along any tips or breaks you might come across that might be the basis for a horse-killer story."

I said, "You want to cultivate us as a source?"

"I want to know who has been killing horses, and I want to know who murdered my father. If you help me crack the case, I can give you some serious airtime. You'll have to hire a part-timer to sort through the inquiries from all your would-be clients. Face it, Denson, Dancer and Sees the Night is a story in itself."

I said, "Despite our unusual credentials and our residence on Whorehouse Meadows, we are not any kind of circus or freak show, Ms. von Bayer. We solve mysteries."

She laughed warmly. "Your being colorful is good but not sufficient for airtime, I assure you. You score only if you're able to help me run the killer to ground. My grandmother and I are in a suite of rooms on the top floor of the Park Place Hotel. Do you know where that is?"

"On Broadway Street downtown."

"Perhaps you and your associate, Ms. Dancer, can come for a chat with my grandmother and me tomorrow night. Would that be possible?"

9 · Pony girls

Outside, a white moon. Inside our cabin, Annie lay on her stomach. She knew I was admiring her. She shifted slightly for my benefit.

"You like this?" She moved again.

I could see her eyes watching me. "Very much," I said. I ran my hand over her rump, catching the edge of her translucent white underpants with my finger.

Saying nothing, she reached down with both hands and slipped off the underpants.

I gave her butt a slap, not hard, just enough to make it bounce. She made a noise in her throat.

She hiked up her rump and spread her knees. Her weight resting on her shoulders, her face turned toward me, she breathed, "Do it."

I slapped her ass again.

Again the noise in her throat. "Yes!" She put one hand between my legs, squeezing hard, and her other hand between her own.

Again I gave her a measured, just-right stroke with the palm of my hand.

She groaned. She was almost hyperventilating. The hand between her legs began to move.

Later, Annie and I lay on our backs with the window open.
The night air was cool on our sweaty skin. Annie flopped her leg
over mine. Life was good. Lying there, I knew in my gut that I
was about to fly spontaneously out of my skin, a disconcerting
phenomenon which occurred with increasing frequency since
Willie, having primed me with a Native American hallucinogen,
first sent me through the existential wormhole to a parallel reality. This other world, having established its grip on my imagination, refused to go away. As Willie warned might happen, I later
began flying without stimulation. Sometimes I landed as an
owl, sometimes not.

For me the question was straightforward: did I literally fly
out of my skin (Willie's assertion) or were my flights inner jour-
neys, hallucinatory explorations of my subconscious (my opinion)?

In these allusive, illusive flights, some longer and more complicated than others, I had more than once encountered my al-
leged creator, an author named T, who lived in the Philippines.
Ours was a bantering relationship in which metaphor, irony,
and paradox flew like shooting stars.

Willie claimed the initial T stood for trickster. T was the
Great Spirit as trickster novelist. Willie believed the most private of private detectives was the investigator who led an exam-
ined life. Who am I? What am I all about? In this pursuit, he
said, the trickster novelist was addressing me directly.

I felt that T most likely referred to *thymos*, Plato's name for
the human spirit or consciousness. T was me. I imagined him as
a writer.

I see Annie's sexy butt. Only my true love's derriere is not in front of me on the bed or bent tantalizingly over the end of the couch, thighs wide. And we are not playing sexy spanking games or check-out-this-target-bub-and-see-if-you-can-still-breathe. No, no, no. Atop a galloping spotted mare in front of me, Annie is naked. She taps the flank of the mare with a leather quirt and digs her bare heels into the horse's ribs, urging more speed.

I'm riding naked too, the only male among some three dozen naked young beauties galloping hard in a valley of clouds. The young women are of all races, and splendid examples of their kind. Their thighs grip tightly the backs of their mounts. Their vulvas are skin to skin against the heat and the power. Their breathtaking bodies shine with a sheen of perspiration that highlights their ribs and spines and the delicate muscles of their shoulders. They ride with joy and aplomb, easy on the backs of their mounts, their sweaty breasts rising and falling with the motion. Their hips move up and back, up and back with the motion of their galloping mounts. They're having a good time, grinning and laughing and calling out to one another in their many languages. Their eyes sparkle and dance.

Puffs of dust rise up behind the hooves of their mounts, who are also enjoying the run. The sound is rumbling thunder.

The happy equestrians are riding every kind of horse imaginable: Appaloosas, buckskins, bays, pintos, sorrels, blacks, name it. The horses, which I recognize as Spanish mustangs, are as beautiful in their way as their riders. Annie is riding Ms. Fab, one of Bob Humping Buck's mares. I am riding Bodan, the leopard appaloosa that also belongs to Bob.

On my left, an African girl with jet black skin has a behind that is nothing short of breathtaking. It is not a timid little butt, hardly a pinch and no damn fun in a pair of tight jeans or thong bikini. It is firm. Fabulous. I whistle in sincere admiration. She grins shyly in response. She knows she's hot. I want leap to leap from my horse and pull her from her mount onto the cloud below us. But am I to choose her over the delicate beauty on my right, who is Chinese or Korean or maybe Japanese? She is petite, delicate, sexy, riding naked on a galloping chestnut stallion. I see a young woman from Southeast Asia, another from India perhaps. All kinds.

Annie is flanked on one side by a Nordic blonde of statuesque physical proportions and on the other by a slender beauty with black hair and the palest of pale skin. The rider to the right of the brunette has fabulous red hair, flowing behind her in glistening waves.

As the lead riders slow their lathering mounts to a walk to give them a rest, a rider joins me, wearing what is supposed to represent the helmet of a knight, but is really a galvanized iron bucket with eyeholes. He is carrying an old broom for a lance. The curious knight is a terrible rider, stiff and uncertain of how to control a horse. He looks like he's Scotch-taped to the top of his mount, an aging gray mare.

He rides his horse alongside Bodan. He removes his bucket helmet and hooks the metal handle over one elbow. As I suspected, it is T. He needs a haircut. His gray hair sticks out every which way. He says, "I slowed the riders down to give their horses a break and so we can talk. What a scene, eh? All these sensational naked young women riding horses. Face it, Denson, female beauty is the juice. What is life without the sensual?"

"Hard to imagine, I have to admit," I say.

He pauses, thinking. "Tell me, Denson, does it strike you as fascinating or in any way instructive that there are as many kinds of horses as women? All with classic lines and profiles and colors. All different. All beautiful in their way. Good that they're not all the same."

"They're lucky, blessed."

"Yes, they are. And so are we when we get a chance to appreciate them. The good-looking ones have been praised since they were little girls and their looks became apparent. By the way, these are what I call 'pony girls' parading their fancy stuff for jerks like you and me."

"Say again?" I ask. "Fancy stuff?"

"You almost fell off your horse staring at that African girl's rear end. With youthful skin, narrow hips, and breasts yet high on their ribs, the pony girls ride into their future laughing and with high hopes. They have years ahead of them in which they'll be admired and courted. Most of those with good conformation will enjoy a fulfilling cycle of whatever turn they choose, work, family, et cetera. Those lacking shapeliness and a pretty face will have a harder time engaging the interest of capricious males."

"Conformation?

"A horse breeder's term," he says. "Conforming to the ideal. Dog breeders carry it to the extreme."

I say, "Come on, T, loosen up."

T remains serious. "Can't be helped. The ranks of *las desperadas* are filled with the nonconforming."

"Outlaw women?"

"Fueled by bitterness, envy, and resentment," T says. "Understandable, all things considered. Tough not to feel a little sympathetic for their plight."

"What happened to ambition, vanity, and narcissism? Isn't the curse of beauty, the reverse of nonconformity? Are you telling me there are no hot-looking numbers among *las desperadas*? I don't believe it."

T pretends to be shocked. "You use your smart mouth on me? I created you!" Then he grins. "Good point. You're right. Just wondering if you were alert."

Looking wistful, T glances about at the naked women. He

replaces his bucket helmet. "To romance! To passion! May it ever flourish!" The doughty knight digs his bare heels into his horse's flanks. T doesn't know how to ride worth a damn. His mount, having no idea what he wants, falls into a jarring, herky-jerky gait. T's stupid white butt bounces up and down. His belly could be smaller. He looks preposterous. Glancing back to wave good-bye, he almost falls off his horse.

When he disappears, the lead riders once again break into a gallop, and we all follow.

Having observed my conversation with T, Annie pulls up slightly, maneuvering Ms. Fab alongside Bodan. We have to shout to be heard. She yells, "Who was that character? Don Quixote?"

"That was T," I shout back. "His loopy idea of being clever."

She grins. "If T imagined this ride, he can't be all bad. This is fun!"

I eye the beauties riding hard on both sides of me. They're aware that I'm admiring their bodies, and they're flattered. The sweat makes them especially erotic. They give me knowing smiles. My grin is so big, it's a wonder it doesn't break my face.

"They're beautiful, aren't they?" Annie shouts.

"T calls them pony girls," I call back. "They're delightful. Look at those smiles! The joy and the delight."

"Don't be bashful on my account. Check 'em out. Appreciate."

"I like all that rising and falling action."

"You see that amazing blonde on the left up there? My God!"

I groan loudly for Annie's benefit. "A sensational rider."

Annie laughs. "You think so?"

"Fun to imagine, what with her being new and different and everything."

Annie laughs all the louder. "I bet. I get to run the camera."

10 · Erika and the Duchess

Annie and I expected to be met at the door by Erika's assistant or gopher, but no. Erika von Bayer, a stunning, tall, lithe beauty wearing jeans and a San Francisco 49ers T-shirt answered the knock herself. Behind her was an attractive older woman wearing a well-tailored dress. Erika said, "Mr. Denson, Ms. Dancer, won't you please come in?"

Annie and I stepped inside.

"Mr. John Denson, Ms. Annie Dancer, I would like you to meet my grandmother, Gretchen Herzogin von Bayer."

"Call me Gretchen, please," said the duchess, who had obviously been a stunner when she was young. She had spent some real bucks on her hair, and her makeup, splendidly applied—that is, almost invisible—looked like the work of a professional.

Call her Gretchen? I didn't feel comfortable with being that familiar. I had no idea what a respectful German would call her. I didn't want to be rude or boorish. That was stupid. I said, "I would be more comfortable with Frau von Bayer." To Erika, I said, "You look like—" I stopped, feeling foolish what with Annie and all.

"Like the French actress Catherine Deneueve?" Gretchen said. "That's exactly what I was going to say."

"Thank you," Erika said. "That's very flattering. I've been told that many times. Younger people have no idea who Catherine Deneueve is, if you don't mind my saying. And my German accent doesn't fit. It should be French." She picked up a small, framed photograph from the edge of the wet bar that was part of the suite. She handed it to me. "This is what my father looked like."

Annie and I shared the photograph with Gretchen looking over our shoulder. Erika was a flat-out clone of Kurt, only female. The resemblance was startling. He had been an extraordinarily handsome man, tall, slender, very elegant, like a young Roger Moore.

Gretchen said, "My son was a gentleman, very polite. Impeccable manners. Very good on a horse. He was captain of the German national jumping team. He won the silver medal at Sydney."

Erika said, "You two found the beached whales. If you saw my report on television, then you know what my mother looks like. I was visiting her when the story broke, so she went with me. If you remember a small woman behind me embracing the dying whale that apparently led the rest onto the beach, that was her."

I remembered the posturing woman hugging the whale, milking the moment for all the attention she could get. Politely, I said, "I remember a woman leaning against the whale, but I couldn't pick her out of a police lineup."

The duchess said, "Erika's father loved horses and so do I. Together we bred Hanoverian jumping horses in the stables that I inherited from my late husband. No matter what you may have read, Kurt did *not* kill anybody's horses."

"Would you like something to drink?" Erika asked. "I have just about anything you want, Scotch, bourbon, whatever."

I said, "A cold beer if you have it."

"As it happens, I have some German beer in the refrigerator. And some Riesling for my grandmother."

While we waited, Annie said, "Your granddaughter is both beautiful and charming, Frau von Bayer."

She said, "Erika travels all over the world interviewing everybody from aboriginal hunters to foreign ministers and heads of state. Our family is very proud of her."

Erika returned with a tray containing bottles of beer and a glass of Riesling for her grandmother. "There are about twelve hundred breweries in Germany, almost all of them local. *Hefeweizen,* wheat beers, are top fermented and unfiltered, so they sometimes have a cloudy appearance, and you'll find yeast sediment at the bottom. My father's favorite was *Schneider Weiss,* partly because it is carried in many specialty shops outside of Germany. That's what I have with me tonight."

Erika sat three tall, graceful beer glasses on the top of the portable wet bar. Their narrow bases widened toward the tops then narrowed slightly again. She held one up. "This is a *Franziskaner* glass. The top is designed to hold a nice head, which the *Schneider Weiss* has. There will be sediment at the bottom, so watch how I pour."

Erika poured the dark, amber beer down the side of the tilted glass. When the bottle was about three-quarters empty, she swirled it to raise the sediment on the bottom and poured the rest of it in. A substantial head rose on top and remained firm. She gave the glass to Annie, then poured one for me.

I sipped it. I could taste the malt and the hops. It was maybe a little sweet. Beyond that, it was hard for me to say, my tongue was probably as sensitive as leather. "I like it," I said.

"This is my little way of remembering my father and honoring him. I am proud of things German. Here you are, Grandma,

some Riesling for you." She gave a glass of Riesling to her grandmother.

It was time for us to get down to business.

Erika said, "There is no credible evidence that my mother
had anything to do with killing horses in Europe. All it does is
make her fair game for a setup here in the United States."

Gretchen shook her head. "The horse killing haunts Marya."

I said, "Can you tell me what is known or suspected to have
happened in Europe?"

Erika grimaced. "Both individual riders and national teams
compete. In some of the larger meets, the Europeans are joined
by teams from North and South America and Asia. In a four-
year period, at least sixteen champion European jumpers met
an early end—falling victim to untimely disease or accident."

"None of the horses were German, I take it."

"Just one," she said. "A horse belonging to my father's rival
for individual honors. The investigation included almost all the
police in the European Union, from Scotland Yard to the French
Surate."

Stiffening, her face grim, Gretchen said, "Authorities eventually questioned Hans Juergen, who once worked in our stables."

"The stables owned by you and Kurt."

"Yes. The theory was that my son hired Hans to kill the horses.
Kurt was crushed by public speculation that he had killed the
horses of his competitors. Then somebody murdered Juergen—
shot him in the face at close range. Kurt was so tarred by public
speculation that he retired from riding." She ground her teeth
together, furious at the memory.

Erika, Annie, and I waited, giving her time to recover.

Gretchen said, "There was no more vile and spiteful thing
anybody could have done than to frame my son for killing

horses. He would never deliberately kill a horse, never."

I said, "How was Kurt killed?"

Erika said, "My father was having problems with the fuel injection on his Porsche, so he took my mother's Jaguar. The Jaguar exploded on an isolated road leading from his estate. His body was burned so badly that he had to be identified through his dental bridge."

Gretchen shook her head. "The Jaguar had been detonated by a bomb. My daughter-in-law claimed somebody was trying to kill her and blew up Kurt by mistake. The police had a new theory: Marya was behind everything, including Kurt's murder."

Quickly, Erika added. "But there was no evidence that she had done anything wrong."

"Do you think Marya murdered your son, Frau von Bayer?" I asked mildly.

Gretchen sighed. "My granddaughter and I have agreed to disagree on that possibility. Everybody knows that Marya and I did not like one another. A wife frequently competes with her mother-in-law over the attentions of her husband. That's not unusual. But now look at what we have happening, Marya is trying to compete with me as a horse breeder. Don't you think that's a little over the top? Yes, I think Marya hired Juergen to kill horses to destroy Kurt's reputation and dishonor him, then murdered him herself to make sure he would never be vindicated."

Erika added quickly, "My mother is temperamental, I admit, but she's not crazy."

"Why would your mother kill horses or murder your father?" I cleared my throat. "Kurt was a ladies' man, was he not?"

Gretchen answered for her granddaughter. "Yes, he was. That's so. Marya eventually dispatched Heinz Steiner, her accountant and longtime personal aide, to document Kurt's assignations. Then Marya began following Kurt herself, catching him once in flagrente in a riotous scene in a Munich hotel that became a staple of German tabloids." Gretchen smiled weakly. "Kurt was titled, handsome, and a champion equestrian. Young women were naturally attracted to him." She glanced at Erika. "I know Marya is your mother, Erika, but if this gentleman is to help solve the mystery, he needs to know the truth."

"I understand, Grandma."

Gretchen said, "The lamentable fact is that Kurt married Marya, a homely little gnome, solely to gain an interest in BioSource. He did not need the money. He had a fortune of his own. He was obsessed with genes and had this idea, considered fantasy at the time, of one day manipulating genes to produce medicine and eliminate hereditary diseases. For Marya, Kurt was a trophy husband. Kurt Herzog von Bayer! A duke! How proud she was! For years she apparently believed, naively, that he was a faithful, loving husband. Or is 'absurdly' the correct adverb?" Gretchen's face tightened. "Shortly after Marya began tracking down my son's infidelities, someone started killing the horses."

I said, "If both the locals and the FBI can't find the mustang killer, what makes you feel that we'll do any better?"

Erika said, "There are no guarantees, I understand that. I'll be out of town on assignments. I'll give you a number to contact me periodically to let me know what you've found. If you need me here personally for any reason, I'll do my best to fly back—depending on where I am and the nature of my assignment."

Gretchen added, "I should tell you also, Mr. Denson, that I have hired a German private investigator, Wolfgang Strehmel, to pursue the murderer of my son. He may come calling. And as for my daughter-in-law, you should go talk to Marya. You can judge for yourself what kind of woman she is."

11 · *Sweaty pink monkeys*

Marya von Bayer's home in Portland's west hills was ultra modern, what appeared to be a haphazard tumble of copper cubes or blocks with green stains running down the sides. The cubes were not at right angles. They were tilted, as though the architect had imagined a pile of kid's blocks transformed into a residence. The windows on the cubes, framed in pink, aqua, and mauve, were likewise placed at odd angles. And the windows were not square. They were rhomboids.

When I parked my bus out front, I stood there looking at the wild house for a few minutes. Then I entered the jumble of blocks and found the front door. I rang the bell.

The door opened. There stood Marya von Bayer, a petite woman, perhaps no more than five feet tall, a kind of canvas of the cosmetic arts, both surgical and chemical, and of curious couture. She gave me a come-hither look with green eyes. She blinked eyelashes thick with mascara. She said, "Well, hello, cowboy! You must be John Denson."

"Yes, ma'am," I said.

"You ready for a good time, big boy?"

Was she drunk? "I've got some questions in mind. Gotta lot of territory to cover."

She gave me a lopsided grin. "I'll just bet you do. What do you think of my outfit? You can call me Mustang Marya." She turned so that I could appreciate her getup and the provocative contents underneath.

Marya's rattlesnake-skin cowboy boots had silver tips and six-inch spiked heels. The wheeled spikes of her silver Chijuajua spurs were tipped with rubies. Her blue silk tights, ersatz blue jeans, were far too small for her tiny body and appeared at first to have been sprayed on. The tights, printed with fake seams, rivets, pockets, and red Levi's tag, were molded into the crevasse of buns that looked like they had been inflated with a bicycle pump. In front, the tights clung so tightly that she was effectively naked between the legs. Her Levi's tights were "held up" by a hand-tooled leather belt with a huge buckle featuring the head of a longhorn bull with blazing ruby eyes.

Over the Levi's tights, the lady wore glistening silver chaps ringed with turquoise studs and fringed with red tassels of tiny, woven bullwhips.

She wore a translucent red cowboy shirt under a white vest. The shirt had snaps rather than buttons and had western-style V tabs over the pockets. The shirt was open two snaps too far, revealing an arroyo of skin between high-riding breasts ordinarily found only on teenagers.

But the sexual drama of Marya's outfit was muted by the fact that she had a holstered, silver-plated Colt dragoon revolver riding low on each hip.

In its way, her face was as chilling as her pistols. She had Faye Dunaway cheekbones. Her perfect little nose appeared to have been inspired by the actress Jodie Foster. Her eyes were genuine imitation Elizabeth Taylor violet, that is, colored-contact-lens violet. Her mascara and eyeliner had been troweled on in the manner of the decadent Liza Minnelli in the movie *Cabaret*. Her skin was so tightly stretched to the top and sides of her head that it was a wonder she could blink, close her mouth, or for that matter touch the floor with her feet. Her scarlet lips, a testament to the silicon arts, were apparent copies of Sophia Loren's sensual wonders. Those amazing reproductions were accurate to the sensual droop of Ms. Loren's lower lip.

Having turned slowly around for my benefit, Marya looked me straight on with knowing eyes that were appropriate to a woman in her late fifties. She was seemingly unaware or indifferent to the fact that she had turned herself into a grotesque. "Well, what do you think?" She ran the palm of her hand over her crotch. "I sent the help packing tonight, so we have an entire pile of copper blocks to ourselves. Beds everywhere. Plenty of floor space."

The first time that I had ever thought seriously about the nature of *thymos* was when I looked into the dying eyes of Sharon Toogood, daughter of the Portland weatherman, Jerry Toogood. Shortly thereafter, Willie sent me flying for the first time, and thereafter I had been contemplating the ancillary issue of what it was that dominated *thymos*. The German philosopher Friedrich Hegel believed it was recognition.

To have gotten dressed in such a bizarre getup, indifferent to excess, there was little doubting that the *thymos* of Marya von Bayer was desperate for almost any kind of recognition.

If Mad Marya wasn't bombed already, she was on her way. Too much alcohol destroyed inhibitions. Whether I was facing neurosis or a woman hosting a monster, it wasn't good.

"Are those things loaded?" I asked.

She slid a hand under one breast. "These?"

What the hell was I getting into? I said, "Those look good, but I was thinking of the others."

"These?" She tapped the pistol in the holster on her left hip.

I nodded.

She removed the pistol and cocked it. *Blam,* she blew a hole in the ceiling. She grinned. "You can call me Mustang Marya, a rich lady who likes a good time. You like a drink?" She slurred her words. She was as loaded as her pistols.

I said, "I'm investigating the killing of the mustang stallions. I've got a lot of questions."

Her face turned sour. She said, "You don't think I had anything to do with killing horses, do you?"

"No ma'am. I didn't mean to suggest that. It's just that in order to find the real killer, I have to sort through a lot of clues."

"You can have a drink and ask your questions at the same time, can't you?" She suddenly turned mean. "Now what're you having, big boy? Whatever you want, I've got. What're you having?"

I cleared my throat. "A beer'll do."

"I figured you for beer," she said casually. As she headed for the refrigerator behind the bar, she said, "Erika looks exactly like her father. He was so handsome it was preposterous. Made the young Prince Philip look like Bozo the Clown. Kurt was a playboy, Mr. Denson. A satyr. He wanted his own BioSource research lab in Bavaria, so he married me."

"A German outpost of BioSource."

"That's all he ever wanted from the moment he set eyes on me. Stupid Bunsen burners and glass tubes and stuff. I thought I was getting a duke. I imagined fancy parties and grand balls. And what did I get? After he had used his title to help snag me, he dropped it, saying it was an embarrassing pretension. So much for Kurt Herzog von Bayer. He wanted to be plain old Kurt von Bayer, research genius. Dr. Gene." Marya apparently viewed marriage as conspicuous consumption; for her, Kurt was a Mercedes Benz husband. Only Kurt wanted to be a Volkswagen. "And so what did he do?" She waited for me to answer the question.

As if I had any idea. I shrugged.

"During the day, he either holed up in his lab or practiced jumping barriers on one of his horses at the stables he and his mother owned. At night, he either drank beer and ate sausage with his friends in a beer hall or humped one of his girlfriends. Never mind that I was a human being with pride and feelings. He must have bedded down every good-looking woman in Germany and in all the adjoining provinces of France, Belgium, and the Netherlands."

She opened the refrigerator door, removed a bottle of Coors, and uncapped it. "It's true we did live in fancy digs on *Kronprinzenstrasse* near *Kaiser Wilhelm Strasse* in downtown Baden Baden. That's where the famous spa is located. I didn't have to put up with smelly barns and horse poop and all of that." She gave me a cold goblet. "Kurt was the captain of the German equestrian team, you know, the jumpers." Her eyes glazed at the memory.

Not knowing what to say, but wanting her to continue, I made a sound in my throat. She was bombed and on a roll, wanting to tell me all about Kurt the bad boy egalitarian.

She said, "Kurt once told me that he was turned on by what he called the power of the 'strange.'"

"The 'strange'?" I asked.

"Having sex with a different female. He said when the sexiness of the 'strange' wore off, his interest flagged. No matter how wild and satisfying it was in the beginning, sex with the same woman year after year got boring. He claimed all men were the same, only few would admit it. He claimed it was part of their genetic burden. The young women followed him from competition to competition. For years I put up with it, pretending I had no idea what was going on. When Erika left the nest, I decided I would take no more."

"And you did what?"

"I started following him. I caught him in the sack time and

again. In Munich once, I was able to get a key to his room from
the desk. I was in a rage, trembling with fury. I got my twenty-five
automatic out of my handbag and threw open the doorway. The
room reeked of hashish. There Kurt was taking on three at
once. Not two. Three! Talk about strange! They were writhing
on top of him like sweaty pink monkeys, crying out, their orifices
in frenzied action. I scattered them. On the way out, one of
them inadvertently raked me across the face with a huge, sweaty
boob. The nipple was big as a silver dollar. I couldn't help but
grab my face. I felt like I had been branded. I was humiliated.
The nipple was chocolate colored. I'll never forget that." She
stopped, remembering. Her Sophia Loren lower lip bobbed up
and down, out of control, then quivered pathetically.

Was she about to weep?

Finally, the lip grew calm. She regained her composure. "The
girls scattered down the flowered carpet with boobs and behinds
bouncing up and down. And the squealing and carrying on!
Other guests opening their doors, peering out at the commotion." Marya rolled her eyes. "And Kurt was laughing, yes, laughing. He was so very European, you see. So cosmopolitan. So
worldly and with it. Men are men. Can you imagine the scene?"

No manner of plastic surgery or colored contact lenses could
mask Marya's bitterness. She poured herself a water glass of
Glenfiddich Scotch. "Kurt must have been popping Viagra like
aspirin tablets and eating ginseng omelets. There was no other
way he could have done it. Left me home with the vibrator. If
they had held a vibrator Olympics, I would have won a gold
medal. It got so bad I got turned on if I heard an electric razor
buzzing. Over the years, Kurt kept adding doodads and whatever to his fancy lab, all on the BioSource tab, mind you. After
getting slapped in the face by that breast in Munich, with him
almost doubled up in laughter, I vowed tat for tit, in a manner
of speaking." Leaning against the bar, she gave me what she

intended to be a coy look. She slipped, barely catching her balance.

If she didn't have loaded revolvers on her hips, her intoxication would have been no concern. All I would have had to do was judiciously retreat. I took a sip of Coors.

"Would you like to see these tits?" she asked suddenly. "They're done right. Men like a natural feel. Cost me a cool fifty thousand dollars each."

"I . . ." I struggled to ignore both tits and pistols. "Maybe we should talk about the horse killings first," I said.

She took a mammoth slug of Glenfiddich, then smiled crookedly. "Okay, I'm game. We'll talk. As long as I get to show you my hundred-thousand-dollar pair of tits. Give you time to think them over. Hell, I even know who the horse killer is. How do you like them apples?" She grabbed her shirt with both hands. "All you have to do is give this shirt a good yank and the rest of the snaps will pop. What do you say, deal?"

No person with a body that small could continue to knock back that amount of high-octane Scotch without winding down. I said, "Sure, why not?"

"But you gotta rip the shirt apart. Part of the he-man thing. I bet Kurt ripped plenty of shirts apart in his heyday. The fancy German stud."

I frowned. "Then we talk. A deal is a deal."

She grinned drunkenly. "Sure, we'll talk and sees what comes up." She arched an eyebrow.

Without ado, I kept my end of the bargain. Grabbing her shirt with both hands, I yanked hard. Out tumbled the hundred-thousand-dollar numbers, splendid examples of the cosmetic art.

"What do you think? Did I get my money's worth?" She weighed her left breast in her hand, examining it like it was a cantaloupe in a supermarket.

"You did indeed. They're very nice." That was a lie. They were off-putting in their excess. They were *things,* somehow not sensual or provocative.

"Very nice! Is that all you can say? They're best damn tits money can buy, barring none. That blonde actress, what's-her-name, went out and bought herself those things that hang like the udders of a Guernsey cow. Yuck!"

"Pretty gross, I agree," I said.

"Why would she do that when she could have bought some great-looking boobs?" Marya shook her head sadly. "How a man would be attracted to those outsized udders of hers is one of life's mysteries."

I didn't want to spend the whole night talking about Marya's mammaries. "I—"

Quickly she said, "You can check them out with your hands if you want. They look right. They feel right." She jiggled her remarkable breasts up and down for my benefit. "You should see my ass."

I shook my head. "No, no. A deal is a deal." No way I wanted to see the lady's inflated butt. Next thing, I'd find myself being invited in for a dip and there was no way in hell I wanted that. I motioned to the leather chairs sitting opposite one another. "You sit there, and I'll sit there. We'll talk. I could use another bottle of beer if you've got it."

She retrieved another bottle of Coors from the refrigerator. "And a tad more Scotch for the lady." She refilled her glass.

The word "lady" was open to a range of interpretation. I sat in my chair. "No reason we shouldn't relax while we talk," I said.

She sat opposite me, casually running a hand over one of her extraordinary breasts. "No reason at all," she said. She drank some more Scotch. Then she took off her shirt and vest, but put the vest back on, coyly arranging it so it covered her fancy boobs. "I don't want you to think I'm cheap or easy."

"I don't think that, I assure you."

"I like you, John. I like you a whole bunch. There's something sexy about a man who buzzes off to an appointment with a millionaire driving a Volkswagen bus that's more than thirty years old. The paint is oxidized. I was watching out of one of the blocks when you pulled up."

"The bus gets me where I want to go," I said.

"I just bet I can throw you a roll in the oats so wild it'll take your breath away. You like that, would you? We're talking real fancy fucking. Give you something to remember." She looked down at her chest. "If I let you eye these things all the while we talk, I risk losing your attention. Better if you know they're right here under this little vest."

"The maintenance of the strange."

She grinned crookedly. "Kurt was right. All men have their brains in their"—*hic*—"balls. Just tell me when you want to take another look at my boobs. Maybe I'll give you a quick peek. They're sensational. They really are."

I said, "Tell me, Mrs. von Bayer, who do you think the horse killer is and why?"

She suddenly turned mean. "Knowing what lies ahead, you insist on calling me 'Mrs. von Bayer.' What's"—*hic*—"wrong with you? You call me Marya." She unholstered the pistol on her left hip and put it in her lap.

"Marya," I said quickly.

"And remember, no t-trying to run. Mustang Marya will put a silver bullet right up your poop chute." Grinning crookedly, she cocked the pistol.

12 · Marya's story

Weaving slightly from side to side, Marya said, "How"—
hic—"how long have you been a private 'dick,' Mr. Denson?"

"About twenty years," I said.

"You've encountered a lot of"—*hic*—"evil in that time, have
you? Lots of ba-ad people."

Some drunks deteriorated slowly. Others seemed to do all
right, laughing and having a good time when without warning
their systems began shutting down, sending them tumbling
over the precipice from being merely being drunk to being totally soused. "I've bumped into a few creeps," I said, wondering
how long Marya would manage to stay conscious.

Grinning, she opened the left side of her vest and looked
down at her breast. "Shtill there." She checked out the other one.
"Thish one too."

"Hard to imagine they'd run away and hide," I said. She appeared to be going fast. I had to get her to focus on something
besides her fancy new body. "You agreed to tell me about the
horse killer, remember? Who killed the horses?"

Marya blinked, then held her eyes wide open. She opened
and closed her mouth. Would she be able to continue? At last

she answered. "A f-female. She is so evil and rotten"—*hic*—"to the core that it makes me shudder. She is v-vile. She is deceitful. She will do anything to"—*hic*—"get her way. Anything. Never trust a w-word out of her mouth. Just when you think she's telling the truth, she's lying. I say again, never"—*hic*—"trust her. She liesh as eashily as she breaths. She's such a liar that she's"—*hic*—"forgotten the truth."

"A liar, got it. Who is she? Who is the horse killer?"

She seemed surprised at the question. "Which horses?"

"The mustangs. Tell me."

She clapped a hand over her mouth. Was she going to vomit? I waited.

"Getting dizzy," she said.

"Tell me."

She sat up, her torso going round and round in a small circle. "M-my former m-mother-in-law."

"Your mother-in-law?"

"The duchess!" she said contemptuously. She spit on the floor. "G-gretchen Herzogin von B-bayer." She puffed her cheeks out, concentrating. She licked her painted lips. "She h-hates me. She w-wants revenge! She is trying to frame m-me. People in this p-piss ass state d-don't like me either. They w-want the mustang killer to be m-me. But even i-innocent people are sometimes not liked. W-would you grant me that, Mr. Denson?"

"Why would the duchess want to frame you for anything?"

She took a deep breath. "I'll be a-all right. Need oxyshun." She began inhaling and exhaling deeply. She motioned me closer with her hand then put a finger to her mouth. She whispered. "The duchess tried to m-murder *me* for allegedly destroying her son's precious reputation, but killed her Kurt by accident. She feels guilty. She b-blames me. She's tormented."

"Gretchen Herzogin von Bayer killed her own son?"

"Shhhhhhhh!" Narrowing her eyes, Marya looked left and right.

"Why?"

"Kurt's P-porsche was having trouble so he took my car that night. His m-mother didn't know that and killed him by a-accident. Isn't that something?"

"What? Say again?"

"I'm t-telling you the t-truth. The venomous, h-hateful bitch Gretchen Herzogin von Bayer blew up her son by m-mistake then hired a private d-detective to try to frame me. Wolfgang Strehmel by n-name. A Kraut private investigator. Can you believe it? No imagination at all. A plodder. Wild, huh?"

I said, "Maybe Kurt was murdered by someone whose horse had been killed. They all had motive."

"Naw. The 'duchess' hired a man who once worked in the von Bayer stables to kill the jumping horses so her precious little boy could win more c-competitions on their h-horses." She giggled drunkenly. "Or maybe Kurt had them k-killed, I d-don't know. What d-difference does it m-make? Kurt went to his grave disgraced, a grotesque, d-dishonorable h-horse killer. Oh, the shame, the shame! The pissing and m-moaning by the von Bayer family. It was wonderful." Marya giggled again.

"What about you? As I understand it, you were also a suspect."

"Of course, they tried to pin everything on me. I was an American. An o-outsider. Very c-convenient. So m-many questions. Blah, blah, blah in their funny accents. W-wouldn't sh-shut their m-mouths. Poor F-fackler."

"Fackler?"

"Rudi F-Fackler, the cop."

"And what did Herr Fackler think was your motive?"

"All the girlsh. The shtrange Kurt needed to k-keep his d-dick hard." Marya was sinking fast. "I hated Kurt, F-fackler said.

I wanted to disgrace him. Blah, blah, blah. All F-fackler had was circumstance. No proof." She grinned happily. She wobbled. She blinked. She opened her mouth wide and held it open.

I made sure I had plenty of room to get out of the way if she suddenly hurled. "Are you okay, Marya? Is there anything I can get you?"

"I can s-see that you're a good p-person, M-mr. Denson. If anybody from G-germany or one of these b-breeders comes to you telling s-stories about me, beware. I m-might be rude and outspoken, but it's true that I'm being framed."

Marya clapped her hand over her mouth. After a moment she took it off. Her eyes turned wide. "Got the spins. I think I need to close my eyes for a few m-minutes and con-concentrate. I'll be all"—*hic*—"right." She closed her eyes.

All right, I thought. *She's passed out.* I waited for a couple of minutes. Seeing no stirring on the part of Marya, I started to get up.

Marya's eyes opened and she blasted a hole in the wall just above my head. "A deal's a deal," she said evenly.

I sat back down. "Sorry," I said.

"Too damn m-much Scotch for me," she said. Again, she clapped her hand over her mouth. She recovered. Again her eyes turned wide. "I'll be"—*hic*—"okay. Give me a little time." She adjusted her vest to make sure her fancy breasts were covered. The strange protected, she closed her eyes again.

I waited ten minutes, then got up and left. Marya von Bayer, who was either passed out or pretending to be passed out, did nothing to stop me.

13 · Kriminalhauptkommissar *Fackler*

The next morning, Annie and I received a call from a man identifying himself as *Kriminalhauptkommissar* Rudi Fackler of the Criminal Investigation Division of the German state of Baden-Wurttemberg in the southern part of that country.

"*Kriminalhauptkommissar*. That's quite a mouthful for an English speaker."

"It means that I am what you could call a captain. I would like to talk to you about unresolved questions having to do with the killing of jumping horses in Europe and two murders. Your name was given to me by a gentleman from the Ad Hoc Committee to Save the Spanish Mustang."

"One moment, Herr Fackler." I put my hand over the receiver and told Annie the deal.

Annie said, "Invite him for supper."

I did and Fackler graciously accepted the invitation. I described how to get to our cabin: west from Portland on Highway 26; north on a back road north through Vernonia to a highway on the north bank of the Columbia River; west along the Columbia to Elk Creek; south along Elk Creek to Jump-Off Joe Creek on Whorehouse Meadow.

"Say again, Mr. Denson?"

"I have no idea how Jump-Off got its name," I said. "There were large mining and timber camps near here in the last century, which explains the likely origins of Whorehouse Meadow."

At two in the afternoon, *Kriminalhauptkommissar* Rudi Fackler parked his rented Nissan beside my VW bus. He got out and stood, stretching, looking out at the expanse of weeds and wildflowers, listening to the clicking of bugs and the distant trill of a meadowlark. He was a small man, perhaps five-foot-four and maybe 130 pounds, looking casual in gray slacks, off-white pullover with a turtleneck and Adidas running shoes. He wore dark glasses and a black beret tilted at a rakish angle. He was dark-complexioned with dark brown hair. His face was dominated by a large nose, nothing to match W. C. Fields's proboscis, but close. He had a high forehead, small mouth, and hardly any chin at all.

Kriminalhauptkommissar Fackler did not look anything like Clint Eastwood playing Dirty Harry Callahan or Warren Beatty playing Dick Tracy. But then again, the German taxpayers were likely more interested in low crime rates than promoting cops who were good-looking studs.

We watched Fackler through an open window, giving him a moment to appreciate the sounds and sights and smells of our mountain meadow. He looked up. Shading his eyes with his right hand, he watched a hawk floating high above looking for a careless mouse below.

Finally, Annie and I stepped outside. I said, "It's a red-tailed hawk, very common around here. We see a bald eagle once in a while, but they're rare."

He smiled. "A most unusual headquarters for a private investigation firm. Nothing like it in Germany, I assure you."

Annie said, "Half of the headquarters." She gestured upstream. "The other cabin belongs to Willie. He's gone. If you'd like to spend the night there, you're welcome."

"We'll see how it goes." He stepped forward, hand outstretched, and we all introduced ourselves. Fackler showed us his credentials, an impressive, ornately cast badge set in a handsome leather folder.

We ushered Fackler inside. He took a seat on an aged wooden chair that we had refurbished. All the furniture in our cabin was fifty years old or more and bought at garage sales. Annie and I loved to browse garage sales. What was one man's junk was another man's treasure.

I said, "Annie and I would like to fix you a supper of elk steaks smothered in wild mushrooms. We've also got some Oddball Ale. We made it ourselves, so it might not be to your taste."

He said, "I'm a German. Of course I would like a glass of ale. I had something called a 'chicken fried' steak yesterday afternoon. I had never heard of such a thing. Meat pounded flat and breaded somewhat in the manner of schnitzel. Beef, I think it was. Served with a kind of sauce or gravy. Unusual. But quite filling. By the way, I know who killed the sixteen jumping horses in Europe and Hans Juergen and Kurt Herzog von Bayer."

"And who would that be?" I asked.

"Erika von Bayer. But it is a complicated story. Perhaps I should wait until after dinner."

14 · *Who tells the tale*

After a late afternoon walk along the creek that meandered through Whorehouse Meadow—during which time Fackler teased us with his silence on the subject of Erika and the horse killings—we took the *kriminalhauptkommissar* inside our cabin for supper.

I poured him a foaming glass of Oddball Ale.

He took a sip. His eyes widened. He held up the glass, looking at it with curiosity.

Quickly Annie said, "If you don't like it, we can get you something else."

"I think we have some commercial lager around here somewhere," I added.

"*Mein Gott!* No, no, no! What *is* this?"

I gave him the empty bottle. "Willie and I make it. We've been adjusting our formula for years. Perhaps we need to abandon our efforts."

He read the label. "'Oddball Ale. 'It makes you drunk.' A straightforward slogan. It's magnificent. The best ale I have ever had."

"We grow our own hops right here on this meadow. It's got

a little elderberry juice in it and a soupçon of wild juniper berry. We want it to be a little sour, a tad hoppy so that it's proper ale, but with a hint of fruit and a suggestion of gin. Perhaps your family would enjoy some. We'll give you however much you can get through German customs."

"Would you really?" He was genuinely pleased.

After a supper of elk steaks smothered in onions and a medley of reconstituted wild mushrooms, it was time to get down to business. I wanted to hear what Fackler had to say about Erika von Bayer.

Kriminalhauptkommissar Rudi Fackler leaned forward, his face grave. "Terrible times that we are forced to address such an outrage." He paused, thinking, then continued. "By the way, I am not here in an official capacity. When the German media carried stories from America about the killing of Spanish mustangs here in the Northwest, I took a leave of absence and bought a ticket to Portland. I don't want somebody to get away with killing sixteen champion jumping horses and murdering two people on my watch. *Nein!*"

I poured myself a glass of ale.

"Contrary to her Zone One television persona, Erika von Bayer finds it impossible to control her runaway emotions. She hired Hans Juergen to kill the jumping horses to humiliate her father, with whom she had been quarreling. She then murdered Juergen. She murdered her father out of that most dependable of motives, plain old greed. She wanted Kurt's inherited fortune and his substantial interest in BioSource. She now has her grandmother believing her mother is the murderer."

"I'm confused here. The German newspapers reported that Marya was the chief suspect."

"She was in the beginning. Marya is an unusual woman,

Mr. Denson. Easy to caricature. The media wanted her to be the guilty one, but in the end we concluded that the murderer was most likely Erika."

"You think Erika framed her mother for both horse killing and murder?"

"Yes, I do. Erika and her grandmother are both in town, by the way. You might have talked to them."

I glanced at Annie. "Yes, we did," I said. "Just last night, as a matter of fact."

"You very likely took them to be gracious and straightforward. Our psychiatrists believe Erika is a pathological liar who will fake every imaginable emotion and will do whatever is necessary to get what she wants. She is greedy. She is ambitious. She will let nothing get in her way. She is the closest thing to pure evil that I have ever encountered."

I said, "Surely, you can't suspect Erika of killing the Spanish mustangs out here. She's off covering the news for Zone One."

Fackler smiled grimly. "Oh, no, no. You are quite right. That would be impossible. She most likely hired Rachael and Willard Leopoldo to do it for her."

"Rachael being the sister of the veterinarian who collected the sperm."

"Correct. They breed mustangs themselves. They have financial problems. I believe Willard is the one who actually killed the horses. He's out and about. Plenty of opportunity. Whether or not Rachael was in on the conspiracy is harder to figure."

"You think Willard was some kind of silent partner."

Fackler shrugged. "The problem is proving the connections. Also, Erika is beautiful and charming. Marya is easy to dislike."

"And possibly easy to frame," I added.

"That too," Fackler said.

The truth, Rashoman-like, depended on who was telling the

tale. Did Gretchen do a number on Marya? Or was Marya in the process of framing Erika?

Alas, even that didn't cover the territory. Before he adjourned to Willie's cabin to spend the night, the judicious Fackler ended his summary of the conundrum by saying, "And it remains possible, of course, that a third interpretation of the facts, perhaps involving extortion or a long simmering hatred, has so far eluded us."

1 5 · Privatdetektiv *Wolfgang Strehmel*

The next day, as I sipped coffee and reviewed the notes of Annie's and my talk with Fackler—looking for telltale intersections of means, motive, and opportunity in the horse-killing puzzler—the phone rang. I picked up the receiver. A gentleman with a German accent said, "My name is Wolfgang Strehmel. I'm a *privatdetektiv.*"

"Wolfgang Spade?"

Strehmel laughed. "In a manner of speaking. I have taken a 'motel' room just outside of Portland. Is that what you Americans call them? I have a small but serviceable kitchen. I have cable television. My client, Gretchen Herzogin von Bayer, tells me you will be expecting me."

I invited him for supper, but unlike *Kriminalhauptkommissar* Fackler, Strehmel had another idea. "Do you have a favorite country pub or tavern? This is the American west. Perhaps we could go there to have some bar food, whatever it is. Perhaps one of your cheeseburgers."

"My partner and girlfriend and I have a favorite place. Timber Jim's. I'll take you there, and we'll talk and have a good time."

While we waited for Strehmel, Annie Dancer settled in at her computer to use the hacking skills that she had learned at the FBI Academy to do what the government forensics nerds could not do without a court order. She hacked her way into the bank records of the three suspects to see if there might not be a clue there somewhere. Which horsewoman was a candidate for *la desperada*?

Marya, the scorned Spanish mustang breeder—Gretchen's candidate.

The duchess herself, the elegant breeder of Hanoverian jumpers—Marya's choice.

Erika, the beautiful, accomplished rider—Fackler's suspect.

What Annie found was not any kind of gun in the literal sense, but plenty of the clichéd smoke. Erika von Bayer had funneled sixteen hits of ten thousand dollars each into a bank account in the name of Willard Leopoldo.

In addition, Annie learned that Erika had inherited more than her father's good looks. Obsessed by the solitary pleasures of the research lab, Kurt had married Marya to get what he wanted. His daughter, exuding ambition, clearly sought fame and celebrity. After her father's death, Erika cashed in the BioSource stocks he had left her in his will. Using that money and part of her father's German fortune—the family title had been given to his grandfather, a steel magnate in the late nineteenth century—she bought a huge chunk of stock issued by Zone One International.

Good things happen to beautiful correspondents who also own a substantial part of the company. The only obstacle that remained between Erika von Bayer and the rest of the BioSource fortune, and possibly the anchor chair at Zone One, was the awkward presence of her outspoken and colorful mother.

16 · Timber Jim's

Wolfgang Strehmel arrived in a rented Toyota. Whereas *Kriminalhauptkommissar* Fackler had been neat and tidy, as Americans had been taught to think of Germans, Strehmel was everything but anal-compulsive. He was a tall, robust blonde with blue eyes and a square jaw, who dressed like he had been on the road for months living entirely on recommendations by the *Lonely Planet* guidebooks. It was easy to imagine that as a young man he might have been a striker on a soccer team. Good-looking women likely took a second look.

Annie and I piled into my bus, and Strehmel followed us up the winding highway that flanked Elk Creek. Two miles later, I slowed at the mouth of Stump Creek and turned into the packed-earth parking lot of an aged tavern. A favorite both of locals and visiting hunters and fishermen, Timber Jim's was built of logs and situated under towering Douglas firs. The tavern had an old-fashioned porch. The shake roof was covered with green moss of nearly luminous green.

I parked at one of the logs that formed the boundary of the circular parking lot, which was empty, and Strehmel did the same. We got out. A wind kicked up, lowing mournfully in the tops of the Douglas firs. I stood for a moment, feeling the cool, piney breeze and listening to the lowing wind. Emerson once said each day was a God delivered unto us.

We tromped across the porch and into the familiar interior of Timber Jim's, which was like a classic old car, a 1957 Chevrolet, say, that had been kept in its original condition. The hardwood floor was worn from years of being tromped upon by fishermen and hunters and loggers. The walls and ceiling were browned from years of accumulated cigarette smoke. The bar had a brass rail at the bottom for customers who liked to stand while they got loaded. Spaced intermittently along the rail were brass spittoons for those gentlemen whose cheeks poked out from gross wads of chewing tobacco. The high stools had tops that spun.

Behind the bar, a handsome mirror was a boon accessory for covertly checking the progress of a peeling nose or the contents of a blouse at the other end of the bar.

And upon the polished hardwood bar there sat gallon jars of pickled eggs, pickled Polish sausage, and long, skinny pepperoni sausages, hard as ropes and tasty as all get-out. The ceramic handles of the draught beer spigots were works of art from days gone past.

Behind the bar where earnest gentlemen ordinarily bellied up was a massive fireplace faced with polished river rocks. The tavern had a shuffleboard. It also had a pool table sans coin slot—one paid by the hour—and a bristle dartboard, not one of those plastic obscenities. Timber Jim's was a place where old-timers from the days of Studebakers and Kaiser Fraziers had told stories of buck fever, flushed ringnecks, and steelies that threw the hook. They regaled newcomers and city slickers with descriptions of Roosevelt elk with racks so big that Baron Munchausen would blush to tell the tale. With rain and snow outside, and the barkeep wooing the fire, the gentlemen in Timber Jim's had enjoyed telling jokes about everything from Tricky Dick's sweaty lip to Billy Clinton's popsicle prick.

The patrons, leaning against the bar, rested their feet on a brass rail at the base of the bar. The proprietor, Timber Jim, periodically polished all the spittoons, except one from which he only occasionally removed the brownish green crud.

Timber Jim's was empty. Upon entering, I spit into the dirty spittoon. So did Annie.

Strehmel looked puzzled.

I said, "It's the custom to spit once in this spittoon upon entering and leaving Timber Jim's. Bad luck not to. Nobody ever told me the history of the spittoon, and I've never asked."

Strehmel spit into the container. Looking at the other spittoons, he said, "It doesn't look like anybody uses the others."

Timber Jim, a large, hulking man with a huge black beard, emerged from the back. "Denson! Annie!"

I introduced Wolfgang Strehmel to Jim, after which we ordered bottles of Henry Weinhardt beer and Timber Jim's cheeseburgers and French fries, big chunks of potato cooked with their skins on. It was time to get down to business.

Wolfgang Strehmel repeated the sequence of events leading to Kurt's murder that I already heard from the three von Bayer women and Rudi Fackler. "Marya framed her husband for killing horses to get even with him for his infidelities and then blew him up, blaming the duchess." He sighed deeply and chomped down on his cheeseburger.

I refilled his wineglass.

"I read in your local newspaper that Marya is despised by the other mustang breeders. They mock her. Is that true?"

"So they tell me," I said.

"I assure you, being ridiculed is more than sufficient reason for her to kill the stallions of other breeders." Strehmel took another sip of Oddball and leaned forward, looking me straight in the eyes. "Kurt had his choice of lady friends. Marya had a collection of photographs of them."

"Beauties, I take it."

Strehmel said, "Extraordinary, most of them. All Marya had to do was look in the mirror to see that she did not have, what is the horse breeder's term?"

"Good conformation. She has poor conformation, the human equivalent of a sway-backed, spavined mare. Who took the pictures of the girls?"

"Heinz Steiner, Marya's passionately loyal accountant and gopher. He will apparently do anything for her. If you discount Erika as a suspect, there are two theories of what happened. One is that Marya hired the stable hand to kill the horses, then murdered Juergen herself. The second is that Steiner murdered Juergen for her. Hard to believe she would know how to rig a car bomb. Most likely, Steiner did that. It's possible that Steiner is bearing a bad case of unrequited love for Marya, but that seems far-fetched."

I laughed. "Knowing Marya."

Strehmel smiled grimly. "If you have enough money, you can find somebody to do almost anything. Kurt's family did not approve of his crass opportunism, but he wanted his own Bio-Source lab in Baden Baden, and he got it. When Marya went to a party with him, she was viewed as an object of curiosity, a kind of freak. Just about the time Kurt's stallions began going under, Marya started flying back and forth to Brazil, the plastic surgery capital of the world, having her face and body rearranged. By any chance, have you ever seen the lady?"

"Once. And more of her than I would have liked, thanks."

Annie, who knew the story, burst out laughing. I repeated the details for Strehmel.

He listened, enthralled. "Mustang Marya! That must have

been something. I have not had such an, ah, intimate meeting with Frau von Bayer, thank God."

We fell silent for a moment, thinking.

Then I said, "In Marya's shoes, I'd likely have gotten a little sore too."

Strehmel nodded in agreement. "Unfortunately, Kurt's chasing women does not give Marya license to kill sixteen European jumpers and two human beings, not to mention twenty-two of your mustangs." He frowned. "If others get in her way, Marya will have them murdered as well."

I said, "Marya might be a monster, but don't you agree that it remains possible, as she claims, that she is the one being framed? Your own client has motive. She ran the von Bayer stables with her son. She knew Hans Juergen. She wanted her son to be a winner on the jumping circuit."

Strehmel frowned. "Kurt was Duchess Gretchen's favorite, that's true. It's also so that she is a forceful and determined woman."

"And judging from my brief conversation with her, she did not take his death lightly."

He suppressed the flicker of a smile. "That's putting it mildly. And yes, in fairness I should add that the emotion and complications of the triangle among son, mother, and wife can sometimes be lethal."

"You might want to think about this." I gave Strehmel a printed summary of Annie's computer research.

Annie and I watched him carefully as he read it. When he finished, he handed it back, sighing deeply.

"Well, what do you think?" I asked.

"I think I will likely find the horse killer and murderer, not you, Herr Denson. Odd that I seem to be the one with imagination, me being a plodding Kraut and you being a clever American and all."

"Oh?"

Strehmel glanced at his watch. "It's late. I have a long drive back to Portland." He stood and scribbled a number on a German language business card. "If you figure out who the killer really is, do give me a call. Perhaps we can work together to bring a little justice to both sides of the Atlantic."

17 · Butt 'em up

We'd no sooner seen Wolfgang off to Portland than we got a cell phone call from Willie, who was with Bob Humping Buck in Bob's cabin in the shadows of Riddle Mountain. "Yo, chief! What are you and Annie up to besides trying to destroy your bed? Those things are made for sleeping too, you know."

"Okay, okay, knock it off. What is it, Tonto? What do you want?"

"Help, if I can get it. After the BLM got curious, the mysterious chopper stopped flying. Bob and I think they've likely reverted to a more old-fashioned way of moving around."

"And that would be?"

"By horseback. The BLM honcho says he doesn't have the people to put in the field on horseback. Besides that, he says, they'd likely fall off their mounts and break a bunch of bones, and there'd be hurt feelings, annoying forms to fill out, and maybe allegations of incompetence in the newspapers. Promotions denied. Lawsuits. Who the hell knows?"

"You're talking Gerald Riggin here?"

"That's him, the guy who manages the two herds down here. How did you know that?"

"We saw him being interviewed on public television."

"Riggin is remarkably sensible for a bureaucrat. Given the horsebleep about the dead stallions, he wants to find out who these people are as much as we do. Bob and I want to go after 'em ourselves, but when we find 'em it would be good to have a couple of riders on our flanks to make sure they don't double back on us. If you can sit in a saddle and focus a pair of binoculars at the same time, you can do the job."

"A couple of riders. You mean Annie and me."

"If Annie doesn't know how to ride, Bob'll teach her."

Willie scorned jeeps, SUVs, and other racket-producing off-the-trail vehicles driven by obnoxious morons. I didn't like them either. They ranked right down there with powerboats as aesthetic puke. Bob had plenty of range for our horses, Bodan and Badgerman, and we tithed ourselves yearly to pay for their hay and such veterinarian fees as were necessary. They were ours, but not really. Mostly, they were ridden by Bob's nephews.

Since Annie had moved in with me, I'd been spending more time with her and less on outings with Willie. Where would I rather be, saddled up and on the trail with Willie and Bob, or in my cabin popping corn with Annie? In the year she had been with me, I had yet to take her riding.

I said, "What do you say, Annie, you want to go play cowboys and Indians with Willie and Bob Humping Buck?"

Annie perked up. She was a gamer, ready for anything. "Really? Sure. I'm anxious to meet Bob Humping Buck. You're always talking about him."

"Bob says the Apache translation is more direct and unembarrassed, but he adopted the euphemism out of respect for us hoity-toity white eyes. Says the usual white eyes wouldn't say 'manure' if his mouth was full of it. When Bob gets to know you, he'll start razzing you. His way of expressing affection. For now let's butt 'em up and move 'em out."

"Butt 'em up?"

"Plop 'em in the saddle. What horseback riders do," I said.
I sang:

> *Well, I'm an old cowhand*
> *From the Rio Grande*
> *My legs ain't bowed*
> *And my cheeks ain't tanned*

"Right," she said dryly.

I dumped the old maids from the popcorn bowl into the trash can, and we set about gathering boots, sleeping bags, and the seasoning mix that I used as the camp cook, a mixture that Willie and I had concocted: dried onions, garlic, carrots, and celery. That plus a couple of cases of Oddball Ale for the cabin. We faced an eight- to ten-hour drive from Whorehouse Meadow through Portland and over Cascade Mountains to Burns, maybe more. Climbing the Cascades was a real grunt for the forty-horsepower engine of my microbus, which is what Volkswagon first called it. After the miniskirt became fashionable in the late 1960s, people started pasting the prefix mini- onto everything, including the hip, buzzing box. Microbus. Minibus. Same dif.

The two cabins that served as the Whorehouse Meadow headquarters of Denson, Dancer, and Sees the Night were in the extreme northwest corner of the state just below Washington. The BLM's Burns District wild horse range was in the southeast corner with Nevada to the south and Idaho to the east—part of what the geographers called the Great Basin. To get there, Annie and I had to leave rainland and pass through the Cascade Mountains.

Annie, looking forward to the adventure ahead, was showing signs of horse fever. Well, good for her. She was likely going to get her fill of horses before the weekend was over.

When we got to Highway 26 the next morning, and I had the bus's engine wound up tightly, she said, "Tell me about riding with Willie and Bob. When have you usually ridden with them?"

I said, "To go fly fishing in high mountain lakes or in inaccessible stretches of river. That and hunting mule deer and Rocky Mountain elk with bows and arrows. Willie and Bob are the bow hunters. I can hardly hit the broad side of a barn with an arrow."

Annie rolled her eyes. "You've got that right." I had a couple of targets that I liked to set up in the meadow where we lived. A week after she moved in with me, I bought Annie a bow, and she learned for herself the viscerally satisfying sound of an arrow going *thump* into its target. There was no explaining the slight gut rush produced by that *thump* other than, possibly, it was a genetic inheritance, a lingering memory of our ancestors on the hunt. A pub dart thumping into a proper bristle board—not wood or plastic—offered a similar satisfaction.

I said, "The truth is I go along so Bob and Willie can fill out my tag. I'm an okay camp cook. On our hunting and fishing trips, they call me John Cooks Good."

"You go along so they can get more game. I see. And what kind of horse is Bodan?"

"A leopard Appaloosa stallion. He likes me. Remembers me from one hunting trip to the next." I glanced at Annie as she poured us both cups of coffee from our thermos.

"And a leopard Appaloosa is?'"

"A white horse with leopardlike spots that can be almost any color. Bodan's spots are black, very dramatic, which is what makes him choice. Lotta folks with Appaloosa mares want a shot at getting a colt that looks like him. A snow Appaloosa is dark with white spots."

We drove for a while in silence. "By the way," I said, "before we left, I looked up 'equicide,' the killing of a horse, in the dictionary. Not there."

She put my coffee in the plastic holder between the seats. "Probably because of the belief that humans have souls and animals don't. If you give preferential status to horses, you'll have nutballs trying to get people prosecuted for killing cockroaches and dung beetles."

I took a sip of coffee. "Bodan is more affectionate, soulful, and deserving of legal protection than some of the scumbags I've encountered."

At two o'clock in the morning, I pulled into an all-night convenience store near Sisters in the high Cascades. We refilled our thermos, and I bought some sugar cubes, a ten-pound bag of potatoes, and Sloan's Liniment. I said, "If I forgot the sugar cubes, Bodan would be disappointed."

"And this is for?" She held up the bottle of Sloan's Liniment.

"You'll see. If Willie was able to score some DMSO, we won't need it."

Annie had no idea what DMSO was. If we had any hard riding ahead, there would be a time when she would likely handle a brown bottle of DMSO like there was a benevolent genie inside.

18 · *Of pintos and Appaloosas*

At six o'clock in the morning, having kept in touch with Willie by cell phone, we pulled into the dirt yard in front of Bob Humping Buck's hunting shack on the western flank of Riddle Mountain. Willie and Bob both had their pickups parked in front of their horse trailers to the right of the cabin. To the left, four horses in a corral, curious about our arrival, crowded up against the lodgepoles.

When I parked the bus under a juniper next to their pickups and trailers, Bob and Willie burst out of the door, grinning broadly.

Annie and I climbed out of the bus, stretching our legs. I had the ten-pound bag of potatoes in hand. We had taken turns driving, but we were still pooped. The second we hit the ground, we could smell the coffee. Well, the coffee and the liver and onions and frying potatoes.

Willie introduced Annie to Bob, a stout, rugged Nez Perce with a broad face and high cheekbones. He was quick with a grin. After he shook Annie's hand, he leaned back, smiling appreciatively, "Why you *are* some kind of good-looking filly, Annie. Here I thought Willie was feeding me a ration. And I'm surprised that you'd have anything to do with a screwup like Denson." He clapped me about the shoulders. "No offense, Dumsht."

"I don't see you turning down my fried biscuits," I said.

Bob laughed broadly. "Sometimes you can be a mean son of a bitch, you know that? Spiteful white eyes. Come on inside and take a load off, you two. Willie and I've fried up a mess of deer liver, and we've got some spuds on too. Brought that liver down in my cooler just for Cooks Good," he said.

I knew that was the truth.

The exterior of the cabin, fashioned from crude, rough boards, was unpainted, but Bob had taken the unusual step of building a covered front porch, transforming it from a windowed shack to a Riddle Mountain villa. From the porch, a sporting gentleman could spit 'bacca without rising from his butt or stand to take a leisurely piss without interrupting the talk of where the pronghorns were grazing in the morning or the mule deer were bedded down in the late afternoon. The roof was covered with black tarpaper. The cabin had small windows flanking the door and one on the left end, facing the horse corral. A length of duct tape covered a crack in the right front window.

Glancing at the horses in the corral, Annie preceded me into the cabin. The single room contained a table with four rickety chairs likely dating from the 1950s, a homemade bunk bed with foam rubber slabs for mattresses, and a wood stove made from a metal barrel cut in half, showing by its seams that it had been made by a beginning welder. For shelves, the resourceful Bob had stacked empty wooden boxes along one wall. Forty years earlier the boxes had been used to ship fruit from Yakima Valley. The boxes held rolls of toilet paper; a cast-iron Dutch oven; a large can, sans label, from which protruded the handles of forks, spoons, and assorted knives, both eating and cutting; gallon jars of pinto beans, navy beans, rice, flour, and jerky; quart

jars of sugar and dried chilies—jalapeno, serrano, and ha-
banero; a can of coffee with a plastic lid; a can of shortening,
also with plastic lid; a basket piled high with onions and bulbs
of garlic; a large can of black pepper; plus cans of chili powder,
baking soda, and baking powder; and a container of Morton's
iodized salt.

The cabin had no electricity. A kerosene lantern hung from a
nail in the ceiling above the table.

I plopped the bag of potatoes next to the makeshift shelves.

Bob cleared his throat. "If you feel nature's call, Annie, I'm
afraid all we have is a pine tree out back. No windows facing that
way though, and you can rest assured we men are all gentlemen."

"And scholars of the first order," I said quickly.

Willie said, "We figured we'd let you two get some rest today.
Gerald Riggin will be over tonight to give us the latest skinny on
where these assholes are."

Annie looked surprised. "The BLM man?"

Bob said, "Oh, hell yes. Gerald's a special breed of bureaucrat. He has the beginnings of a brain. If it hadn't been for Gerald, the BLM hotshots would have torn down this cabin a long
time ago. You got boots? You'll need boots."

Annie blinked.

"A horsewoman's gotta have proper boots," Bob said. He got
up and retrieved a package from the top level of the bunk bed.
He gave the box to Annie. "Try these."

Annie opened the box and found a beautiful pair of boots
that looked brand-new. The leather was hand-tooled with an
elaborate pattern stained turquoise, yellow, green, and red. "My
God, they're beautiful." Annie held them up, admiring them,
her eyes wide. "And spurs too."

Bob said, "Chijuajua spurs. Silver. Try 'em on. If they don't
fit, we'll drive into Burns and get another pair."

Annie slipped on the boots and stood, looking pleased and proud. "They fit. Perfectly," she said. She strode to and fro, looking at her feet, the spurs jingling. "How on earth did you know my size?"

"Ask your friend Cooks Good," Bob said.

I said, "Those are handmade boots made by a friend of Bob's. A month ago, I ordered a pair for your birthday. I thought we might go see the Round-Up in Pendleton and take in Happy Canyon."

"You! They're beautiful!" Still admiring them, she said, "And what, may I ask, is Happy Canyon?"

"It's a kind of western theater or pageant, I guess you'd say, that retells the story of the settling of the West. The stage is huge, large enough to accommodate horses and wagon trains. It begins with Indians camping and hunting and holding powwows and so on. Then the fur trappers arrive. There is a trading rendezvous. Then come wagon trains bearing settlers. The cavalry arrives to herd the Indians onto reservations. Action ensues."

"We Injuns didn't want to live on any damn reservation," Willie said. "Who the hell would?"

I said, "There are fights with rifles and pistols loaded with blanks. George Armstrong Custer goes down at Little Big Horn. All this cowboy and Indian stuff is where Bob and some of his friends come in. Bob and Thunderballs are stars. Tell her, Bob."

Bob grinned broadly. "Some of my friends and I play warriors. Fun fighting the cavalry every year. For decades the cavalry routed us easily at Happy Canyon. Now they've rewritten the script to let us get the upper hand once in a while. Affirmative action victories for the redskin. We get to yip and yelp and carry on."

Laughing, Bob slapped his thigh in merriment. "Anyway, a

half dozen of us have trained our horses to go down in battle. At the right time, when one of the cavalry actors fires his rifle behind me, I give Thunderballs a special slap on the neck and bark in his ear. Down he goes just like he'd been shot, and I tumble off. My friends and I fight on behind the bodies of our 'dead' horses, but lose the scrimmage. It's fun and the crowds love it. Thunderballs is the best of the trained horses. His dive is so realistic you have to see it to believe it. He even throws in some death throes. He's the star of the show, and that's the truth."

"A high point of the pageant is an Indian actor giving Chief Joseph's 'from where the sun now stands I will fight no more forever' speech. Bob has played Crazy Horse for, what is it, Bob, something like twelve years now?"

"Thirteen years coming up. I love wiping out those pony soldiers. Nobody knows for sure which warrior actually put George Armstrong Custer down at Little Big Horn. But since Crazy Horse led the charge, we take a little dramatic license and claim it was that great Oglala Sioux himself."

"And you get to be Crazy Horse?" Annie asked.

Bob grinned broadly. "What an honor! Each September I get to blast that asshole Custer off his feet, never mind how it actually happened or that he's really a wheat rancher and a member of the Pendleton Chamber of Commerce. When I gallop across that stage I'm *him*, Crazy Horse. He's in me. I've got Sitting Bull in my heart and Wounded Knee on my mind." Bob paused in his narrative, then said, "George Armstrong finished last in his class at West Point. In the history books you see this great hero posing for the daguerreotype artist in his fancy blues and long, golden locks. But when they found his body at Little Big Horn, he was wearing buckskins and had his hair cut short. Put 'em together and what do you get?"

"I dunno," Annie said.

"A stupid chickenshit," Bob said, slapping his thigh as he laughed broadly.

Annie was pumped. "I want to go see Crazy Horse in action."

"A cowgirl has gotta have some snazzy boots if she's going to Happy Canyon," I said.

The boots had cost me a bundle, but the look in Annie's eyes and the joy on her face were worth a million bucks.

Annie gave me a look. "We're going to the Pendleton Round-Up and Happy Canyon this September. No arguments."

"Consider it done," I said.

Watching the horses, feeling good in her new cowboy boots, she leaned over the cast-iron skillet on the wood stove. "Don't think I've ever had liver and onions for breakfast. Smells good."

As we sat down to eat, we knew that Annie was watching the horses through the window behind the stove, wondering which one of the four she was going to ride. As a form of tease, we pretended not to notice. We were all used to horses. No biggie for us.

"Either of you two remember to get some DMSO?" I said.

"Got it," Bob said. To Annie, he said, "You know what DMSO is all about?"

"No idea," she said. "And my bet is you're not going tell me either."

Bob winked at me. "She's smart too. They tell me that can be a good thing in a woman."

"Sometimes," I said.

"Oh, shut up," Annie said. Finally she made a face and said, "Okay, you guys. I got my fancy cowboy boots. You all know I'm dying to see which horse I'm going to ride. We've finished with breakfast. Enough already. Stop the delaying. Dammit, let's go out to the corral."

Bob burst out laughing. "By God, Denson, you better watch out she doesn't use those spurs on you."

————

The second Bodan spotted me walking around the cabin, he came galloping to meet me at the edge of the corral. I leaned over the top lodgepole and gave him a half dozen cubes of sugar in the palm of my hand. His velvety soft lips scooped them up eagerly. I said, "Well, what do you say, Bodan, ready to cover a little ground?"

I was making Annie wait to find out which was to be her horse. Finally, she said, "Aw, come on, you jerks. Give me a break."

Bob opened the gate to the corral, gave a whistle, and yelled, "Yo, Ms. Fab!" A beautiful little filly came running. She had an irregular patch of rich brown down her back. She had patches of brown running down her rump and rear legs. The patches of brown continued down her shoulders and front legs, and under her throat. The sides of her torso and neck were white. She had three white legs beneath the knees and one solid leg.

Bob said, "Annie, this is Ms. Fab, a frame overo. Ms. Fab, this is Annie Dancer, who used to be an FBI agent. As you'll note, Ms. Fab, Annie doesn't weigh more than a sack of feathers, so you can cover a lot of ground without working up a lather."

Eyes wide, pleased in the extreme, Annie snatched some sugar from me and gave it to Ms. Fab. "You're spectacular, Ms. Fab. Truly."

Ms. Fab accepted the sugar with gratitude, looking up at Annie with blue eyes. She had a white blaze on her forehead.

Bob said, "Ms. Fab is two generations removed from the wild. You sometimes get those blue eyes in an overo."

Willie said, "An overo is either predominantly dark or white, Annie. The white can cross over the mane, but not the back. At least one of their legs will be dark. Their tail is one color. Also, the frame pattern on both sides is identical, although the markings on their face are sometimes asymmetrical."

Willie then greeted his own horse, a buckskin stallion. Willie said, "Badgerman is one generation removed from the wild."

"He's beautiful."

Willie shook his head. "His daddy was from the Sulphur herd in Utah's Needle Range."

"He's the real deal," Bob said.

Willie said, "Badgerman is slightly smaller than most of the horses you're used to seeing. He also has a shorter back because he only has five ribs, not six. But take a close look at his ears. If somebody tells you he has a mustang descended from the Kiger or Riddle Mountain herd or from the Needle Mountains, the first thing you do is take a look at his ears and face. Go ahead, he's friendly."

Annie studied Badgerman's head, which was slightly convex on top rather than straight. The tops of his ears, rimmed with black, were notched on the inside with the tips leaning toward each other. The interiors were a light cream color, but the top third of the outsides were dark buckskin, close to black. He had black under his jaws. His face, a kind of "mask," featured a black pyramid from nose to forehead, and parallel black lines from eyes to mouth. A black line ran up his spine, and there were thin black stripes on the front of his legs and chest and on the bottom of his ribs.

Willie said, "Badgerman has a heavier mane than your usual western horse. His chest is more narrow and more deep. The legs of most horses are parallel where they join the chest. Badgerman's form a slight A. See there."

Annie walked around front and looked at Badgerman's chest.

"His back is shorter because he only has five lumbar vertebrae, not six." Willie ran his hand down Badgerman's left lower leg and lifted his hoof. "He has what we call a 'mule' foot, thick walls and concave soles to resist bruising from rocks." He put the hoof back on the ground and patted the horse's neck.

Bob said, "You want to see a real horse, watch this!" Bob put two fingers to his mouth and whistled shrilly.

Annie's eyes widened. A white stallion came running. He had a patch of black over his ears, a black blaze on his chest, and a black mane and tail. Grand, he was. Dramatic.

Running an arm under the the his horse's neck, Bob said, "Thunderballs is a 'medicine hat' tovero, a predominantly white horse with both overo and tobiano characteristics. The black over his ears is the chief's war 'bonnet.' The black blaze on his chest is his 'shield.' We redskins have always believed a medicine hat has magical powers to protect the rider from harm."

"A horse for a chief or a great warrior, neither of which describes Bob Humping Buck," Willie said dryly. "Call him Chief Bunghole maybe."

"Easy, easy. You know damn well flattery will get you everywhere," Bob said.

Willie said, "Can't take anything away from Thunderballs, though. Bob shows him off every year in the Pendleton Round-Up, the Cheyenne Frontier Days, and the Calgary Stampede. That's not to mention the Rose Parade in Portland and the Tournament of Roses Parade in Pasadena."

Bob said, "Those folks down there in Pasadena endure such mindless shit and huckster's assertions of quality, all that plastic and contrived drama, that it was a treat for them to see something truly beautiful. The guy on the loudspeaker describing the parade had a rich, deep voice. 'Now ladies and gentlemen here comes a horse you won't soon forget, the Nez Perce rider Bob Humping Buck on *Thunnnnnnnderballs.*' He held that *N* for what seemed like a full minute. The people just went out of their minds cheering for Thunderballs. You should have seen him prance, head up, saying to them: 'Here I am, folks, a fabulous stallion. Take a look at my war bonnet. Check out my shield. Ain't I some kind of hot damn stud?' "

"I bet they knew he was talking to them," Annie said.

"Sure they did," Bob said. "The street was a din. The moment belonged to Thunderballs. Gave me goose bumps. I'll remember it to my grave."

Overcome by the sweet memory, Bob Humping Buck gave his horse's neck an affectionate squeeze.

19 · *Padre Eusebio's legacy*

Annie and I stayed at the cabin, giving us a chance to rest and for Annie to get acquainted with Ms. Fab, while Willie and Bob took twenty-gauge shotguns out to rustle up some supper. We agreed that Bob would teach Annie how to ride in the morning when we got underway. For me to teach her how to ride was not good. I wasn't the best rider myself, and for me to try to teach Annie was like a man attempting to teach his wife how to drive a car.

Just before sundown Willie and Bob came back with a pheasant, four grouse, and a half dozen quail.

Willie and I cleaned and plucked the birds. I whacked them up with the cabin's meat cleaver and rolled them in some flour mixed with salt and pepper. I threw them into a cast-iron skillet to fry along with some chopped onions and garlic and a judicious crumbling of dried chilies for flavor, not heat. Then I put some water on to boil for the potatoes. When the birds were starting to crust up nicely, smelling good and with the onions browning, a Toyota SUV rolled into the yard.

I looked momentarily alarmed. It was off-season for game birds. Bob waved off my concern. "Not to worry," he said, and rose to meet our guest.

I looked out of the window and saw that it was Gerald Riggin.

Riggin walked through the door without knocking. "Welcome, Gerald," he said loudly. "Boy, oh boy, something smells good."

Bob and Willie both shook his hand, after which Bob introduced Annie and me.

When the introductions were finished, Gerald leaned over the skillet, inhaling deeply. "No better smell than chicken frying with onions."

"Poached," Bob said. "Not chicken either."

"Poached? Really? I could have sworn they were frying. Does that chicken look poached to you?" Gerald winked at Annie and me.

Bob said, "Willie and I promised you a good meal. That's why we had old Chief Cooks Good come up with a real mess."

After supper, we all pitched in to clear up the dishes; even Gerald helped out.

When the table was free, Gerald spread out a BLM map on top, explaining to Bob and Willie where the Riddle Mountain herd was currently grazing, where the helicopter had previously been seen in relation to the herd, and where three unknown riders had recently been spotted. The lines that measured the elevation and contours of the geography were confusing to me. I watched, uncomprehending, as Gerald ran his finger along the map. Bob and Willie followed his narrative intently.

When they were finished, Gerald folded his map, put it back in its folder, and gave it to Bob. "You want it, it's yours."

"Appreciate it," Bob said. "Anything that will help."

Gerald said, "I'm putting my butt on the line, helping you out like this. But there are some times a guy has to take a chance. We should put wild horses before rules and regulations. Until we know for sure, we do what we have to do."

"We'll ride them down," Willie said.

Gerald grimaced. "There's one other thing I should tell you.

Earlier tonight, somebody calling herself Mustang Mary posted a drawing on multiple Internet Web sites, claiming to be the horse killer. I downloaded it and brought it over." He dug into another folder and pulled out a piece of paper and laid it on the table. We all gathered around.

The paper contained a drawing of a naked beauty with outsized breasts and rump riding a twisting, bucking mustang. Smoke rose from the area of the nude cowgirl's genitals.

Below the drawing, a message in tiny block letters:

HE SURE WAS A FROG WALKER—HE HEAVED A BIG SIGH

HE LACKED ONLY WINGS TO BE ON THE FLY

TURNED HIS OLD BELLY RIGHT UP TO THE SUN

HE SURE WAS A SUN-FISHING SON OF A GUN

THIS STRAWBERRY ROAN IS NEZ PERCE NED, LATE OF BOISE, A HAND-
     SOME MUSTANG. I SLIPPED A NEEDLE BETWEEN TWO RIBS,
     STRAIGHT INTO HIS HEART. TURNED HIS OLD BELLY RIGHT UP TO THE
     SUN.

CALL ME MUSTANG MARY, A HORSE-KILLING BITCH.

I RODE THAT OLD BRONCO WITH NARY A STITCH.

"Jesus!" Bob said.

"Wonderful," I added, suddenly remembering that when I had my wild meeting with Marya von Bayer, she had referred to herself as Mustang Marya. A coincidence?

Gerald said, "I talked to the FBI guy Sheb Goodall a few minutes before I drove over this afternoon. He says the FBI is wondering how a crackpot would know about the needle. It's never been reported in the media that Nez Perce Ned took a needle between the ribs, which he did, straight into his heart."

Gerald put the Mustang Mary printout back in its folder, and we adjourned to the porch, taking our chairs with us. It was a starry night with a big white moon. We lit up joints to go with our Oddball Ale. Since we only had four chairs, I sat on a Yakima Valley peach box, as I had at supper.

Bob said, "In all the TV coverage of the killing of the mustang stallions, I never heard anything at all about just how in the hell it was they wound up out here in Oregon. To hear most folks talk, you'd think these horses meant more to white eyes than us redskins." He smiled. "Sorry. We 'Native Americans,'" he added sarcastically.

"Tell 'em, Bob," Willie said.

"Yes," Annie said quickly.

"Of course, the Spanish brought the horses to the Caribbean and Mexico. The Catholic padres wanted to turn us all into Christians, even if they had to shoot us to save our souls. Well sir, a certain Padre Eusebio Kino started breeding mustangs on a spread outside of Sonora. He pushed north, handing out crosses and teaching us dumb redskins to genuflect and the rest of it. To encourage us to listen up, he gave us horses. We Apache liked the horses, to hell with the Pope and that Jesus, Joseph, and Mary crap. With horses, we could follow and hunt game. And with horses, we could defend ourselves against you white eyes."

I said, "I take it a well-trained Spanish mustang was worth a whole lot of wampum."

Bob laughed broadly and gave Willie a whack on the shoulder. "Valuable ain't the word for it. We started riding south to get more horses. And when we got back, well, let me put it this way, we weren't stupid. We had to fight for those horses, so we worked a hard deal to anybody who wanted one."

"Until you were eventually breeding your own."

"Oh, hell yes. Us. The Kiowa. The Sioux. You name the tribe. Lewis and Clark got some ponies from the Shoshone. The Texas Rangers had a hell of a time with Comanche riding horses. And ask George Armstrong Custer what some hard-riding braves on fast ponies can accomplish if they put their minds to it." Watching me over the fire, he grinned broadly. His ancestors had fought the good fight against an overwhelming foe. Not a little pride there. In his moccasins, I'd have felt the same way.

He said, "A thoroughbred is bred for racing. A quarter horse is fast over short distances and are good for roping and steer wrestling. But these Indian ponies have a little skill of their own. A white eyes named Frank Hopkins rode a mustang from Galveston, Texas, to Rutland, Vermont, in thirty-one days, two weeks ahead of his next competitor. Emmett Bislawn won the 1966 Bitterroot endurance race on a sixteen-year-old buckskin stallion named Yellow Fox who had been retired and put out to stud for years."

Grinning, Bob slapped his thigh. "Why the hell you reckon those cavalry pricks had such a hard time running us Injuns down? Yellow Fox's granddaddies just rode those horse soldiers straight into the ground. Those horses were our way of life. If anybody wants to keep the breed in business, it's us."

We lit up another joint and passed it around, taking thoughtful draws.

"Maybe Willie can tell us what this is really all about," Bob said.

Willie grunted.

We waited. Was Willie really Coyote in human form? Was he a sorcerer? Or was that all nonsense? There was something about Willie that made him special, but just what was hard to define. Although he looked like he was in his robust fifties, his anecdotes and references to his past made him far older than that. He was seemingly ageless. He was wiry and fit, tough as rawhide.

The Coyote part, in my opinion, was horse dumplings. A shaman? I could give him that. A sorcerer? No way.

Finally, Willie said, "Koonran maybe."

Bob's chair scraped on the porch.

"Koonran?" Annie asked.

I knew who, or perhaps more accurately, what Koonran was

supposed to be, but it wasn't my place to try to explain what I thought was a fantasy of the American Indian. It was their mythology, not mine.

Annie glanced at me. "Well?"

I shrugged.

She wasn't about to accept silence for an answer. "Who is Koonran?" she said again.

I sipped some Oddball. I took another toke on the joint. I flew.

20 · *On the good ship* Peculiar

I am in a sandstorm. I look up at the sun that is pale yellow and barely visible. I see the rigging of a huge sailing vessel with towering masts. I hear the snap and pop of sails as the ship tacks. There is shouting. About me, cowboys are scrambling through the blowing sand, their boots clomp, clomp, clomping on the deck, spurs jingling. Boots? What is this?

I lean over the rail. We are plunging forward, but not on water. We are just above the ground. Below me, passing by the hull of the vessel, are sagebrush and clumps of stunted cacti. I am on a ghost ship sailing an invisible sea that's just above the desert.

A gust of wind slams against me. I grab for the rail. I cling to it for all I'm worth.

Beside me, with a kerchief tied across his face, is Willie Sees the Night. "Hold on, Dumsht," he cries. He is wearing leggings and moccasins, but is bare from the waist up. He is covered with tattoos. He is holding an outsized spear with a line attached to the butt. It is a harpoon. Willie with a harpoon?

Forward, I hear a thumping on the deck. "Denson! Denson!"

I am being summoned by whoever is making the thumping sounds.

"It's there. Right in front of us. Dammit, Denson, where are you? I want you and your redskin pal up here now!"

"We better do it, Dumsht," Willie says.

I follow Willie forward, clutching the rail so as not to be swept overboard onto the desert.

At length we arrive at the bow. I see a figure striding to and fro in the fury of blowing sand. T has a peg leg. The leg goes *thump, thump, thump* as it hits the deck.

I draw closer, squinting my eyes. His leonine mane of nearly white hair is whipping in the wind. He's sore as hell. He brandishes a knobby stick that he uses as a cane. The stick has a polished burl on the top.

Leaning against the knob on top of his stick, he cries, "Denson! Willie! Where the hell have you two been?"

Suddenly the vessel pitches sideways. I sprawl face first on the deck, which is strewn with horse dumplings and blowing straw. It reeks of horse urine.

T grabs me by the scruff of the neck. He yanks me erect. "On your feet, damn you. We've got her now. *La desperada!*"

I glare at him. What the hell is this all about?

He yells at me. "Whales! Wild horses! Wind storms! Ships plying the desert sands! All this confusion piss you off, does it?"

"Damn right it does," I shout. "Screw this nutty crap."

T looks contemptuous. "Oh, grow up, Denson. You wanted to fly, okay. I had Willie send you flying. And this is what you found. Life is full of the incongruous and the unexpected. Just who in the hell do you think led those whales onto the beach? Do you think that was just a leviathan oopsie? What's wrong with you?"

"Look there!" Willie shouts.

Clutching the rail, I see it. A white whale with leopard Appaloosa spots rises from the desert and rolls, disappearing back into the earth with a loud slap of its wide, paddle-shaped tail. It is a beaver's tail. It has a hideous face. It is part whale, part beaver, but all monster. It exudes unfathomable malice. Its eyes are feral and hateful. It has two huge front teeth like a beaver. Streams of frothy green trail from its mouth, blown from the wind. Lipstick. It has lipstick around its mouth. A monster with lipstick. Is it Marya, Gretchen, or Erika? Impossible to tell.

I join Willie at the rail. We pile into a whaling boat with a crew of young cowboys in chaps, cowboy hats, boots, and spurs. They grab the oars, and we are off after the leopard Appaloosa monster whale with lipstick and the teeth and tail of a beaver. They sing lustily as they dip their oars into nothing at all and row hard.

> *I ride an old paint, I lead an old Dan.*
> *I'm going to Montana to throw a hoolie han'.*
> *They feed in the coulees, they water in the draw.*
> *Their tails are all matted, their backs are all raw.*

They're supposed to be singing sea chanteys, the dumb bastards. What's wrong with T? He's got everything scrambled. A ship of the desert. An Appaloosa whale with the teeth and tail of a beaver. There is nothing about this that makes any sense.

> *Ride around little dogies, ride around real slow.*
> *For the Firey and the Snuffy, they're a rarin' to go.*

Behind us on the bow, T, nearly hysterical, is fully into his Ahab persona. "Get it! Get it! Get it! Get that evil!" he screams at us.

The surreal cowboy sailors, heeding their obsessed, maddened captain, still singing, bend their backs to the task at hand.

Old Bill Jones had a daughter and a son.
Son killed a man, and his daughter went wrong.
His wife she died in a poolroom fight.
And still he keeps singing from morning 'til night.

Willie readies his harpoon. He knows what the monster is, even if I don't. And he wants it as much as does T.

Ride around little dogies, ride around real slow.
For the Firey and the Snuffy, they're a rarin' to go.

Concentrating on the beast, arm cocked, Willie shouts at me. "This is gonna be a high desert sleigh ride, Dumsht. Grab your nuts!"

Above the howling of the storm and the shouting of the maddened T behind us, the rowers dig their oars into the blowing wind, pulling as hard as they can. Loudly they sing, lustfully.

When I die, take my saddle from the wall.
Lead me to my pony, take him out of his stall.
Put my bones on his back, point our faces to the west.
And we'll ride the prairie that we love the best.

Above the fury of the sandstorm, I can hear T shouting, "Horse killer! Horse killer! Take it under! Take it under! Do it! Do it! Do it!"

Ride around little dogies, ride around real slow.
For the Firey and the Snuffy, they're a rarin' to go.

The air is green with slime from the monster's hideous, foaming mouth. All malice it is. Hateful. The stench is enough to knock a dog off a gut wagon. I want to vomit. But I know in my gut what this is all about. We are in battle. Epic struggle.

I glance back up at T. Beneath the bowsprit of the *Peculiar,* a carved maiden plunges into the sea and emerges with water trailing from her wooden breasts.

Behind us, above the fury, having committed himself to taking the Appaloosa whale under, T screams, "You can do it, Willie. You can do it. Throw it! Throw it!"

Poised on the bow of the whaling boat that plunges into invisible swells, Willie is a warrior of warriors, proud and unafraid. He waits for the spotted beast to rise once more from the floor of the desert. Next time up, he will hurl his harpoon. It is not right for me to stand and dither. It is fitting and becoming that I join battle with this vile presence that rises inexplicably from the desert floor and sinks again.

I join in the singing, screaming the lyrics lustily, manfully as I can, at the top of my lungs:

> *I ride an old paint, I lead an old Dan.*
> *I'm going to Montana to throw a hoolie han'.*

"John! John! All you all right?"

I came around. Annie had her arm around me, her face concerned. "You had us spooked there for a moment. What happened?"

"I'm okay. Just went into a little zone there. I saw—" I shut up.

"You saw Koonran, did you?" Willie asked.

Feeling stupid, I licked my lips. "It was nothing," I said. Just how in the hell was I supposed to tell them that I had just flown out of my skin to join Queequeg and Captain Ahab in a sandstorm on a square-rigged sailing ship a couple of feet above the desert. That's not to mention the malevolent, leopard Appaloosa white whale with a beaver's tail and giant beaver teeth, wearing lipstick and with putrid green slime streaming out of its mouth. And those vile, hateful eyes!

"He saw Koonran," Willie said with finality.

Bob blinked. "You think so? Jesus!"

"Koonran being?" Gerald asked mildly.

Willie didn't say anything. Bob too remained mute.

To me, Annie said, "You tell me then, John. Dammit, you know the story. No reason to leave Gerald and me in the dark."

I didn't say anything either. This was Willie's turf, not mine.

Willie looked distracted, as though he were remembering something that happened a long time ago. Finally, softly, his face serious, Willie said, "Koonran is a shape-changer, just like me. He is evil and spiteful. We have been struggling against one another since the beginning of time. To explain him fully is complicated. Someday I'll tell you the story, Annie. You too, Gerald. You're both in this fight. You have a right to know the nature of your adversary."

Willie looked out into the starry night. "But not tonight. I need to think about this turn of events." Willie fell silent. He didn't want to talk about it anymore.

To change the subject, remembering the cowboy sailors rowing the whaleboat, I sang:

The stars at night are big and bright,

Rhythmically, I stomped my boots four times on the porch.

Deep in the heart of Oregon.

My companions, understanding what I was trying to do, all joined me for a second verse, singing lustily:

The stars at night are big and bright.

Stomp! Stomp! Stomp! Stomp!

Deep in the heart of Oregon.

Laughing, we passed the joint on another round and un-capped more Oddballs. The night air was turning chilly. In the Great Basin the days were hot and the nights were cold.

Koonran!

21 · *The perfume of DMSO*

We got an early start the next morning with Willie and me at the point. Since we expected to be traveling fast, we decided not to take a packhorse, which would slow us down. I was no fan of living on the trail without gear, what with the bugs and the cold, no showers, and having to sleep on the ground. Far better to have packhorses loaded with the accoutrements of reasonably civilized living. We packed our saddlebags with a few basics for cooking on the trail: hard-cured slab bacon, jerky, flour, baking soda, salt, pepper, Ziploc bags of sugar and coffee, and our mix of dried vegetables.

All that and both digital and 35mm cameras and lenses we needed to collect evidence on the mystery riders if they turned out to be miscreants.

We headed for the place where Gerald Riggin's BLM range managers had last seen the mysterious trio of riders. Bob and Annie fell back. Bob was to teach Annie how to ride. When she and Ms. Fab were comfortable with one another and understood one another, they would catch up. Beneath me, Bodan was full of energy, feeling good, and ready for action. I suspected few horses worth their salt were content to roam around a pasture all day waiting for their ration of hay. John Cooks Good was in the saddle. For Bodan, this was a form of play, not work. He liked it.

An hour later, Willie found the sign he was looking for. Or said he found it. I didn't see anything. After that it was slower going, with Willie staring at the ground in front of us.

After following the sign for another ninety minutes, Willie reined in under a juniper saying it was a good place to take a breather while we waited for Bob and Annie. We each took a swig of water from our canteens.

Gravely, Willie said, "We need to talk about what you saw when you went flying from the porch last night, Chief."

"It was my subconscious at work, a mild form of madness."

"Tell me what you saw."

"Ah crap, Willie!"

"Tell me."

I described my vision. When I finished, I said, "Easy enough to explain what I saw. When I was a kid, I read a novel about an obsessed captain pursuing a white whale named Moby Dick. I had to write an essay on the meaning of the whale. Was it simply revenge against a beast that had taken his leg, or was its meaning more complicated? I greeted Bodan, a leopard Appaloosa, a few minutes before we went to the porch. Then you mentioned the possibility that we were facing Koonran. You've told me before that Koonran is a beaver monster. Put them together and you get Captain Ahab chasing an Appaloosa white whale with the teeth and tail of a beaver."

"Put them together and you get coincidences," Willie said. "Tell me, did everything seem real to you? Did you really believe you were riding a sailing vessel in a sandstorm just above the desert? No feeling of being in a dream or anything."

I was reluctant to admit how real my vision or whatever it was had been. "Aw, come on, Tonto!"

"I was right. Tonight I have to tell you more about Koonran.

Annie needs to know too." He stopped. "Hear that? They'll be here in a few minutes."

I didn't hear anything. I leaned against the juniper, enjoying the fragrance. As Willie had predicted, few minutes later Bob Humping Buck and Annie Dancer emerged from the growing heat. Annie was in the lead and doing just fine on Ms. Fab.

Bob called, "She' a quick learner. Ms. Fab took to her immediately. Easy to tell if a horse likes its rider."

Annie reined in Ms. Fab. "We're best friends already. I can tell."

"She's yours," Bob said.

Annie's mouth dropped. "What?"

"She's yours. I give her to you."

Annie was stunned. "I don't have any place to keep a horse."

"I'll keep her at my place. 'Course you'll have to share her with my niece, Ellie. She has her own horses, but she likes to ride Ms. Fab too. And I get her foal."

"Wow!" Annie said.

Bob was pleased. "Done then. As long as you agree to ride her in the Westward Ho parade in Pendleton come September. If you own a special horse like Ms. Fab, you have to let others enjoy her too. Not good to keep beauty like that to yourself. Selfish."

Annie looked at me.

"Tell him hell yes, Bob," I said. "The Round-Up is fun. We'll go to Happy Canyon and watch Bob and his friends do battle with the cavalry."

Annie beamed. "Hell yes, Bob. Thank you." She gave him a high five.

I said, "Of course that means you'll have to send him hay money, come winter. You being the official owner and all. Nobody ever accused Bob Humping Buck of being dumb."

She gave me a look. "Hey! Of course, I'll send him hay money. And of course you'll share the driving so I'll get a chance to ride her more than once every six months. And when you go hunting, I go too so Ms. Fab and I can have fun."

Bob liked that. "That'll teach you to flap your mouth, Denson."

Willie cut in on the banter. "Our mystery riders were through here late yesterday. We've got a lot of ground to cover."

"I saw where you picked up the sign," Bob said.

As darkness set in, after fourteen hours in the saddle and still on the trail of the three riders, we decided to camp in the bottom of a narrow gulch to help keep us out of a chilling wind that had picked up. When Annie and I dismounted neither of us could stand up straight, much less walk without crying out.

Wincing in pain, Annie grabbed the insides of her thighs. "My God, what's happened?"

Grinning, Willie finished removing the saddle and saddlebags from Badgerman's back. Bob too looked amused. "Give me a minute, and I'll take care of Ms. Fab for you, Annie. Just hang tight." He removed the gear from Thunderballs as Willie dug out the bottle of DMSO from his saddlebag.

Willie said, "When we get the horses taken care of, Bob and I will take a hike to collect some firewood so you and Dumsht will have some privacy to do what you gotta do."

I said, "We'll get it taken care of, but there'll be side effects, Annie."

Annie said, "That sounds ominous." She tried walking, her legs bowed, her face twisted with pain.

"You'll see," I said. When Willie and Bob had disappeared, I said, "What Willie said was right. We have to rub this crap on our thighs tonight and in the morning."

"What's that stuff used for?"

"Bruises. Stiff joints. Sore muscles. Can't get it from a pharmacy. Gotta find a vet."

"Vet?"

I dropped my trousers. "You drop 'em too."

"What do you mean vet?"

"Just do it. I can rub it in for you or you can do it yourself."

"I think I can manage," she said dryly. She peeled off her jeans.

"Cup your hands." I uncapped the DMSO and gave us both a ration.

"Smells sort of like garlic," she said, rubbing the colorless fluid into her thighs.

"Comes now the side effect," I said.

"*Ugggggggggggghhhhhhh.*" She made a face.

"Tastes like your mouth is a sewer, I know. It'll go away after a while."

As the taste disappeared in our mouths, so, slowly, did the pain and stiffness in our thighs.

Later, when Willie and Bob returned with armloads of dried sagebrush and dead juniper branches, they let out a howl and clapped their hands over their faces. Bob dropped to his hands and knees, pretending to vomit.

Willie said, "You two smell like you've been swimming in garlic juice. Disgusting."

Swimming in garlic juice roughly described it. Disgusting was insufficient. Repugnant was maybe a little better. But we were also walking normally and the excruciating pain was gone.

"What is that stuff?"

I said, "Willie turned me onto it originally. I couldn't believe how well it worked, so I did some research. It's dimethyl sulfoxide, an industrial solvent made from wood that was originally discovered by a doctor researching fluids to preserve transplant organs. It was the first anti-inflammatory discovered since aspirin that wasn't a steroid of some kind, and it has a remarkable ability to pass through membranes."

"So what's the catch?"

"If you mean side effects, there aren't any that anybody knows about except for the taste in your mouth, and you'll get a headache if you take too large of a hit. The real catch is that since it's widely available, no drug company can get a patent on it. To get FDA approval to market it, a company would have to commit millions of dollars on blind testing that's impossible by the nature of the drug."

Annie frowned. "Why is it impossible?"

I grinned. "The subjects getting the placebo wouldn't get the taste in their mouths, would they?"

"Oh no!"

"Oh yes. The drug companies are in business to make money, not help people. No monopoly, sorry, no testing. They're also afraid nobody would want to buy anything that gives them such a taste in their mouth. So people all over the world use DMSO to treat sprains and strains and bruises except for Americans. Germans and Japanese physicians routinely prescribe it. We use it to treat the muscle strains of racehorses."

Willie said, "Rodeo cowboys use it too, and we redskins who aren't as preposterously stupid as your FDA and drug marketing system. You'll have to use it again in the morning, though. It doesn't cure. It only relieves the symptoms."

22 · *The vagaries of Koonran*

We built a fire. As John Cooks Good, I set about doing my thing. I warmed some water to soak my mix of dried vegetables. I whacked off some thick slices of bacon with my hunting knife. While the bacon fried, I worked the onions, garlic, carrots, and celery into some biscuit dough. I fried the biscuits in the bacon fat. When I finished, we had a supper of bacon sandwiches washed down by tepid canteen water, a meal that could easily have been topped in any MacDonald's or Burger King franchise.

Bob was an enthusiastic and appreciative eater. "You outdid yourself this time, Cooks Good. Be damned if these aren't the best bacon sandwiches I ever had. I like the onions and vegetables in the biscuits."

I said, "You'd say that if these were cow pie sandwiches, long as somebody else did the cooking."

After we cleaned our tin plates, we huddled around the fire, sipping sweet pine needle tea. After a long day on the trail, we were pooped, but our bellies were full. Nobody wanted to go to bed. There was a white moon above. The white stars blinked like Christmas tree lights. In front of us, the fire popped and crackled.

This was a time for talk. Willie leaned forward, the shadows of the fire flickering across his face. "We've got to talk about Koonran," he said.

We waited.

"Each time, Koonran takes me by surprise. Few people have ever witnessed him in his elemental form. You did last night, Dumsht. Unusual for a white eyes to be so honored. If you can call seeing Koonran an honor."

"I hallucinated," I said.

"You want to tell Bob and Annie what you saw?"

"Sure. No reason why not, other than it was a trifle bizarre." I described my flight, and the reasons why I thought I had taken it.

When I finished, Willie shook his head, looking grave. "Koonran and I have been having at one another since the beginning of time. Like I said, he's a shape-changer, just like me."

"You want to tell Annie what animal spirit he actually is."

"I first encountered him as a beaver monster. But he appears differently, and under numerous names, to different tribes. The Yakima have also seen him as a beaver monster, but call him Wishpoosh. There is an Iroquois story in which he is a crow. Pima sorcerers have seen him as a Gila monster. But his name and the manner in which he has appeared is irrelevant."

"Just one Koonran."

"Correct. And while I call him a beaver monster, I saw him as a beaver just once, and that was at the beginning. He is the Dark Force. The Sinister One. You might recognize some of his incarnations. Among others, I believe he was likely Vlad the Impaler, Torquemada, Idi Amin, Pol Pot, Ed Gein, John Edgar Gacey, Geoffrey Dahmer, and Ted Bundy. Remember all that Bundy charm? Every mother's son, Bundy was. Pure Koonran. When he is among us, his essence is invisible. The Internet simply multiplies his ability to do mischief. Who else but Koonran would post that sick Mustang Mary cowflop on the Web? He wanted you to know he is Mustang Mary, which is why he wore lipstick on his ugly mug."

Looking thoughtful, Willie pulled off his boots and began massaging his feet. "I have won some of our confrontations, or thought I won, but Koonran always pops up again. Each time I'm surprised. Stupid. You'd think I'd learn. You can give Koonran the deep six, but he'll start out again as bacteria and work his way up the food chain until he reaches humans and finds himself a host with a rotten soul."

"It was a silly hallucination," I said.

Bob said, "Listen to Willie. He's right. You flew out of your body."

Willie said, "You know it's so, but you won't admit it, Dumsht. In posting as Mustang Mary and appearing to you in an out-of-body flight, he's offering us a challenge, taunting us. 'Screw you and the horse you rode in on,' he's saying. He's not finished yet. Whether or not anybody around this campfire believes me, I beseech all of you, I beg you, please, please know that Koonran might be inhabiting the body of anybody we encounter. He delights in the unexpected. Until we take Koonran under once again, we can't be lulled into trusting anybody."

"Even Gerald Riggin?" Annie asked. She really didn't mean Gerald Riggin. She liked Gerald. She was just testing Willie.

"Sure, Gerald Riggin. If Koonran is inhabiting his body, that's no bum rap on Gerald. But I don't think it's Gerald. Koonran is a spiritual parasite who regards a human body as a kind of vessel. He moves from person to person or animal to person, transferring his malevolent spirit by touch, until he settles into the most malignant, vile person he can find. He's looking for a character in decay or a misguided imagination. We should not allow ourselves to be deceived by exterior beauty or apparent charm. Koonran works his mischief from within."

I said, "The monster I saw was a combination of Moby Dick,

Bodan, Mustang Mary, and your Koonran blather, welled up from my subconscious. Nothing more."

"Moby Dick, was it? What about that demented old bull that led forty whales including cows and little calves onto the beach? I remember you pissing and moaning, asking yourself how that happened. Did the bull whale simply lose his bearings? Maybe Koonran appeared as an Appaloosa whale so he could take credit for what he did on the beach. He's proud of himself."

It was impossible to defeat Willie with mere logic. He had an answer for everything. I said, "Those names you mentioned, Torquemada, Pol Pot, and the rest. They were all male. Now we're dealing with Mustang Mary and a leopard Appaloosa wearing lipstick. How does that follow?"

"It doesn't, which is all the more reason to believe we're dealing with Koonran. He's devious. Maybe he thinks he's ridiculing feminists. They want equality, he'll show them equality. Begging your pardon, Annie, I don't mean to be disrespectful here, but you have to understand how Koonran thinks."

Annie grinned. She liked it when Willie explained his beliefs.

I said, "Oh, for Christ's sake, Willie!"

"You asked a question, Dumsht. Don't object to the answer."

"You two!" Annie sounded disgusted, but she really wasn't. She enjoyed our banter. Willie liked to call me Dumsht, short for dumb shit. I frequently called him Tonto. But I was no dumb shit, and he was no Hollywood Indian. When Willie called me "Dumsht," he meant anything but. This companionable form of irony, a kind of masculine repartee, wasn't common among female friends. It was possible that females did do that, only not within earshot of males.

"I don't want to talk about it," I said. I tossed some more wood on the fire.

————

We fell silent, watching the fire, each of us considering Willie Sees the Night's belief in the existence of the evil, shape-changing Koonran. If I was right, the makings of Koonran lay within us all, the evil lurking in our reptilian brain stems. But there remained the nagging possibility, however remote, that Koonran was not within. He was out there moving freely among us, an evil parasite ready to take over the body of whomever he pleased.

The corporate religions with their churches, temples, and mosques had their many embodiments of evil. There were numerous religions, mainstream and esoteric, that had rites of exorcism to purge the Dark One, by whatever name, devil, Lucifer, Satan, Shaitan, and the rest, including Koonran. How was one to pick from among them? Were we to vote, with validity and authenticity for a particular Lucifer figure to be conferred by majority rule? Hands up, all you Christians! You Muslims! You Hindus! You Buddhists! You Bushmen of the Kalahari! You Yamanano isolated out there in the Amazon basin. You Umatillas. You Apaches.

In the end, all devils were based on faith. Who was to say whose Evil One existed, and whose did not? Were the shamans and medicine men and sorcerers to be scorned simply because they did not build magnificent cathedrals and gilded mosques and splendid temples? They had no sacred texts or holy books. They neither tithed nor passed the collection plate. They did not establish schools. They did not send forth missionaries. Did the wormhole of creation necessarily pass through Bethlehem, or could it not just as easily have opened in the great expanse of the American West?

Willie Sees the Night claimed that he, the shape-changing Coyote, and his shape-changing opposite, Koonran, the beaver monster, had battled for supremacy since the beginning of time, an unending Manichean struggle between good and evil. In this struggle Koonran casually skipped from host to amenable host.

I was a show-me kind of guy. I would plod, donkeylike, into the tangled, thorny thicket of evidence. The poisoned fruit of motive was somewhere in the thicket. Was it plain old greed that led to the killing of the mustang stallions? Envy? The fury of a scorned lover? A desire for rough justice? One of the above, or perhaps none? Maybe simple madness?

What if Willie had it right and I was wrong? Willie was my partner. Out of respect, I would leave open the possibility of Koonran. After all, in flying out of my skin, I had seen an Appaloosa beaver monster in the shape of what appeared to be a whale. Was that Koonran? Until a premise was disproved, the question of its validity remained unanswered.

With the blinking stars and cold moon above, my back was freezing. The fire leaped and twisted in front of us, a dervish swirling in ecstasy, hot, hot, hot amidst the ice of midnight. In those flames I saw huge rodent incisors. The teeth of a beaver.

For me, the question with regard to sleeping on the trail was always the same: to sleep in my clothes or not to sleep in my clothes? In the first hour, a sleeping bag was always comfy and cozy, if not downright hot. But if I had learned anything in my hunting trips with Willie, it was that as the warming campfire waned, the frigid night would follow with a vengeance. In the morning, I would be tucked tightly in the fetal position, conserving every calorie of warmth. If I left my shirt and jeans on the ground, they would be brittle as ice and just as cold.

But this trip, I had Annie. We had sleeping bags that zipped together. When it was time to bed down at last, Annie and I zipped our bags together. No sooner than we had gotten settled in, all warm in our cocoons and still reeking of DMSO, than

Annie proceeded to work her way down my neck and across my chest doing her sensational thing with her tongue and teeth.

"Stop that," I whispered.

"Shush, they'll hear you," she breathed. She continued on her way south.

Shit! I wiggled. Couldn't help it.

Her mouth was at my ear. Her tongue darted in, then out. "Be still, or you'll embarrass yourself."

So that was the game.

I went rigid. "Damn you," I murmured.

"What's going on over there, you two?" Bob asked.

Her mouth was directly on me, giving me a passionate Monica.

"Nothing," I gurgled, sounding half strangled. A devil she was, but wonderful.

Bob said, "You two need to get some rest. We've got a long day ahead of us tomorrow."

"Can't take Denson anywhere," Willie added.

Holding two fistfuls of Annie's hair, I squeezed tightly, holding on for the ride.

I woke up, cold. On the next ridge, leading up the flank of Riddle Mountain, coyotes were yipping and yelping. Also, I had to take a leak. Reluctantly I crawled out of my cocoon and slipped on my boots. The campfire had been reduced to ashes. Bow-legged, I walked a respectful distance from our campfire. As I did, the coyotes began howling.

As I unzipped and let fly, the frigid air, bracing but invigorating, clutched my balls. *Ooooh!* It occurred to me that taking a leak on the side of a mountain in the high desert was one of life's sweet pleasures. There were those males, poor bastards, who spent their entire lives pissing on porcelain. Urinating into somebody's hedge or bouncing it off the side of a building in an urban alley was malt liquor. Pissing on Riddle Mountain was Jim Beam. One crassly guzzled malt liquor, one sipped Uncle Jim, appreciating the moment.

When I got back to our camp, I noticed that Willie's sleeping bag was empty. Willie liked to hike in the night, doing what, I had no idea. That's the way he was.

I crawled into my bag. Both Annie and Bob were awake too, listening to the howling.

"Where do you suppose Willie is?" I asked.

Bob said, "With his friends on the next ridge, talking it up. Why do you think they named him Sees the Night?"

"Fun to think that's where he is," I said. The howling was grand and wonderful.

"Enjoy, Willie," Annie said.

As if they were aware of our sentiments, the coyotes howled even louder. *Hear this, you moon, you stars, you distant burning galaxies. Koonran is among us. Hear our reckoning, beckoning call. Be warned! Beware the danger, the deception, the treachery!*

23 · Sylvia and Charlene

The effect of the DMSO wore off during the night. Annie and I awoke stiff and sore as all get-out. Once again, we swabbed the insides of our thighs with the clear fluid, bracing ourselves for the foul taste in our mouths. Yuck!

Our breaths coming in frosty clouds, we shifted from foot to foot to keep warm as Willie and Bob got a morning fire going to thaw us out. I fixed a breakfast of jerky, fried biscuits, and coffee.

I took a sip of coffee, watching Willie over the edge of the plastic cup. "Coyotes were howling last night the next ridge over."

Willie chewed on a chunk of jerky, saying nothing.

"Made a helluva racket, didn't they, Annie?"

"I'll say," Annie said, repressing a grin.

Bob joined in. "Yipping and yelping and putting up a helluva racket. Woke us all up, of course. You were gone, Willie. We wondered where the hell you were that hour of night. We have a hard day's riding ahead of us. A person would have thought you'd be getting some rest."

Willie grabbed another hunk of jerky and began gnawing on it. "I was out to take a leak. Denson's mommy taught him never to get too far away from camp at night on account of the spookies and boogies, so we wake up having to smell his piss. I've got better manners than that."

We got no more out of Willie. After we finished the pot of coffee, we saddled up and picked up the trail of three riders where we had left off the day before. Willie and I again rode up front. Behind us, Bob paired off with Annie, still giving her tips about riding and taking care of a fine mare like Ms. Fab.

As we rode, with Willie keeping a careful eye on the hoofprints we were following, Willie said, "Lot of trails for us, eh, Chief?"

"A whole bunch," I said.

"Remember what I taught you about hunting mulies."

By "mulie" he meant mule deer, so called because of their lar-gish "mule" ears. A mule deer was considerably larger than the while-tailed deer found in much of the country. I said, "They feed largely after dark, which is why some assholes are able to pin them in a spotlight and shoot them at night. They're active shortly after dawn and shortly before sunset. They like to sleep in the afternoons."

"We hunt them by finding their favorite trails to water, the meadows where they like to feed, or the places where they like to bed down. What's the difference between finding a fingerprint on a doorknob or a series of hoofprints leading to a stream?"

I said, "Your point being?"

"Same skills required to hunt mulies and run down horse killers. To reassure the white faces footing the bills, we call our-selves 'private investigators.' The truth is we're a helluva lot more than hunters, Dumsht. We're eternally at war with Koon-ran's progeny."

"Koonran's progeny?"

"He's the granddaddy, Chief. The original bad seed. We've all got a little of his blood mixed in somewhere. Every once in a while he decides to show up himself for a little entertainment.

This is one of those times. We're warriors." He gave me a wry look, arching an eyebrow. "We wouldn't score a whole lot in the way of jobs if we called ourselves 'warriors for hire.' Warriors? Ha, ha, ha."

Willie reined in at a trickle coming down the mountain. I reined in beside him.

Behind us, Bob said, "Good thinking. They've got to be getting a trifle thirsty."

Willie and I dismounted. While Badgerman and Bodan sucked up some water, Willie said, "Koonran can be whatever he wants to be, slipping into and out of such human bodies as he takes a fancy. I take him under, and he pops right back up again like a crooked cop or a CEO with too many stock options. No matter how much we change the rules, his progeny will figure a new scam. We can never get rid of them. Never."

The horses had drunk their fill. We mounted up and continued on our way.

A few minutes later, behind us, Bob shouted, "Willie!"

Willie said, "I see it, Bob. I've been keeping an eye on it for the last ten minutes."

"See what?" I asked.

"Look down there." He pointed downhill.

Annie said, "Ah, I see it now."

So did I. I twisted quickly and retrieved my binoculars from my saddlebag.

How could Willie have been watching the terrain so carefully and talking to me at the same time? He had given no hint, none.

We continued down the ridge on foot, leading our horses so as to give the riders below us less of a profile to spot. I dropped back with Annie, so Bob, a veteran hunter, could take my place beside Willie. Bob and Willie knew what they were doing. Better they call the shots without a white face making silly suggestions.

After about a hundred yards, Willie waved us to a stop. We tied up the horses and continued on foot. Ever since she threw in with me and Willie, Annie, who had been trained by the FBI, was in charge of working the computer and all things technical. I helped her lug her gear: a parabolic microphone in case we got close enough, plus a 35mm Nikon and Sony digital cameras with long-distance lenses and a folding aluminum tripod.

Twenty minutes later, we stopped again.

Willie came back and murmured. "There are three of them. Two women and a boy or a small, fit female, hard to tell which. They've got a six-horse trailer hitched to a Ford double-cab. Annie, do you want to do your thing before they're outta here?"

"Too far for the parabolic, but I should be able to get us some good shots with my cameras," Annie said.

Willie and Bob found Annie a good spot to set up her gear at the edge of some trees. While she unfolded her tripod and shot pictures, I focused my binoculars on the distant figures. I said, "Well, well!"

"What you got, Chief?" Willie asked.

"You remember you asked me to interview that veterinarian in Sheridan?"

"The lady who milked those studs dry before they were killed."

"She's the one on the left."

"You mind if I take a look-see," Bob said.

I gave him the binoculars.

Bob refocused the glasses for his eyes. "By God, you're right, Cooks Good. The other woman is Charlene ReMillard. She's Bonner's partner. She's also Bonner's lady friend or significant other, or whatever it is they call themselves."

Then a flash. Light reflecting off glass. We all ducked. Charlene was scanning the hillside with a pair of binoculars. Had they seen us or was she just being careful? Impossible to tell.

With Annie still shooting pictures, Sylvia and Charlene loaded three riding horses onto the trailer, which had stalls for six horses and no license plate. Stalls for six horses. Had they already loaded three mustangs on? Impossible to tell. But if they had nothing to hide, why had they removed the trailer's license plate?

Their chores completed, they climbed into the Ford double-cab and drove off, leaving a rooster-tail of dust on the fire road leading away from Riddle Mountain.

A few minutes later, we took turns looking at the images in Annie's digital camera. The gender of the third person remained impossible to determine.

We rode down to the spot where Sylvia and Charlene had loaded their horses. Bob and Willie studied the hoofprints around the trailer. They counted the hoofprints of the same three shod horses that we had followed. No more. If Bonner and her companions had loaded any Riddle Mountain mustangs into the three remaining spaces, they had done it somewhere else.

We decided to split up. Annie and I would return to Whorehouse Meadow while Willie and Bob followed the trail of the horses to see what Sylvia Bonner and Charlene ReMillard had been up to.

As Annie and I were building our campfire that night, I got a call from Gerald Riggin on my cell phone asking what we had found. I told him we had caught a glimpse of what appeared to be two women and a boy or three women, depending, adding quickly that we would appreciate it if he could keep it under his Stetson for the time being. I said, "We don't have any evidence that they broke any kind of law. If we tell the FBI, we risk seeing it on the tube news."

After a moment's pause, Riggin said, "Were you able to get any pictures of them?"

"Naw," I said. "Before Annie could get her gear set up, they were gone." I hated lying to Gerald, but I wanted to talk to Dr. Sylvia Bonner again before the FBI or the Oregon State Police.

"Speaking of females. Remember the artist and wannabe novelist who busted the editor's jaw in New York a couple of years back?"

I laughed. "Hard to forget that one. Toni Lindemann. After she did time for assault and battery, Portland State hired her. The sisterhood came through. Or somebody."

"She's made the news again. This time she's claiming that an anonymous correspondent, communicating by e-mail, hired her to render a series of drawings with mythological and sexual themes and Spanish mustangs. Mustang Mary on Nez Perce Ned is the first in a series. Lindemann claims her mystery client promised to eventually give her the details of her life as the basis for a book."

"We get to be treated to more drawings, I take it."

"Lindemann held a press conference, saying she gave the FBI a list of drawings, which they asked her not to reveal. She was shocked, shocked at this Mustang Mary business! How awful!"

"I take it she loves the attention."

"*Loves* the attention? She revels in it."

24 · A casual lie

Annie and I arrived back at our cabin in Whorehouse Meadow totally exhausted. We were at the table eating our breakfast speculating about what Dr. Sylvia Bonner and her partner had been doing on the BLM range when Willie called. "Bob and I followed the horseback trail of Sylvia Bonner and Charlene ReMillard and their female friend. They appear to have been watching the Riddle herd from a distance."

"How do you know the third person was female?"

"All God's children take leaks, Dumsht. All three were squatters."

"Well done. What are you going to do now?"

"Hang with Bob to make sure they really are gone, then come back to the meadow. And you?"

I told him I'd talk to Sylvia Bonner again, followed by the artist at Portland State. I called Dr. Sylvia Bonner, but she wasn't back from whatever she was doing at Riddle Mountain. I decided to take a nap to rest up from three exhausting days in the saddle. I would try again later.

I woke up late that afternoon, finding Annie bent over her computer working on an insurance fraud case. She was younger than me and had gone right back to work while I was passed out.

She glanced my way, saying, "Well, the exhausted cowpoke emerges from his slumber. Dreaming of Sweet Betsy from Pike were you?"

"It'll take me a week to recover from that horseback crap," I said. "I'm not getting any younger." I sat on the edge of the bed and stretched, my joints popping. After all those years of going it alone, it was nice to have someone around who gave a damn about me. There were younger men, unable to imagine the day when they would stiffen up after a few days on the trail or that their joints would ever pop and crack, who did not appreciate their mates. Annie was so damn fine, I could hardly believe it.

She said, "You got enough energy to look at two more Mustang Mary postings? Turns out the Portland State professor was telling the truth."

I grabbed a chair and put it beside Annie's. She called up the first posting in which the naked young woman who had ridden Nez Perce Ned was now in a cloud, on her back, legs wide, with a young man on top of her. They were doing the old huckle buck. The in-out. Hiding the salami.

Underneath, a message in the same handprinted block letters as before:

YES, YES, THE PORTLAND STATE PROFESSOR DID THE DRAWINGS FOR ME JUST LIKE SHE SAYS. I HAVE A WHOLE PILE OF THEM. I CHOSE HER BE- CAUSE I LIKE HER SPUNK, KNOCKING THAT MORON OF AN EDITOR ON HIS ASS. THE MUSTANG STALLIONS WERE JUST HORS D'OEUVRES. NOW I START THE MAIN COURSE. MMMMM. YUM, YUM!

"That's wonderful," I said. "I take it she's going to tell us what that all means besides a quickie on cloud nine."

"You wait." Annie punched up the second posting.

Mustang Mary was still in the cloud, which had thinned. A grin on her face, her left hand over her twat, she stood over a skeleton, presumably the young man who was on top of her in the first drawing.

HE WAS A HARD RIDER, I'LL GIVE HIM THAT. A MUSTANG MARY KIND OF GUY. I'VE GOT A SET OF TEETH ON ME YOU JUST WOULDN'T BELIEVE. PEARLY WHITES THEY ARE. SOME DAY SOON, I'LL SHOW THEM TO YOU. RIP AND TEAR. GOBBLE, GOBBLE, GOBBLE. OOOOWWWWWEEEE!

"Sweet Jesus," I said.

Annie remained silent for a moment, then said, almost absently, "I don't think any real woman ever had boobs like that unless they were stuffed with silicon. Makes a person wonder what on earth Toni Lindemann was thinking when she read the descriptions of what she was supposed to draw."

Annie was right about that. Hoping Dr. Sylvia Bonner was back from her adventure, I tried her number again. She was back. Reluctantly, she agreed to talk to me a second time.

I carried a large manila envelope with me as Dr. Sylvia Bonner ushered me into her office. I put my envelope on the corner of her desk without a word of what might be in it.

Bonner couldn't dodge what she had done for the horse killer, so she had apparently determined to do whatever was required of her under the circumstances. That didn't mean she had to like the intrusion on her life or that she had to kiss the ass of every cop or private investigator that showed up. As before, she poured coffee from an urn on the table in front of her desk.

On my first visit, I hadn't paid a whole lot of attention to the photographs on the walls. This time I put a little cream and sugar in my cup and, sipping my coffee, browsed the photographs.

She took a seat at the coffee table in the middle of the room. Following her lead, I put my cup on the table and also sat. I took a sip, looking out of the window. "Nice Appaloosa," I said, referring to a white mare sprinkled with black spots.

Sylvia looked out at the mare. "She belongs to a woman in Eugene. An Appaloosa that dramatic is rare. When she's ready, we'll find her the right stallion and see what happens."

I said, "You must be getting tired of talking about this horse-killing business. I apologize for asking you to go through it one more time."

She sighed. "I've loved horses since I was a little girl, Mr. Denson. That's why I studied veterinary medicine at Oregon State. Bad enough that I was an unwitting accomplice for a killer of prime Spanish mustang stallions. Worse that I know that I'm likely suspected of knowing the identity of the killer." She took a sip of coffee and fell silent, watching the mares in the pasture. "Can you tell me why I'm a suspect? I find that bewildering. No, I take that back. I find it outrageous." Her face grew tight.

"Lots of people with motive. You have means and opportunity."

"Opportunity to do what? Means? Why on earth would I kill horses?"

"Opportunity to learn about barns and pastures that the killer would need to know. As for means, you have the technical skill to handle the semen and use it to impregnate a mare. You're an insider, like a bank employee. Why? *Cui bono?* Who profits?"

She shook her head in disgust. "I've gone over that repeatedly with the Oregon State Police and the man from the FBI. But maybe you picked up on something that escaped them."

I reached over and snagged the envelope containing the photographs from the corner of her desk. Bonner pretended to be uninterested.

I said, "I'm told you and your sister raise horses in Southern Oregon."

"My sister Rachael and I own a spread on the Rogue River. We inherited it from our parents." She retreated to her desk and retrieved a business card that she gave me. The card contained a winged-BR brand, plus the words "Bonner Ranch, Champion Spanish mustangs." It also had a telephone number and an e-mail address.

Watching me read the card, Bonner said, "Rachael's gonna love having to rehash this again."

"If she doesn't have anything to do with whoever it was who killed those stallions, she doesn't have anything to worry about."

"Wait until you meet Little Willard. He's a real case."

"Little Willard?" I asked.

"Willard Leopoldo, Rachael's husband. By the way, Charlene and I are lovers," she said mildly. "I assume somebody told you that or you figured it out."

"Somebody told me. I don't spend a whole lot of time thinking about what other people do under the covers."

She said, "Rachael doesn't like it one damn bit. In fact, she professes to loathe Charlene. She's embarrassed, most likely. I think she's very likely more comfortable with horses than human beings." Bonner smiled ruefully. "Between the two of us, I'm glad Rachael is down there on the Rogue, and Charlene and I are up here in Sheridan with our work. Rachael and I both love horses, but beyond that—" She stood. "Will that be all? I've pretty much covered the territory, haven't I?"

"Oh, sure," I said.

As Bonner walked me to the door, I opened the envelope and retrieved the photographs, from which Annie had removed all the shots that contained the smaller, third person. "Oops, almost forgot. You want to tell me what you and Charlene were doing at Riddle Mountain!"

"You *almost* forgot. You and Columbo," Bonner said dryly. She glanced at the photographs, then slipped them back into the envelope. "So it was you up in the trees. Charlene said somebody was up there."

I nodded. "If you don't mind my asking, what were you doing?"

"Long before the FBI made its conclusions public, Charlene and I suspected that somebody was killing the stallions. The BLM manages four herds of classic mustangs, two in Oregon, one in Utah, and one in Montana. With those herds and the horses on the ranches of various breeders, one would think the lineage is safe. But is it?"

I said, "You wanted to inventory the stallions and mares with the best conformation."

"We may need them to preserve the bloodline. The first time you talked to me, you mentioned a sperm bank. That was our idea as well, but first we had to do some research. Nobody knows for sure what this horse killer is up to, do they?"

"They sure as hell don't," I said. "What about the BLM? Gerald Riggin and the BLM people are ultimately responsible for maintaining the integrity of the herds."

"The BLM is a government agency. Their people do their best, I won't quarrel with that. But there's an old saying, 'Good enough for government work.' Have you ever heard that phrase?"

I had, unfortunately. I said, "By the way, who was the third person with you?"

She blinked. "I . . . It was Willard Leopoldo."

Willard Leopoldo was small, but it was my bet that he stood when he took a leak. Marya von Bayer most likely didn't.

25 · *To frolic naked down Broadway*

The story of Portland State University's Dr. Toni Lindemann was well known to Oregonians. After years of trying to get a novel published, Lindemann typed Sinclair Lewis's *Babbitt* word for word and gave it to an agent, claiming she had written it. The agent failed to recognize the story, then passed it on to an editor, who rejected it. In a rage, Lindemann flew to New York, stormed into the office of the editor and slugged him, breaking his jaw and knocking out most of his teeth.

Charged with assault and battery, Lindemann used her day in court to go on a tirade against the publishing industry, claiming New York editors and publishers were morons. Before sentencing, Lindemann told the judge she would one day score a New York publisher for one of her novels. There had to be a way to get an editor to listen up, and she would find it. She served six months of an eighteen-month sentence. And now she was an assistant professor of art, famously hired by Mustang Mary to render those crazed drawings being posted on the Web.

While Annie Dancer did her thing with the computer, I went to see Lindemann. When I say Annie 'did her thing,' I mean that she embarked on her own version of what Internet enthusiasts

call "Google-whacking." A Google-whacker entered a combination of two words into the search engine Google, then hit the
search key to see if he or she could come up with just one result,
a whack. Two or more results didn't count. It had to be a single
hit to be a whack.

What Annie did was to take the FBI's list of breeders of Spanish mustangs and enter their names plus combinations of words
and phrases having to do with mustangs into Google, hoping
for a luck-out whack that could be a clue.

Portland State University was one of those urban schools that
had always been forced to take a backseat to the land grant colleges farther down the Willamette Valley, Oregon State University in Corvallis, and my alma mater, the University of Oregon in
Eugene. Located just south of what were popularly called the
park blocks at the southwestern edge of downtown Portland,
PSU was not at all second rate. But colleges and universities were
not entirely for learning, they were also for drinking beer and
humping—breakaway time for young adults.

Dr. Toni Lindemann turned out to be a large woman with an
outsized bosom that looked like it was stuffed with foam rubber
pillows and the kind of rump that most people associate with
mountain mamas and ladies who eat too many potatoes. She
squeezed her behind onto the seat of her swivel chair with some
difficulty. She had a round face and wore round eyeglasses with
gold wire rims. She wore a comfortable dress patterned with
tiny daisies.

There were three large black-and-white drawings of animals
in her office, one of a tiger peering out of jungle foliage, a second of a solitary penguin floating on an ice raft looking out to
sea, and a third of a running herd of Spanish mustangs. All
three, signed T. Lindemann, were like Mustang Mary's images
on the Internet—that is, almost photorealistic.

Lindemann appeared amiable enough as she read my business

card. She ran her tongue over her teeth and said, "Denson, Dancer, and Sees the Night." Her tongue slid over her teeth again. "And who is it you're representing?"

"The Ad Hoc Committee to Save the Spanish Mustang."

"I'm the lunatic wannabe writer who busted an idiot's jaw six years ago, I suppose you know that. I'm preceded both by my reputation and my boobs." She burst out laughing, a loud, raucous *haw, haw, haw*.

I grinned.

She ran her tongue over her teeth. "The day I walked into that editor's office I was suffering from a wicked bout of PMS. I was so twisted by hormones you just wouldn't believe. Super bitch, I was. I could have played defensive tackle for the Green Bay Packers. You should have seen the look on that poor bastard's face when I doubled up my fist. Busted him square in the chops." Lindemann burst out laughing. *Haw, haw, haw!* "Before that happened I was just another frustrated wannabe writer who could draw, a fat lady with a Ph.D. I couldn't get a job teaching. I was going nowhere. Spending six months in jail was a revelation . . ." She stopped, savoring the memory.

She was drifting. I jogged her memory. "A revelation."

She shook her head to get herself back on joint. "Why yes, I got hundreds of letters from people who couldn't get published. They hated agents and editors with a passion. To them, I was a hero. Yes, a hero! I did what they all wanted to do." She looked amused.

"One night in my cell, I had a kind of pot flash without the pot. I got to thinking about all those writers out there who get wonderful reviews but can't pay the rent. Book buyers think authors on the best-seller lists are there because they write the best books. That's the logic. Right?"

"Well, I guess. But if you're trying to tell me that all best-selling authors are lousy writers, that's not true. It has to be far more complicated than that, what with deals, connections, powerful agents and editors, and the rest of it."

She frowned. "Of course it's more complicated. What I *am* saying is that for most readers buying a novel is like buying a new pair of shoes or a new car. They want to be fashionable. They want to wear the same shoes and drive the same SUVs as everybody else. The fact that the shoes look stupid and the SUVs are overpriced and guzzle gas is irrelevant."

"So?"

"So the fashionable reader wants to buy the same books as everybody else. It doesn't make any difference if a novel has cardboard characters or is long-winded. What self-respecting reader who seeks the approval of the herd would want to read a novel by a nonfamous author? A publisher wants something more than a good book."

"I see. So you face a paradox. The trick is to become a celebrity author without getting published. How do you do that?"

"You frolic naked down Broadway." She broke out in a peal of guffaws that would have shattered the speaker cones at a Rolling Stones concert. *Haw, haw, haw, haw!* Finally, recovering, she said, "That's in a manner of speaking. I was the woman who broke an editor's jaw, so when I got out, I had my pick of jobs. I came here to Portland State because I have family here." She gestured toward the drawing of the running horses. "When my anonymous client turned out to be Mustang Mary, I saw the future." She slapped her thigh. *Haw, haw, haw!*

"And?"

"I went straight to the police, of course. Then I was invited to write a piece for the *Oregonian,* speculating on the identity of Mustang Mary. After the *Oregonian* piece, *USA Today* came calling. Pretty soon I had reporters queued up waiting to interview me." *Haw, haw, haw!* "I was famous once again without even having to break anybody's jaw. Portland State liked it so much the dean has recommended me for promotion to associate professor." *Haw, haw, haw!*

"All right," I said. "Good on ya!"

"But that isn't the best part. The best part is that I've gotten a contract to write a novel. Maybe not as much of an advance as Tom Clancy or Stephen King, but I'll take it. I had publishers bidding for the manuscript. None of them wanted to take the chance that I wasn't telling the truth about being Mary's artist. Maybe I'm the real Mustang Mary, horse killer. Yes!" *Haw, haw, haw!*

I joined Toni Lindemann in laughing, braying like a donkey while she kept haw-hawing.

She wiped tears from her eyes. "If you want, we can look at some Mustang Mary drawings. I hasten to add that I didn't have anything to do with the choice of subject matter or the narrative. My client told me exactly what she wanted in each drawing. I'm beginning to get a clearer idea what she is up to, although her motive still escapes me."

"'She.' You think she's female then."

Lindemann sighed. "I use the pronoun 'she.' I can't prove her gender, but her obsessions became clear when she described the drawings she wanted. At the time, I thought it was pretty wild, but hey, what's to account for taste, right?"

"Let's look at the postings, sure," I said.

I slid my chair next to Toni Lindemann's facing her seventeen-inch computer monitor. She cocked her head. "This is pretty crass stuff. You smoke?"

After we each had a couple of hits from Toni Lindemann's flowered ceramic bong, she tapped in some instructions to her computer. Exhaling a cloud of pungent smoke, she said, "This drawing of Mary and her lover in a cloud, followed by her standing over his skeleton, I've traced to a Sioux myth. Just spread her legs and gobbled him up."

"Mean lady."

She giggled. "Wait 'til you see this one." She reloaded her pipe then called up a drawing of Mary squatted atop a male.

Lindemann said, "She hasn't posted this drawing yet, but I believe it depicts the Hindu goddess Kali sitting atop her dying lover, Shiva. She's devouring his penis with her vulva."

"Whoops," I said, squirming slightly in my chair.

Grinning, Lindemann gave me the pipe. "Horses, sex, eating, and teeth are recurring themes."

"So?" I took a final, modest hit.

"So to get a better idea of the clues Mustang Mary is giving us, you need to consider this one." Up popped Mary, naked as usual, standing beside a gravestone in a sand dune. "I might be wrong, but I think it illustrates a Muslim aphorism."

"And that would be?"

" 'Three things are insatiable: the desert, the grave, and a woman's vulva,' " Lindemann said. "So far, she's not using all the drawings I sold her. But eventually she's almost sure to use this one." She called up a drawing of Mustang Mary naked except for cowboy boots and chaps, on her back, legs parted. Her vulva was shaven. Her vaginal lips were tattooed with evil-looking little teeth.

Lindemann said, "Here she gives us *vagina dentata,* a pussy with teeth. The female as one who devours with her vagina is a familiar theme in mythological literature. In the Amazon basin, for example, the Yanamamo word 'to eat' and 'to copulate' are the same. There are those feminists who assert that controlling men secretly fear being consumed. That's what ails those Muslim men in the Middle East, morons that they are. No damn wonder they're suicidal lunatics."

Lindemann turned off her computer and swiveled in her chair, facing me as I retreated to my previous spot in front of her desk. She said, "This mythological hocus pocus is sophomoric nonsense. Nothing esoteric about *vagina dentata*. It's shocking only if you've never heard the phrase before. It's simply, uh . . ."

"Graphic," I said quickly. "And amusing in a sick sort of way."

She grinned. "And far-out. There you go. An illustration for all the stupes who don't get it. All you have to do to find examples is paw through Sir James Frazier's *The Golden Bough* and you can come up with all kinds of examples. By the way, do you like my tiger and my penguin?"

"They're very well done."

"When I learned my client was Mustang Mary, I called the cops. What more can anybody do? She paid me a thousand dollars for each drawing. It was like she had money to burn. I'm supposed to turn that down? It was fun. I had no idea what she was going to do with the drawings. That was up to her. Do you think Mustang Mary killed the stallions?"

"There's a case to be made for it," I said.

"Just like everybody else, I want the horse killer caught pronto. If it's Mary, maybe she'll feel compelled to tell me the whole story, just like she promised. If it's not her or she doesn't deliver on her promise, I've still got my contract. I'll invent some sick shit, and it will be published anyway. After all this publicity, my publisher will still sell books." Looking pleased, Lindemann gave me a sly wink. "Then again, I could be making all this up, couldn't I? A clever opportunist. A far-out put-on artist."

"Your way of frolicking naked down Broadway."

Her bosom shaking, she burst into another round of *haw, haw, haw*.

Toni Lindemann, frustrated author, clever as all get-out, was running naked down Broadway, passing 42nd Street with her behind bouncing and bosom flopping. Was Mustang Mary her lucky break? Or had Lindemann gotten stoned one day and glanced up at her hip little penguin standing on his chunk of ice and suddenly burst out in one of her fits of guffawing? She would transform herself into Mustang Mary and have fun with the credulous masses. More fun than doing time for knocking an editor on his behind.

26 · Entrance of the Lawyers

What happened next can be fully be appreciated only by somebody familiar with the "Entrance of the Gladiators," a song popularly associated with a steam calliope heralding the entrance into the Big Top of a parade of clowns, freaks, acrobats, lion tamers, ladies wearing too little, and gentlemen with jockstraps stuffed with cotton socks. Circuses and press conferences. Very often the same thing.

In this case, Marya von Bayer had chosen to turn the Pioneer Square Plaza in downtown Portland into the center ring. Annie and I watched on television, the best seat in the big tent.

Marya von Bayer wore a soft, aquamarine dress molded over her pumped-up butt and teenage breasts. Whether the dress was transparent, or merely translucent, was open to question. For some reason, a senior moment perhaps, madame had forgotten to wear a bra. Her tattooed nipples looked like the brown eyes of a strange beast peering balefully out from an aquarium. Milady displayed her surgically sculpted globes, fascinating under see-through blue. Had she forgotten to wear underpants as well? Or was she wearing thong underwear? Hard to tell.

To make up for any perceived deficiencies in her dress, she

wore a wide-brimmed hat, straight from the mythical South, from which dangled a lacy fringe. This was a Sunday hat, appropriate for a tea party of proper ladies. Judging by her retiring and demure body language, she was nothing if not a lady. Very feminine. Fragile. Vulnerable. Vivian Leigh in *A Streetcar Named Desire. I have always depended on the kindness of strangers.*

She was about to face the rapacious reporters, who did not include "kindness" in their vocabulary.

Marya was represented by celebrity lawyer Gerrold Parker, a man in his early fifties and a veteran of media hoo-hoo. Thrusting himself before the cameras at every opportunity, Parker had become the mouthpiece of choice for flagrantly guilty clients with too much money. A favorite of Larry King and the morning talk show circuit, he was famous for coining amusing, if cynical, legal aphorisms. For this occasion, he wore a blue power suit, black wing tips, and pale yellow shirt. His bourgeois noose was powder blue, tied into a tidy double Windsor. Parker appeared earnest and grave, a pose necessary to make absurd legal stratagems appear respectable to juries and people who watched the drama on television.

Behind Parker, two young suits jockeyed to get into the range of the cameras. These were Parker's legal gophers, wannabe celebrity lawyers, apprentices to the famous one. As individuals they were as nondescript as male models, but their eager eyes blazed with ambition. Neat and tidy, they were, wearing Italian suits. Very pretty.

When the Cyclops eye of the video camera turned red, Parker said, "I would first like to make a short statement, then I will take questions on behalf of my client, Mrs. Marya von Bayer."

The cameras shifted briefly to the demure Marya, who blinked shyly.

Parker said, "I would like to announce the successful recovery, by my client, of the frozen semen collected from the twenty-two dead mustang stallions. An anonymous woman calling herself Mustang Mary called Mrs. von Bayer at ten o'clock yesterday morning threatening to destroy the semen if she was not paid one point five million dollars. She instructed Mrs. von Bayer to electronically deposit the money in a numbered account in the Cayman Islands, saying she would know immediately if Mrs. von Bayer contacted the police or the FBI. If Mrs. von Bayer did that, Mustang Mary would destroy the semen.

"My client is a breeder of Spanish mustangs. She loves mustangs and understands their importance as part of our historical legacy and to the culture of Native Americans. She was unwilling to let the bloodlines of these magnificent horses be wasted by a moral monster. She is a wealthy woman, able to accept the loss of a million and a half dollars in a hoax. After several hours of personal torment, she decided that if she lost the money, she lost it. Some things in life are more important than money." Understanding the correct pacing of television drama, Parker paused.

He then said, "Accordingly, at one o'clock yesterday afternoon, Mrs. von Bayer took a deep breath made an unselfish if calculated gamble on behalf of all lovers of the Spanish mustang. She wired the money. After two hours, during which time the distraught Mrs. von Bayer concluded that she had been swindled, a Federal Express truck delivered a refrigerated container containing the straws of frozen semen. Marya then contacted Dr. Sylvia Bonner, the veterinarian who originally collected the sperm. Late last night, Dr. Bonner confirmed that the bar codes on the straws indicated they were genuine. The seals were unbroken."

The gullible might have concluded from Parker's solemn manner and apparent sincerity that he was telling the truth. But the reporters, some of whom were veterans, needed a moment to digest the turn of events.

A young man reporting for the *Oregonian* asked the first

question. "Is the stallion sperm being held by the police as evidence?"

Parker looked startled at the question. "Evidence? Evidence of what? The sperm wasn't stolen. It was purchased from the owners. No law violated there. My client simply bought equine sperm from its current owner, a straightforward commercial transaction."

At Parker's side, his client, the erstwhile innocent, blinked her Elizabeth Taylor eyes. *Such a question! Oh my!*

Undeterred, the reporter said, "But isn't it true that somebody calling herself Mustang Mary has been posting drawings on the Internet, claiming responsibility for killing the horses?"

"Yes, the woman identified herself as Mustang Mary, but my client had no way of knowing whether or not that was true. Also, I should point out that nobody knows for a fact that 'Mustang Mary' killed anything. Mrs. von Bayer welcomes police forensic examiners to check the shipping container or her phone records for fingerprints or other evidence they might find. What she does not welcome is any examination of the straws and shipping container under conditions that might allow the semen to thaw. If that should happen, lawsuits will follow that will take your breath away, guaranteed."

Another reporter asked if Mrs. von Bayer would, if asked, share the sperm with those breeders who had lost stallions.

Parker said, "Perhaps you didn't understand my earlier answer. Let me try again. My client is of course sympathetic to those breeders who lost their stallions. But those breeders sold the sperm. My client bought it from the buyer. The fact that it was purchased under the threat that it would be destroyed is irrelevant. The straws filled with semen are hers. Her property. She owns them."

Marya leaned forward and said in a husky whisper, "What happened to those breeders was awful. Just awful. I know many of them personally from horse shows and competitions. They're good, hard-working people. They loved their stallions. My heart goes out to them. It truly does. One can only imagine how they must feel. My heavens to Betsy." So very sympathetic was Marya von Bayer. Gracious. A lovely lady.

Another reporter said, "What do you propose to do with the sperm now, Mrs. von Bayer?"

Marya looked surprised. "I became interested in breeding horses from my late husband, whose stable produced numerous champion jumpers in Germany. Everybody knows that it is my ambition to become the premiere breeder of Spanish mustangs in the United States."

Parker didn't like the direction of his client's response. "My client—"

Marya pressed forward, eyes blazing. "I own the sperm. I will not yield to whiners or the righteously indignant. Let them buy their own semen. I will use the contents of these straws to impregnate mares with superior conformation. I am not interested in breeding ordinary horses. Only the best. Rather than challenging me, you should think of honoring me for public service."

"Who do you suppose killed those stallions?"

Parker tried again. "My client—"

"I have no idea," Marya said. "My guess is no better than anybody else's. Why on earth would you ask me that? Are you accusing me of killing those stallions?" She glared at the reporter, waiting. When he said nothing, she pressed forward, abandoning her feminine persona. "I don't accept that kind of question from a pipsqueak. Would you like to be sued? Would anybody else like to ask that question?" She looked around angrily, challenging the reporters.

Parker interrupted more forcefully. "My client is a breeder of mustangs, not an officer of the courts. She has already said that she will cooperate fully with the police. She has made public what happened. I have answered your questions. I believe that will be enough for now."

Gerrold Parker's history suggested that he would eat an excrement sandwich if the price was right. Suing a reporter would be a dill pickle on the side. When Parker said the press conference was at an end, it was finished. Full stop. No more.

Marya von Bayer quickly reverted to her feminine, demure look. Knowing the cameras were tracking her, she dabbed at her tightly stretched face with a lace hankie. Her heels were too high. Her ankles wobbled. She allowed herself to be escorted to a stretch limousine with dark windows. Looking as stern and important and commanding as their youth and inexperience allowed, the wannabe celebrity lawyers cleared the way.

On arriving at the limousine that stretched ostentatiously over two parking slots, Marya turned toward the cameras and batted her Elizabeth Taylor eyes. She nearly swooned, poor thing. "You reporters are horrid. Horrid!" she exclaimed. She held up her chin to demonstrate her wounded pride. Poor suffering Marya. "The nerve, bringing up the nasty subject of those dead stallions. I am a lady, for heaven's sake. My word!"

The gallant Parker opened the door of the limousine for the abused heroine. "Mrs. von Bayer," he said unctuously.

Marya pretended to have a hard time getting in the fancy vehicle. First, she bent far too low, the better to demonstrate that she didn't require any kind of high-tech push-'em-up. Then she "accidentally" hiked up her dress, flashing her behind to the folks at home, a momentarily awkward moment inasmuch as the lady wore no underwear. Giggling nervously, pretending to be embarrassed at having aimed her southernmost chute at the cameras, she demurely pulled the bottom of her dress back into place.

"Oh my goodness gracious!" she exclaimed. "Whatever did I do?" She put her hand over her heart. *Pat, pat, pat. Bat, bat*, went her Elizabeth Taylor eyes. She wrinkled her Jodie Foster nose. The people wanted to see justice, let them see her bum hole. If the police wanted to arrest her for indecent exposure, let them.

She puckered her Sophia Loren lips and gave the cameras a sweet kiss. She slid onto the seat. The network's parabolic microphone caught her laughing uproariously as one of Parker's assistants, giving the cameras a how-dare-you look, closed the door with a righteous flip of his wrist.

The limousine sped off. Were Marya, Parker, and the two pretty-boy lawyers peering out of the tinted windows at the curious onlookers, glasses of preposterously expensive wine in hand, toasting the mooning of credulous morons? Those who had heard her laughing had to wonder.

27 • *Vagina dentata*

If ever there was a moment that I wanted to accept Willie's assertion that he had spent millennia battling the evil, shape-changing Koonran, it was when the limousine disappeared around the corner.

If Marya had intended her mooning as payback for being ridiculed as Mustang Mary, she had done one hell of a job. Having successfully washed the semen (if that phrase was not too awkward) that she had likely bought in the first place, she was now free to use it as she pleased. She could deliver the offspring of dead stallions and enter the correct lineage of their foals in the Spanish Mustang Registry. Perfect conformation they would have. Beautiful horses.

Was there a single word that adequately described Marya von Bayer's performance?

Cheek? Anatomically appropriate perhaps, but not strong enough.

Gall? Too sweet.

Chutzpah? Insufficient.

Effrontery? Again, not sufficient.

None of that made her guilty of any kind of felony. Rudi

Fackler said the German media wanted the murderer to be Marya. After her so-called press conference, it was easy to see why. I brought myself around. Wearily, I punched the remote, silencing a commercial break.

I retrieved two bottles of Oddball and popped the caps. "Well, what do you think happened, Annie? Assume Marya is the horse killer and murderer. Give me the theory."

"Marya, furious at her husband's philandering, transformed herself into a bizarre image of his playthings, then framed him for horse killing. She murdered him and vowed to compete against his achievements as a horse breeder. She moved back to Oregon and secretly bought semen from the best studs of the most successful breeders of Spanish mustangs."

I gave Annie her Oddball and settled back in a Goodwill chair. "Then hired somebody to kill the stallions."

She took a sip. "Marya 'bought' the semen from an 'extortionist,' that is, from herself, and hired Gerrold Parker to help her explain what happened. Everything else is for sale, why not justice?"

I said, "The Strehmel premise. The Fackler premise is that Marya's calculating daughter, having an advantage because she's attractive and people like her, wants to score the rest of the BioSource fortune. She's playing her mother's rage and ambition like a Stradivarius. Framing her. How about some popcorn?"

"Popcorn sounds good."

I got up to snag the popper.

Behind me, Annie said, "The awful truth is both mother and daughter have so much money they might very well be untouchable."

Just then the phone rang. I snagged the receiver. It was Toni Lindemann.

Toni said, "Did you happen to see Marya von Bayer's press conference on the box?"

"Annie and I watched it, yes."

"She's the inspiration for Mustang Mary. Has to be. Did you see those crazy boobs?"

"How could anybody miss them?"

"And that ridiculous behind!" Lindemann laughed broadly.

I said, "None of which gives us a clue as to the identity of your mystery client."

"Mustang Mary is back on the Web."

"She is? Which drawing?"

"My long awaited and much anticipated masterpiece, *Vagina dentata.*"

Annie called up the latest Mustang Mary image on her computer. Naked except for cowboy boots and chaps, a grinning Mary lay back with her legs spread wide, revealing her shaven vulva. The lips of her vagina were tattooed with evil little teeth. Under the vertical mouth, a rivulet of blood flowed.

Under the drawing she had neatly printed in her usual block letters:

> *SNARFED UP TWENTY-TWO FANCY MUSTANG STUDS. YUM, YUM, YUMMY IN THE TUMMY AND SWEET TO EAT. NOW I'VE SCORED A MILLION AND A HALF BUCKS, AND NOBODY KNOWS WHO I AM. OR CAN PROVE WHO I AM. DRIVE YOU ALL CRAZY, DO I? FIND THE WOMAN WITH THE TEETH, AND YOU'LL FIND ME. YOUR HUNGRY CORRESPONDENT, MUS-TANG MARY.*

28 · Rogue River Rachael

In my experience, being laid-back and civil, a soft-boiled dick, worked far better than the clichéd hard-boiled variety. Confrontation only made people defensive. Better to ease into the territory of motive, especially if it were true, as Rudi Fackler asserted, that Erika von Bayer had hired Willard Leopoldo to kill horses.

On the phone, I told Rachael Leopoldo that Denson, Dancer, and Sees the Night thought the horse killer might well be a breeder of Spanish mustangs. In pursuit of clues, I needed to learn more about horse breeding and horse breeders, and she was one of the best.

I had a five-hour drive south to Rachael's ranch on the Rogue River. There were times when it felt good to be alone, buzzing down the road in my Volkswagen microbus. On those rare occasions when I drove with the radio on, I cruised the stations looking for golden oldies. If a song was adolescent shouting or noise, I moved on. If the lyrics were poetic or told a story or the rhythm made me move, I loosened up. Humping was what rock and roll meant. Life. When I moved to a thumping, humping beat, juices flowing, I felt good.

I finally punched off the radio and drove in silence, thinking about the horse killer and counting red-tailed hawks perched on fence posts just off I-84. The interstate highway was a boon to the red-tailed hawk. I once counted forty-four of them on a run between Roseburg and Portland. It was difficult to tell whether this was because of roadkill or because the passing traffic flushed startled rodents.

Two more hours and twelve red-tailed hawks, I turned off near Medford and headed down the Rogue on the highway that led to the Flying B, a ranch that looked far more prosperous than I had expected. It sported tightly stretched barbed wire fences around lush green pastures, and a new barn, a replica of one of those huge, grand, traditional barns with a spacious hayloft, the originals of which had long since rotted, crumbled, or burned down. The red barn was flanked by splendid white stables with red roofs.

The house was not one of those awful ranch-style houses made popular by the booboisie in the 1950s. It was a two-story Victorian that had a modern, retro look about it. I pulled in to a gravel parking lot in front of a rolling green lawn bordered by irises. I parked my VW beside a black Cherokee that needed washing. Since I grew up on a farm, I wore boots for the occasion, not because I expected to do any riding, but because on the phone I had asked Rachael Leopoldo if she would show me some horses. I knew about barns and barnyards. When the hay went in, just like the truth, it had to come out somewhere.

When I hopped down from my bus, it was late afternoon with a warming summer sun. A tall, long-legged woman wearing cowboy boots stepped out of the house onto the sprawling front porch. Rachael Leopoldo slapped a weathered cowboy hat on her head and strode across the lawn to meet me, a long red ponytail flopping on her shoulders. She had a pair of well-used Levi's stretched across broad hips and a shapely rump, and a western shirt with snap tabs over the pockets. She was all woman and then some. She had high, broad cheekbones and intelligent gray eyes.

Was this the face of a horse killer? Hard to believe.

Rachael thrust out her hand and we shook. She had a firm grip and a big smile. "I'm Rachael. The Big R, Willard calls me. Willard being my husband."

"John Denson. I have to say you don't look anything like your sister."

She laughed broadly. "Boy, oh boy, I like a man who isn't stingy with the flattery. It's all in the genes, Mr. Denson. In humans and horses. I'm a clone of my dad. Sylvia is Mom all the way. Biologists have figured the probabilities for inheriting almost every characteristic imaginable, both in horses and human, did you know that? Stocking feet. Blonde hair. Blazed foreheads. Dimples. You name it. But in the end there is no way in advance for anybody to know how a foal or baby will turn out."

"A biological crapshoot," I said.

"Ain't that the truth? It's a long drive down from Portland. Won't you come in and have a cold one and let 'em hang for a few minutes? Gotta refrigerator full of Henry Weinhardt's beer. After that I'll show you some horses, and I'll tell you everything you want to know." She turned and cupped her hands around her mouth and shouted, "Willard!"

I followed her onto the porch out of the sun. An earthy kind of woman, she was.

She said, "He's out back somewhere pooping around. Finished with his happy tap-tap for the day."

"Happy tap-tap?"

"After Willard hurt his knee, he learned all about computers, and now he has his own business keeping records for veterinarians all over the country. There's probably more money to be made in sick people than animals what with the boomers turning creaky, but there's more people setting up data systems for their records too."

Just then an athletic-looking man who couldn't have been a bunch over a hundred pounds soaking wet, strode around the corner of the house wearing cowboy boots and jeans, same as Rachael. He sailed his cowboy hat onto the porch, looped his arm around Rachael's waist, and gave her a little hug. She was a whole bunch bigger than he was and eight or ten inches taller.

As we shook, Willard said, "I used to be a jockey, Mr. Denson. Screwed up my knee in a spill at Santa Anita."

Rachael said, "Modesty prevents him from telling you that he rode Bobby's Luck to victory in the Preakness eight years ago. Just came flying around that last turn, flogging the ass of Bobby's Luck most proper. What a ride! We've got it on tape."

"The past is past," Willard said.

Willard and I took our seats at a table on the porch while Rachael went inside to fetch the beer.

When she was out of earshot, Willard said, "Rachael and I love horses. If I ever catch the son of a bitch who killed those studs, I'd show him what a pissed-off hundred-and-six-pound jock can do."

"I think you'd probably have to get in line."

"Anything we can do to help, just ask."

"For starters, I need a primer on the business of raising mustangs. There's gotta be a clue in there somewhere."

"No *problema.*"

Rachael arrived back with a huge tray containing a six-pack of Henrys, a bag of corn chips, and a bowl of Mexican salsa. "After we wet our whistles, I'll show you some horses, and we can talk about genes and semen and all that good stuff." As she sat, she said, "Willard and I know that people enjoy speculating about us. Willard says that when he was growing up, all the other boys got bigger and taller, but Willard went straight to dick. Isn't that right, love?"

Willard grinned.

"Other times he claims he raised it by hand. It's a shame I never got to see him in those tight riding silks. Oooh!" Grinning at Willard, she fluttered her eyelashes.

"My God! Enough!" Willard said. But he was pleased nevertheless.

Rachael said, "Better than my sister Sylvia getting off stuffing horse's cocks into rubber pussies. I swear that gets her juiced. Can you imagine?" She took a slug of Henry Weinhardt's beer. "You have to feel some sympathy for the stallions, right, Willard?"

"Right," Willard said dryly.

I said, "Nothing like a cold beer on a summer afternoon. Maybe now I should have a chat with Charlene ReMillard. See what she has to say."

Rachael grimaced. "The vile little bitch. You'll hear it from other people, so I might as well be up front. I cannot abide that cunt, begging your pardon. And it isn't because she's a lesbian. There was a helluva lot more to it than that, I assure you."

"What would that be?" I asked mildly.

Glowering, eyes blazing, lips tight, Rachael glanced at Willard. "Never mind. Suffice it to say I'd be pleased never to lay eyes on that slut again." She stopped, thinking about what she had just said. "We've got a bunkhouse out back. Stupid to drive back to Portland this late in the day."

I said, "Thanks, but I better get on back."

"I'll take my fly rod along when we go see the mares," Willard said quickly. "Maybe I can catch a couple for the smoker."

Rachael said, "Let's go see the mares. Good idea."

29 · *The tyranny of conformation*

With Willard carrying an ultralight fly rod in a day pack and a wicker creel on his hip, we strolled out into the main pasture where Rachael and Willard kept their mares. A meandering creek wound lazily through the pasture, leading to a draw flanked by Douglas fir. This was where the mares grazed. To prevent the inevitable quarreling over the favors of the mares, the stallions were kept in separate pastures.

Willard said, "In the afternoon, the mares like to drift on up the creek. There's shade up there, and it's cooler. This is Siskiyou Creek. Float a bucktail nymph on the water, and you'll have a trout on in seconds."

Rachael fell silent as we all watched a hawk high above soaring on an updraft, its wings spread. "Most wild horses are a duke's mixture. Working horses got loose, and the ranchers released any number of breeds, Hambletonians, Morgans, Irish stallions, Shires, Percherons, you name it. The mustangs the Conquistadors took to the New World were bred from North African horses brought to the Iberian peninsula by the Moors. The Kiger and Riddle Mountain mustangs and those found in the Pryor Mountains and Needle Mountains look very much like the modern-day Spanish Sorraias."

She fell silent, thinking. "The color of all horses is determined by seven genes. We've got the white gene, W, but if you match two dominant W genes, you get a dead horse, one of the reasons all-white horses are rare." She gave me a wry grin. "You know, Mr. Denson, I could take you through a complicated explanation of dominant and recessive genes and their alleles and what kind of foal they produce. Will knowing about the agouti gene and the TO gene help you in any meaningful way? I don't think you need to know all that."

"I just want to find the person who killed the stallions."

Willard gestured up the draw. "The mares are not down low. Looks like we'll need a little hike."

"I don't mind a little exercise," I said. "Skip the details of the genetics, but I want to know more about breeding mustangs. Maybe you'll say something by accident that will help out."

"You got it," she said.

Saying no more, we continued on until we came upon a lazy bend in the creek. Willard said, "There are some big old lunkers who hang out here in the afternoon."

Rachael and I retreated to the shade of a Douglas fir and sat, watching Willard ease carefully up to the fishing hole.

A few minutes later, a half dozen mares came walking down the trail that followed the creek.

Rachel said, "Baba Girl, the mare in the lead, is a tobiano. Note that she has white on the bottoms of all her legs. All four of a tobiano's legs should be white below the hocks and knees, and the white should extend over the back. Her tail has two colors, also found on most tobianos. Right behind her are Riddle Smiddle and Tyger Syl, buckskin mares descended from Riddle Mountain stock."

"There he is!" Willard shouted. He had a fish on.

"Don't try to horse him in," Rachael called.

"Nag, nag, nag," Willard said, concentrating on the trout burst from the water, struggling to rid itself of the barbed fly in its mouth.

"Riddle Smiddle and Tyger Syl both have extraordinary conformation. If you have a male with all the classic markings, you never geld him. You use him as a stud. It's okay to breed father to daughter or father to granddaughter, but not brother to sister. Among humans, conformation can be a kind of tyranny. We horse breeders thrive on it."

We fell silent, listening to the bugs pop and snap in the waning afternoon heat.

I said, "Who do you think killed those stallions?"

She waited, then said, "I have no idea."

I said, "Are you going to help your sister and Marya von Bayer with their mustang sperm bank?"

She furrowed her brows. "Sperm bank? With Marya von Bayer? Who on earth told you that cock and bull story? Sylvia would never work with that bitch on anything. She hates her as much as I do, if not more. Marya von Bayer is *the* bitch of the western world. You have only to set eyes on Marya, and you'll know for a fact who Mustang Mary is. You won't have to ask her a single question."

"I only have to see her?"

"You ever been to a freak show? Geeks and pinheads and stuff?"

I sailed a question at her that was a kind of verbal beanball. "A German cop showed up on my doorstep claiming that Erika von Bayer is trying to frame her mother. He believes Erika hired Willard and you to kill the horses."

Rachael exploded, her eyes wide. "What a crock of horseshit that is! Willard and I love horses!"

30 · *Cardinal gossip*

After withdrawing as gracefully as I could, amid many apologies, I drove along the Rogue River upstream, pulling into the gravel parking lot of the Cardinal Tavern about a mile from the entrance to the Flying B. The tavern, which had a huge neon cardinal out front, was flanked by the Sportsman's Café on the left and an Exxon gas station and the Quik Stop convenience store on the right. A sign outside the Quik Stop advertised fishing tackle and bait. About fifty yards upstream from this rural oasis, the Tillicum Motel overlooked the Rogue River. Till I Come. Get it? Ha, ha, ha.

As I climbed out of the bus, I wondered what motivated the owners of the convenience store to call it the Quik Stop, instead of Quick Stop. Over the years I had seen dozens of rural and small town cafés named the Koffee Kup, and each time I wondered about the spelling, which in my mind was stupid, not clever.

Was Cardinal Tavern named for the bird or the baseball team? I hopped up onto the porch and stepped inside. Looking around, I almost groaned out loud. Baseball. Yes!

On the walls were photographs of famous St. Louis Cardinals.

Most of them were old-timers, including Dizzy Dean throwing
a heater, Red Schoendienst turning a double play, and Stan Mu-
sial in his nutty batting stance, coiled like a snake and with his
bat held high. But there were some moderns too: Bob Gibson,
Curt Flood, Ozzie Smith, and Mark McGwire.

I took a seat on a bar stool, grateful that for the time being
I was the only customer. The bartender, a slender redheaded
woman in her midthirties, wore jeans and a blouse inadequate
to the task of concealing the contents of her push-'em-up bra. A
name tag perched at the top of her cleavage said her name was
Edna. With a little luck, Edna would be one of those country
bartenders with not a whole lot to do but speculate on the com-
ings and goings of the locals.

Surveying the row of ceramic handles, I said, "A pint of
draught Rainier sounds good. And a couple of those beef jerkys."

Edna unscrewed the lid of the jar and stabbed two strips of
dried beef. "These're real good. Gotta little flavor. A lot of 'em
taste like cardboard."

Sitting there sipping my Rainier, I had a gut feeling that
Rachael and Willard Leopoldo couldn't have had anything to
do with killing mustang stallions. But then again the German
cop seemed certain of his charge, and I had been wrong before.

I also thought about Rachael's remark about conformation.
She incessantly mixed and matched dominant and recessive
genes until she got the kind of foal she wanted. Dog breeders
did the same thing. I had seen Australian sheep dogs so smart it
was nuts. They got that way because their breeders were after
smart dogs. There were big dogs, cute dogs, cuddly dogs, mean-
as-hell dogs, all ultimately bred from just one dog, the wolf.

In the Cardinal Tavern with a glass of Rainier, sitting alone, I
arranged and rearranged the possibilities. I believed Sylvia
Bonner when she said she and Charlene ReMillard had been in-
ventorying the stock at Kiger and Riddle Mountain. Yet, she had

accepted my assertion that the third person was Willard Leopoldo when it was clearly female, possibly Marya von Bayer.

Outside, a black Cherokee raced by at high speed.

"Who in the hell is that?" I asked. I had seen clearly who it was.

Edna put two strips of jerky on a napkin and put them in front of me. "That was Little Willard. The chase is on. Hold onto your stool. Rachael will be coming along in a few minutes."

"Little Willard? Rachael?"

"They're from the Flying B Ranch a little west of here."

"I think I saw it off the side of the road. Big house. Fancy place. Lotta bucks there."

She pulled my beer. "Rachael's sister is a veterinarian. The one who collected the semen of those mustang stallions that were killed. You might have read about it in the papers."

Edna was a gossip. I'd lucked out. "Big piece about it in the Sunday *Oregonian*. Yes, I read it."

Edna said. "The Flying B looks prosperous, but the truth is complicated. The two sisters inherited the place when their mother died about ten years ago, and they started breeding mustangs. About five or six years ago, they got into an awful row and after that they fought like cats and dogs. But Rachael needs Sylvia's skills as a vet to keep the breeding business going, so they have to see each other whether they liked it or not. Then Rachael fell in love with a jockey named Willard Leopoldo. And she married him!" Ah, romance. Marriage. Edna grinned expansively.

"She tied the knot with a jockey."

"Former jockey, little fart. He was actually well-known before his horse balked and sent him over a rail. Fouled up his knee. Rode a lot of winners. Won the Preakness one year. At about the same time Sylvia took up with Charlene, who runs the business end of Ames and Bonner. Sylvia and Charlene paid too much for their practice in Sheridan, so Sylvia had to continue yo-yoing back and forth to the Flying B to make money off breeding horses."

"Ah, the old cash flow problem raises its ugly head."

Edna grinned. "Cash flow is one way of putting it, I suppose. Meanwhile, with Charlene helping him understand veterinarians' accounting problems, Willard designed some record-keeping software and set up a business using what came to be the bunkhouse as his office, which brings us to the fun part."

Edna was on a roll. Ah, sweet gossip! "Oh?" I said.

"Well, Sylvia and Charlene are lovers, you know, lesbians. When Sylvia came down, she always brought Charlene with her. Trouble is, Charlene spent too much time with Willard in the bunkhouse-office developing computer software. She started testing his personal hardware, if you know what I mean."

"I'm shocked! Shocked!" I said.

"Every time they get a chance, they rent a room in the Tillicum for a little poke-poke. It's a real kick watching them. Even if they're on a run for beer and potato chips, they'll head for the Tillicum for a quickie." Edna giggled. "What a pair! Regular squirrels. It's like she's in heat, and he's constantly rutting. Give 'em five minutes and they'll go for it. Willard's a tiny little squirt, but he must really be something in the sack, taking care of both Rachael and Charlene."

"Oh, oh," I said. "Another beer, please."

Pulling another pint of beer, Edna said, "Rachael eventually found out, of course. You can't keep a secret like that in a place like this. And you have to understand that Rachael is a woman with a real temper. A lot of us can be real bitches when we've got the rag on, but if somebody pushes Rachael too far or crosses her, she goes flat out of her skull. It's like she's on steroids or something. She's famous for it." Edna laughed. "When Rachael loses it, we just keep our distance. We know she'll get over it. Ordinarily, she's a whole lot of fun. Likes to laugh. She and

Willard come in here all the time for a couple of beers and a cheeseburger."

"What happened when she found out about Willard and Charlene?"

"What happened?" Edna laughed even louder. "It was a real show, let me tell you. It was just after the mill shift let out, so I had a full house. Willard and Charlene were in the Tillicum testing the mattress one more time. They parked their vehicles in back, but we all knew they were in there. Then Rachael's Cherokee came flying into the parking lot, sliding sideways on the gravel. Somebody shouted, 'Rachael's figured the action.' By the time we got to the window, Rachael was coming out of the office all worked up and in a lather. We're talking maximum pissed here. She strode directly to the room where the action was going on and put her shoulder to the door."

"Knocked it down?"

"I told you she's got a temper on her. A few seconds later Willard came flying out of the door buck naked with Rachael right after him. She planted a right cross on him—the boys all tell me it was a right cross—that you just would not believe. Caught him flush in his face with a hell of a *craaaaack* and knocked him off his feet. It was like in the movies or something. Sylvester Stallone lands punches like that in the *Rocky* movies but not a tall, redheaded broad decking a gimpy little jockey."

"Whoa!" I said.

"She hurt her hand, so she started shaking it, her face all bunched up in pain. Then she began bawling, at the same time kicking Willard as hard as she could. She tried to kick him in the crotch, but he curled up to protect himself, so she switched to his head. All the time she was weeping and wailing. My God, the racket that woman made! Poor little bastard Willard, still dizzy from the punch, was trying to defend his crotch and his head at the same time. But Rachael wasn't about to quit. She laid the toes of her cowboy boots in there as hard she could. Willard's nose was bleeding like a stuck pig. Keep in mind that he was naked as a jaybird. Wasn't wearing a stitch."

Edna was right. That was a real scene. "Are you bullshitting me?" I said.

"No, no, no, this is a true story. Then Charlene came outside hysterical and wailing and everything. Rachael must have caught 'em in the act because Charlene was wearing only underpants. She jumped on Rachael's back, wrapped her legs around Rachel's waist, and chomped down on her neck big-time. We're talking bared teeth bearing down hard. She was like a rat terrier. But Rachael ignored her and kept on kicking Willard. We all thought she was going to break his skull or something, so a couple of the boys ran across the lot and pulled them all apart. Rachael screamed that if she ever caught Willard and Charlene in the sack again, she'd kill both of them."

"Threatened to kill them?"

"Yes, she did," Edna said. "The lady was in a real bad mood."

"What happened then?"

"Rachael tried to slap Charlene, who was bent over Willard, but only got her on the shoulder. Then she burst into a fit of sobbing, clapped her hand to the back of her neck where she had been bitten, and jumped into her Cherokee. Spinning her tires, she fishtailed out of the parking lot, sending gravel everywhere, and headed upriver. I took a bucket of bar ice over to Willard for his face. We carried him inside to his motel unit. Both of his eyes were swollen shut. He had a broken nose, and his lips were swollen as big as sausages. He also lost a couple of teeth. And the blood! My God, there was blood everywhere. It was like he had gone fifteen rounds with Mike Tyson. The motel manager was painting one of the units so he had a sheet of plastic to throw over the bed."

Remembering the scene, Edna shook her head. "That was probably the most fun this place has had in fifteen or twenty years. A real show. The boys even got a freebie tit shot of Charlene. A nice pair, they all say."

"Did Sylvia ever find out about the melee?"

"You know, that's interesting. Sylvia has never had anything to do with us locals, other than to buy gas or a Coke in the convenience store. She's certainly never came in here. None of us here have been able to figure whether she found out or not. Maybe she did. Maybe she didn't. Charlene didn't have any bruises or anything. On the other hand, Rachael broke her knuckles on Willard's face. She had her hand in a cast and a bandage on the side of her neck when she and Willard dropped by for a beer a few days later. His eyes were still slits. Since everybody had seen what happened, they pretended it was all just a little tiff and everything was hunky-dory. That's the last time Charlene came down. Sylvia's been here a couple of times to inseminate a mare or collect semen, but Charlene stays up in Sheridan. Don't blame her."

"When did all that happen?" I asked.

"Oh, I don't know. Must have been four or five months ago." Glancing out of the window, Edna did a double take. "There Rachael goes now."

I swiveled on my stool, but I was too late to see anything.

"Whole lot of heat on at the Flying B these days, let me tell you. But Willard had enough of a lead that she won't catch him. He'll be all right."

"You think he's headed for Sheridan."

"I think that's likely it, yes. Makes a person wonder how much longer Rachael and Willard are going to keep their act together."

31 · *Worrying about Willard*

When at last I parked the bus and flopped down on the Goodwill couch in our cabin, I told Annie about my day. I knew I wouldn't be able to sleep so we decided to continue our ongoing chess tournament in which we played several games daily with nobody counting wins and losses Annie was a flamboyant attacker. I was a by-the-booker. Stolidly, I developed the middle, seeing to the chores of defense while I watched for an opportunity to counterattack. Our chess styles reflected our styles as investigators. Annie went straight to the guts. I circled quietly as possible, observing.

An hour later, the phone rang. Studying the position of her rook, Annie grabbed it without looking up from the board. She listened for a moment then handed me the receiver. "It's for you. A woman. She doesn't sound happy."

I took the phone. "John Denson," I said.

A woman sobbed.

I waited.

"This is Rach—this is Rach—this Rach—" She began wailing.

"Rachael Leopoldo. Take your time," I said. "No hurry." That was a mistake because Rachael wept unabashedly. Dammit, I just hated it when people cried. Women. Little kids. Hated it.

"Easy. Easy. What happened?"

She started to say something, then broke down again.

Finally she said, "Do you know where Willard is?"

"Well, no," I said. "Last time I saw him he was racing by the Cardinal Tavern with you in hot pursuit."

She made a noise in her throat. "We had a little tiff. You know how those things go. Willard is one of those men who likes to take off once in a while. Air out his shorts is the way he puts it. I don't know what he does when he takes off, and I don't want to know. If he doesn't come back right away, he always calls to tell me when he'll be back. Always. This time he hasn't called."

I had a good idea what he did when he disappeared, but I didn't say anything. I said, "If he always comes back or calls, he probably will this time too. Maybe all you have to do is be patient."

"I'm afraid something has happened to him. That he's in trouble or something. I thought maybe you might be following him."

Ah, so that was it. The hysteria was likely bogus. Rachael was curious about my visit. "What reason would I have to follow Willard?"

"You said yourself that Willard and I are suspected of murdering those mustangs."

I didn't say anything.

She waited, then said, "You think Willard is shacked up with that little whore Charlene?"

"Everybody in the Cardinal saw that set-to you had with Willard and Charlene outside the Tillicum."

With that, Rachael went ballistic. "Who told you that?" she screamed. "Edna? The slut. She's got nothing better to do than flap her mouth. She'll fuck anybody for a ten spot, did you know that? Ten bucks! The bitch! It's like she's in heat or something. Who told you? Was it her?"

"A logger," I lied.

"I bet. I just bet. It was Edna. Had to be. She's bored, and she's got nothing better to do than tell strangers about my little disagreement with Willard. Yes, Mr. Denson, I caught him on top of Charlene, his ridiculous little butt going up and down. And don't tell me to call Sylvia. Sylvia is my sister, for God's sake. She thinks she's in love with that little witch Charlene. What she doesn't know won't hurt her."

I said, "She'll find out eventually. Has to."

"She can learn from somebody else, not me. Wait 'til I get my hands on Edna. I'll rip those fancy tits of hers right off her chest."

Eyeing the chessboard, I advanced a Denson gambit. "Okay, Rachael, you want to know the truth? There are those people, police among them, who believe Willard killed those Spanish mustangs on these trips of his."

"What?"

"Hired by Marya von Bayer or her daughter Erika, depending on whose theory you believe, a cop's or a private dick's."

"You dirty son of a bitch," Rachael said evenly.

"Or maybe Willard and Charlene did it themselves to score money for their own ranch. A million-and-a-half-dollar semen scam will buy a lot of hay." I hated doing that to her, but in the heat of passion, people sometimes blurted out unexpected truths.

Rachael Leopoldo slammed the receiver in my ear.

32 · *Sperm conference*

The next day there was another press conference about the deaths of the mustang stallions. It was a traditional media event, minus the outlandish theatrics of Marya von Bayer's performance. A sober, serious Dr. Sylvia Bonner, dressed in a tailored suit, appeared before a podium holding a prepared script. At her side, FBI agent Sheb Goodall looked equally sober and serious.

Public relations types advised their clients to establish eye contact with the camera and to appear casual and earnest, not stiff or nervous. But Sylvia was not a celebrity. She had no professional advising her on the requirements of public theater. She was a veterinarian caught up in public drama.

Reading from a script on the podium in front of her, she said, "My name is Dr. Sylvia Bonner. I am the veterinarian who collected the sperm from the mustang stallions that were later killed. I have been in the business of artificial insemination of horses ever since my graduation from Oregon State University sixteen years ago. In all that time, I never once had an anonymous client hire me to collect sperm. Secrecy is inimical to the proper tracking and registration of bloodlines. Only when both sire and damn are known and their bloodlines are properly recorded can we maintain the purity of this breed, which is a form of national treasure. When an anonymous person offered to pay me triple my usual fee to collect sperm from a champion stallion and ship it to an equally anonymous drop box, it made no sense whatsoever. I got immediately suspicious." Sylvia looked up from the script, glanced at the camera, then continued reading.

"So I did something that was at the time unprofessional, but in retrospect, I think, judicious. I stored the sperm that I had collected and sent sterile semen to my client's specified drop box." She paused, clearing her throat. She looked up, then back down at her script. "My logic was that if this unknown person had a legitimate, benign reason for the secrecy, I still had the frozen sperm, safely stored. I am a lover of horses. As a veterinarian my larger responsibility is to the horses. When this anonymous client gave me a second and yet a third assignment, jobs in Idaho and Montana also involving prime stallions, I resolved to continue my deception until I was given a good reason for the secrecy."

Sylvia paused and took a deep breath, exhaling through puffed cheeks. "In all, I collected sperm from twenty-two stallions before my free-spending, anonymous client fell silent. It was then that the killing of the stallions began. I had no idea that any of these horses had died mysteriously until I read a small article in the *Oregonian*. At that point, I went to the FBI field office in Portland."

Sylvia stepped to one side. Special Agent Goodall took her place. "Our problem from the beginning was the horse killer chose ranches that were widespread geographically. In all but four cases, the breeders had no idea that stallions other than their own had died. The stallions were killed within a space of four weeks. And the deaths all appeared to be accidental or from natural causes. When Dr. Bonner contacted us, we were conducting a preliminary investigation into the possibility that the horses had been deliberately killed. On the basis of her story, we ordered the exhumation of the dead animals and began a forensics examination of their remains."

Goodall started to step aside, but quickly reclaimed the mike. "I should add here that the FBI is investigating the deaths of the horses because the killer or killers traveled across state lines. At this point, we don't know if the anonymous buyer of the semen was aware that it was sterile."

It was Sylvia Bonner's turn again. Still reading from the prepared script, Sylvia said, "If the anonymous buyer will step forward and confirm details of his or her contact with me, I will surrender the frozen sperm forthwith. No problem. Mrs. Marya von Bayer bought the semen as a public service, growing from her love of the Spanish mustang and her dedication to see that their bloodlines are preserved. I feel very sorry that she paid a million and a half dollars for sterile semen. As Mrs. von Bayer said, she had no way of knowing she was dealing with a possible horse killer. Neither did I." She turned, giving Goodall his cue.

Goodall said, "As Mrs. von Bayer said in her press conference, the semen is now hers. She paid for it. She is correct when she says she is not obliged to share it with anybody. The attorney general of Oregon State tells me that Dr. Bonner is likewise under no legal obligation to turn over the good semen to Mrs. von Bayer. Her contractual obligation is to the anonymous client who paid for her services. Since Dr. Bonner still has the straws of frozen equine semen, the attorney general is satisfied that she has not committed fraud."

Marya had resorted to mooning as a gesture of contempt. Now it was Goodall's turn. Blandly he said, "I, for one, think Mrs. von Bayer is a special person. We owe her a tip of the hat for her courageous and unselfish, if ultimately costly, attempt at public service. Thank you, Mrs. von Bayer. We appreciate it. Let's give it up for Marya!" He began clapping his hands.

After an uncertain moment, the onlookers joined in, and the

applause grew with whistling and crying out. "Viva Marya! We love you, Marya! Keep up the good work, Marya!"

When the applause died down, amid giggling and laughter, Goodall looked around, suppressing any hint of emotion. How he managed to do that was beyond me. "Are there any questions?" asked.

The assembled again exploded with applause. This time it was for Special Agent Sheb Goodall, who demonstrated that not everyone in the Federal Bureau of Investigation was a humorless suit.

33 · *In the big little city*

While one of the von Bayer women was most likely responsible for the crimes in Germany, the circumstances surrounding the mustang killings pointed directly at Willard Leopoldo and Charlene ReMillard. There was only one reason a former jockey and a horse lover would agree to kill mustangs: money for their future. Either Marya, Erika, or Gretchen had somehow found out about their affair and their mutual dreams.

Where?

My bet was the National Wild Horse and Burro Show in Reno, which promoted itself as the biggest little city in the world. The competition in Reno was the high point of the year for breeders of the Spanish mustang. If a stallion won a prize, his stud fee went up. If a breeder had a good-looking mare for sale, the Reno competition was the place to show her off. Marya, Rachael, and Willard almost certainly made an annual appearance there, showing horses, talking horses, watching horses, and perhaps buying horses. Dr. Sylvia Bonner and Charlene ReMillard would also have been there promoting the artificial insemination services of Ames and Bonner.

The next morning, Annie and I buzzed south on I-5, a thermos of coffee in the holder between the Volkswagen's seats. As we drove, we counted red-tailed hawks sitting on the fence posts on either side of the freeway. We would spend a night in Ashland. The next day we would continue south over the Siskiyou Mountains into northern California and across the Sierras at Lake Tahoe, dropping down into Nevada late in the afternoon.

It was almost dark when we got to the eastern outskirts of the city, built on the desert beside the Truckee River just east of the Sierra Nevada. Las Vegas, with its theme park casinos in the shape of pyramids and Spanish galleons, was a city as might have been imagined by Salvador Dali. Gamblers from Southern California were apparently charmed by the surreal. Reno still had an element of a frontier western town to it, entertaining such gamblers from the Bay Area that were not siphoned off by the casinos at Lake Tahoe. Not too far outside of Reno, real cowboys still did their thing.

Of the two, I preferred Reno.

Annie and I were too tired to scout for an older motel, perhaps owned and managed by Hindus, that was not a budget-breaker. Those motels, with threadbare carpets and beds that sagged, still existed, but they were getting harder to find with the passing of years. Increasingly, travelers felt self-conscious if they did not spend an absurd sum to get a night's sleep. Besides, I was not spending my own money. The Ad Hoc Committee to Save the Spanish Mustang was paying. The committee members were not rich and I didn't want to foolishly waste their money. In the end, I popped for a seventy-five-dollar room in the Bunkhouse Motel that was all done up in a cowboy theme.

The room had a refrigerator. It also had a twenty-five-cent slot machine mounted on the wall by the toilet. The television set could likewise be turned into a form of slot machine. If a person got bored with Sunday night baseball or listening to politicians flapping their jaws on cable television, he or she could slip five-dollar bills into a slot and use the remote to stop the spinning fruit on the monitor or use it to watch the posting of Keno numbers. By such devices, the management of the Bunkhouse Motel drained money from their patrons' wallets like a leaky faucet, likely turning a seventy-five-dollar room into a one- or two-hundred-dollar trick.

Annie and I had a supper of hot roast beef sandwiches, an old-fashioned rural and small-town western favorite. Easterners knew their pizza and subs. Out west, the hot roast beef sandwich was ubiquitous on the menus of all manner of greasy spoon diners and cafés in truck stops, podunk burgs, and jerkwater towns. Hot pork and hot turkey sandwiches were also good.

It was my bet that one could buy an overpriced rib steak of Kobe beef in Las Vegas, but not the classic western concoction: slices of overcooked beef on Wonder Bread, smothered in brown gravy slopped artfully over a pile of mashed potatoes. Throw in some boiled corn or peas and carrots at the edge of the plate for those folks who just had to have their veggies, and there you had it. Once in a while, I stumbled onto a prideful boondocks cook who served slices of beef that were slightly pink and who took the time to make the gravy from the roast drippings, not a packet of commercial powder supercharged with monosodium glutamate. Whenever I ate a proper hot roast beef sandwich, I got downright sentimental.

Annie and I took some Coors beer back to our room for a game of chess before we got a good night's rest. The next day we would find the Reno Livestock Event Center, where the annual wild horse show was held. We would separate and fan out, looking for a bar or nightspot where somebody might remember Charlene ReMillard and Willard Leopoldo having a tête-à-tête.

Then too we would do our best to find the fancy digs where Marya von Bayer stayed.

The hotel and casino district, the heart of central Reno, was located just north of the eastward flowing Truckee River that had its origins in the Sierra Madre Mountains, the summit of which was the border between Nevada and California. Just east of Reno, sitting cheek by jowl with its more famous twin, was the city of Sparks. In downtown Sparks, as in downtown Reno, a cluster of gaudy gamblers' sirens, all dazzle and neon and brightly colored plastic, blinked and flashed their beckoning call. *Come here, lady! Over here, pal! Be a sport. Leave your money here! Give it to me! Give it to me! Give it to me!*

The famous arch proclaiming Reno "The Biggest Little City in the World" faced north. South of the arch and the Truckee River, Virginia Street bore slightly to the southeast, headed for the Reno Convention Center and east of the convention center, to the Reno airport.

The Reno Livestock Events Center, a clean, modern, covered arena, was used for rodeos, horse shows, cutting competition, dog shows, and even track meets held by the nearby University of Nevada, Reno. The center was located on Wells Street, a couple of blocks north of the downtown area.

Where I had grown up, a rodeo was an outdoor kind of thing with spectators, armpits reeking of sweat, using cowboy hats to shade their beaks from the summer sun. The Eagles, Elks, Lions, and other animal clubs used the smell of fried onions to lure customers. If you felt the urge, you strolled across ground soaked with horse urine and littered with fresh dumplings to a portable toilet, fender, or back tire. The queen and her court, smiling until their cheeks ached, rode around on farting horses.

In spiffy, odorless indoor venues like the Reno Livestock Events Center, all those smells were gone. Porcelain toilets flushed. Professional caterers had replaced the plain old hot dog with German sausages on fancy buns, and added designer beer and espresso coffee. And the untidy fact that horses let farts, no surprise considering their diet, was to be forever kept from the masses.

All that was not a bad thing, I suppose. Or at least some of it. There would come a time, perhaps, when real horses would be replaced by holograms, and future generations would look back with nostalgia at places like the Reno Livestock Events Center where cowboys tough as rawhide, wearing big hats and with crap on their jeans, rode real Brahma bulls and bucking broncos.

In looking at the map of Reno, it seemed likely that Marya von Bayer would likely have stayed in one of the fancier hotels in the downtown area, which was close to the events arena. Willard Leopoldo and Charlene ReMillard wouldn't want a re-peat of the scene outside the Cardinal Tavern. If they scored a few minutes for some sweaty fun, they would likely split for downtown Sparks or for one of the motels on Virginia Street. We flipped a coin. I got the downtown area and Marya. Annie got Virginia Street.

The batteries in our cell phones were fresh. We had work to do. We set out to do our thing.

It took me less than an hour to find out that when Marya von Bayer attended the National Wild Horse and Burro Show, she stayed at a fancy suite on the top floor of the Reno Hilton. She was a big tipper so everyone knew her well, from the doorman to the elevator operator. I grabbed a cab to downtown Sparks to help Annie run down the place where Willard and Charlene mostly likely met for their assignations. Halfway there, I got a call from Annie on my cell phone.

"Got it," she said triumphantly.

"Tell me," I said.

"A black man named Leo Monahan used to train horses in Southern California. He now plays at a piano bar in the lounge of the Motherlode Hotel, where I am now. A blackjack dealer tells me an ex-jockey and his girlfriend used to come in and talk to Monahan every year during the wild horse show. That was for three or four years running. Monahan and the jockey knew each other from the days when they were involved in racing horses. He plays from eight o'clock to around four in the morning, she says, but he comes in early to score a freebie supper before he starts."

"Gotta be Willard and Charlene. We can try to talk to him when he comes in to eat."

"That's what blackjack dealer says."

"What do you think, rendezvous back at the Bunkhouse and maybe take a little nap before we talk to him? After all that driving the last couple of days, I'm pooped."

"Face it, you're getting a little long in the tooth for all this kind of running around."

I smiled to myself. Maybe she was right, but I didn't want to admit it. I was glad I had found Annie. I said, "I wonder what a Reno bartender would do if I sat down on the stool and asked for a Tom Collins?"

"A what?"

"Oh, shut up," I said.

34 · What Leo heard

Annie and I learned from Leo Monahan's friends at the casino in the Motherlode Hotel that he always ate his supper in the little lounge where he played the piano. It was a piano bar in the literal sense. The piano had seats all around it so those customers who liked to chat with the musician and request songs could get up close and personal.

The harvest of greenbacks at the Motherlode was reaped at the gaming tables and the slot machines. Sodden, dysfunctional brains offered maximum profit. In an effort to keep people at the roulette wheels, slot machines, and blackjack tables, busty girls dressed in not a whole bunch served freebie cocktails on the casino floors. But even drunks got hungry once in a while and a gambler with a buzz on was more profitable than a sober one. The lounges adjoining the casino floors offered good, relatively cheap food so people could eat without leaving the premises.

In my opinion, as casinos went, the Motherlode was very hip. The furniture was either the original carefully preserved or artfully copied, likely the latter. The designers had scorned the colorful, computer-operated modern slots, retaining the old-fashioned machines with yank-on-it handles. The décor dated from the 1950s. To walk through the Motherlode was like admiring a restored 1949 Studebaker. It was to casinos what Timber Jim's was to taverns.

Annie and I sat in chairs cushioned with red plastic, nursing glasses of draught beer, narrow at the bottom, wider at the top, while we waited for Leo Monahan to show up. While everything looked dated in the Motherlode—from the cocktail outfits the waitresses were wearing to the beer glasses and the floral design on the carpet—it also looked new. The gambler who wanted to take an amusing trip back in time threw away his money at the Motherlode.

When Leo Monahan finally arrived, he was easy to spot, being not a whole lot bigger than a jockey. A good-looking black man in his early forties, he wore a pair of casual gray slacks and a light turtleneck pullover. He looked remarkably like Sammy Davis, Jr., right down to Sammy's rich, mellow voice. Leo took a table, and I introduced myself and Annie, telling him what we were after.

He said, "I read where Willard is missing. I'll help you any way I can, sure. Sit, both of you. Join me."

We sat.

Leo said, "Have you eaten? Why don't you eat with me while we talk?"

I said, "Do they have any hot roast beef sandwiches on the menu?" This would be my second hot roast beef sandwich since arriving in Reno. I was on a roll.

He grinned. "My good man, you're talking the Motherlode. No foo-foo food here. The menu is straight from the 1950s. We've got fried chicken with mashed potatoes and that obscene-looking yellowish gravy. We've got chicken fried steak. We've got roast beef sandwiches *au jus*. A blue plate special. Roquefort dressing for the tossed salad. The works. All the plates have a little sprig of parsley on the edge for garnish."

I said, "Where's Dean Martin and Frank Sinatra and the rest of 'em?"

Leo laughed. "Yeah, yeah, I know. Sammy Davis, Jr. Why do you think I got the job? The owners promote the Motherlode as being 'authentic' Reno. Lots of celebrities pop in just to tell their friends they've been here. The television people like to use it for background, what with all the retro furniture and slots. I fit right in with the décor. I'm not bad on the piano, and I'm a good singer, but unfortunately I can't dance like the real McDavis."

A waitress showed up, one of Leo's friends, and took our order. While we waited, he said, "Willard Leopoldo and I were good friends in the days when he was a hot jock. I owe him. Ten years ago, it wasn't easy for a black man to score a job as a trainer, but Willard spotted me giving a horse a workout in Seattle and recommended me to his boss. That's how I got to the big time, at least the big time for me. I was good at my job. My horses won races. I'd still be doing it if my joints hadn't started acting up."

The waitress arrived with our food. The edge of the roast beef peering out from the gravy was overcooked, which was the fashion with such western fare.

When Leo saw the expression on my face. "I knew you'd go for it. But my meal is on the house, hence the prime rib."

While we ate, I filled Leo in on the story so far and why, exactly, we had come to Reno.

Thinking a moment, Leo dug into his prime rib. "Willard and Charlene come here at least once during the wild horse show every year. Willard and I like to talk about old times. Willard is married to a woman who owns a mustang ranch in southern Oregon. Charlene is a two-way kind of gal. She has a girlfriend who is a veterinarian. Or maybe had a veterinarian girlfriend. Or something."

Annie showed him a photograph of Marya von Bayer. "You ever see this woman?"

Looking at it, Leo grinned ruefully, shaking his head. "That one, oh yeah, I've seen her. One of Teddy Burgoine's Janes."

"Oh?" I said.

"Teddy's a gigolo. He's a friend of mine. The hookers call their customers johns. Teddy calls them Janes. We keep our customers happy." Leo took a sip of water. "Teddy likes to bring his Janes in here. They're generally rich, and this is their idea of slumming with a handsome bad-boy gigolo."

Annie said, "When did Teddy bring that woman in here?"

"It was on a day that Willard and Charlene were here, as a matter of fact."

"Did they see Teddy and his Jane?"

"Oh hell, yes! It was the day Erika von Bayer shot the nostalgia piece on the Motherlode—the way casinos used to be in Reno and all that. We were bullshitting between sets when Charlene spotted Teddy and this crazy Jane on the casino floor. Willard and Charlene started to split, but the Jane showed up, leering and saying, 'Well, well, well, fancy meeting you two here! Like this place, do you?' Then she steered Teddy back to the casino floor."

I said, "What happened then?"

"Willard and Charlene took off. They were shaken."

"Did they say why they were leaving?" I said.

Leo shook his head. "I think they were afraid the crazy Jane would rat them out. I remember the Jane had this nutty body. I've seen her somewhere since then, I know. In the news or something." Leo glanced at Annie then me. "That help?" He could tell by the expressions on our faces that it did. He added, "When Willard and Charlene came back a couple of hours later, Erika von Bayer and her camera crew were here. Erika joined them at my piano, and they had a passionate conversation about a telephone call and somebody named Martha or somebody."

"Marya," Annie said.

"Marya, that's it! I remember Erika telling them it was definitely Marya who hired that stable hand to kill those jumping horses in Europe. Is Marya the name of the crazy Jane?"

Annie said, "Yes, it is."

"Teddy could tell you what she said, if anything, but a rich lady from San Francisco hired him to go on a Caribbean cruise with her." Leo shook his head. "The money's good, I know, but I don't know how Teddy does it." He furrowed his brows. "Wait a minute, now I remember where I later saw the crazy Jane. She was the lunatic female who gave that press conference about the mustang semen and then mooned everybody."

"A charming lady."

Leo blinked. "Marya von Bayer. Erika's mother!"

"There you have it," I said.

35 · *Mademoiselle Marie*

After we had a supper of chicken mole in a Mexican restaurant, Annie drove me back to the Bunkhouse Motel, saying she had to attend to some errands.

"Errands?" I said.

She gave me a lopsided grin. I had been with her long enough to know she was up to something. "I won't be long," she said. "An hour maybe. A little longer. I might give you a call. Watch a ball game or something."

"A ball game?"

"No dirty movies. You need to save your strength." With that, she put the bus into gear and buzzed off.

No dirty movie was a clue, I knew. I did find a ball game, the Atlanta Braves and the Los Angeles Dodgers. I settled in with a bottle of High Sierra beer to watch a developing pitchers' duel. An hour later the phone rang.

I answered it, and a woman said, "Mr. John Denson?"

"Me," I said.

"Are you the private investigator pursuing the horse killer?"

"I am," I said. "Along with my two partners," I added quickly.

She said, "I am calling from the Mustang Ranch. We have a gratis take-out order from one of your admirers."

The Mustang Ranch, a legal brothel just outside of Reno, was one of the most famous whorehouses on the planet. "I see," I said, wondering what Annie was up to.

"You have your choice of girls, Mr. Denson. We can offer you Annie Oakley, no relation to the original, out of Cut and Shoot, Texas. She's quite skilled with ropes."

"Ropes? Ah, no. Not tonight."

"And we can give you Ms. Cassie Craven out of French Lick, Indiana. She's quite talented with her—"

I interrupted. "And my third choice?"

"That would be Mademoiselle Marie."

"And Marie's specialty?"

The woman hesitated. She put her hand over the receiver. I could hear her talking to someone. She removed her hand.

"Mademoiselle Marie says she never tells her customers in advance what she's going to do. There is no drama in that. They must discover it for themselves."

"I'll take Marie," I said.

The doorbell rang a half hour later. I knew it was Annie. By then wild with anticipation at the arrival of Mademoiselle Marie, I opened the door. There stood Annie, dressed in a black plastic raincoat and black high heels. She had a shopping bag.

She cocked her head, looking at me as though she had never seen me before. "Monsieur John Denson?"

I smiled.

"I am Mademoiselle Marie."

"From Mustang Ranch."

"That's right." She stepped inside.

"And who is footing the bill?"

"A lady named Annie. She wishes for me to give you a drama of passion that you will never forget." She looked around. "This will do quite nicely. You will remove your clothes, please."

I started undressing. "You going to take off that raincoat? Fair is fair."

She walked around me, looking me up and down. "No prize there, but it will do. On the bed, please."

I did that too. Annie removed restraints from her bag and set about tying my wrists to the headboard. We had done tie-down games before, so that was not unusual. I said. "When are you going to take off that raincoat?"

She cocked her head, smiling. "In a hurry, are we, monsieur? Anxious to get on with the action. With Mademoiselle Marie, you will learn patience." She tied my ankles.

Finally, Annie removed her raincoat. She was wearing black net stockings, a red garter belt. A silver chain joined modest nipple clamps on her breasts. Naturally double-jointed, she turned slowly for my benefit, twisting her limbs this way and that in the manner of a Kama Sutra model.

Then she reached down and held me lightly with her hand. Watching my reaction, she said, "You like that, monsieur?" She squeezed me gently.

"Very much," I said.

"Oh, oh. Too bad." She removed her hand.

"Come on, Annie," I said.

"Please. I am Mademoiselle Marie." She went down on me with her mouth.

I did my best to arch my hips. "Damn you, don't stop," I breathed.

Annie sat up, grinning. "You like that too much as well. I suspect, Monsieur Denson, that you are going to have a long night ahead of you."

With that, she sat on me. "Ah, ah, don't move now. If you move, I'll get up."

It was contrary to the nature of the male not to move. She was so warm inside it was maddening.

Absently, she flipped the chain between her breasts. "Feel good, does it? Warm." She moved gently up and down, her butt brushing lightly against my thighs.

"That's very nice," I said.

"I can see you like it." Up and down she went again. Then she sat there, all heat. Burning.

I forced my hips up. Couldn't help it.

"Monsieur! I told you not to move." She stood, giving me a look of reprimand.

Annie came up to me and flicked the tip of her tongue in and out of my ear. She blew into my ear, then breathed. "You are a detective, no, monsieur? You want to know how to solve a mystery, monsieur? This is how a mystery works. A mystery evades you. It teases. It tortures you. Thus the answer, when you find it, is very, very sweet. The more you want it, the more it eludes you. This will be a long, long night. A lesson for an impatient detective."

I was damned near ready to explode. She stood above me and bent, the better for me to see the wetness between her legs. She ran a finger lightly over it.

I groaned.

"You like that too," she said. "But then you like just about everything, don't you?" She sat on me again, grinning as she flipped the chain. "Fun sitting on you like this. I want to move too, but I've got discipline. You don't. If you want to appreciate the full measure of my drama, you have patience, monsieur. Patience, patience."

I knew if I moved, she would get up. I didn't want that. Neither could I stand being immobile inside her. I was in for a prolonged, erotic tease. "You damned bitch. Wait until we get back home. Then it's gonna be your turn."

"Oooh! You promise? You nasty, nasty man." She moved slightly.

I moved in response. Couldn't help it.

Annie got up again, frowning. "Ah, ah. I told you, no moving around."

36 • *Breakfast at Tessie's*

We got up at four o'clock the next morning for the long drive back to Portland. As I buzzed up the highway toward Lake Tahoe and the California border, I said, "We've got a nine- or-ten-hour drive ahead of us, and I'm pooped from your Mademoiselle Marie stunt. I'm getting older. You need to give me a break now and then. Think a little."

Annie knew I was teasing her. I had loved it. Giggling, smelling good, she leaned against me. "Fun working you to the edge then stopping. You suffered so much. How you wanted it all to end, poor baby."

"When it's my turn, I'll make you lose ten pounds before I'm finished, I swear. You've got biological repeating action. You'll beg for mercy. Beg!"

Annie laughed. "Talk, talk, talk. We'll see if you're any good or if you just like to run off at the mouth."

"I'll show you mouth and a whole lot more."

"Oooh! Really?" She unscrewed the top of the thermos. "Coffee?"

"Coffee'll do for now," I said.

As I drove, I wondered about the puzzle of Leo's story. Want

to know what was said on that eventful day in the Motherlode?
Ask Marya and Erika.

I punched up Marya's number on my cell phone. Before I
could tell her why I had called, she interrupted, "You're not part
of this at all, are you, Mr. Denson? You and your Injun pal really
are trying to find a horse killer. Straight arrows, both of you."

I said, "From the beginning. I *am* working for the Ad Hoc
Committee to Save the Spanish Mustang. Nobody else. I have
no idea who is behind Mustang Mary. I don't know who pulled
the sperm scam."

Marya fell momentarily silent. "You know something, John
Denson, I liked you the first time we talked. I like you even better now."

The lady liked me! I cleared my throat.

"I mean *really* like you. Too bad you're such a Boy Scout.
Such a waste." Then she added, "Mr. Denson, I'm the butt of a
conspiracy, and I can prove it. Will you talk to me? If you want
the truth, please."

"I'm on my way back from Reno. When I get back this afternoon and answer my calls and sort out my mail, I'll call you
back. Will that work?"

"That will work just fine, Mr. Denson. Thank you."

I tried the number that Erika had given me. An assistant
answered the call, telling me she would pass on my message to
Ms. von Bayer.

By one o'clock in the afternoon, we came upon the billboard
advertising Tessie's, a well-known restaurant in a remodeled
Victorian mansion south of Portland. We were getting groggier
by the moment. Annie was a good traveling companion, neither
grumpy nor naggy.

Seeing the billboard, Annie said, "What do you think?"

Being foo-foo and feminine, all dainty and doily, Tessie's wasn't my idea of a good place to eat. It was popular with yuppie females, making it unacceptably bourgeois in my opinion, but Annie had endured plenty of John Denson greasy spoons since throwing in with me. "Lunch at Tessie's? Why not?" I said. I slowed for the exit ramp.

Tessie's was famous for its omelets stuffed with all manner of exotic fillings, from goat cheese and truffles to crawfish and shad roe. But its vegetable omelet was most popular with the ladies.

Thinking goat cheese omelet, I followed Annie into the foyer that was decorated with delicate watercolor landscapes. Tessie's did not have a single, large dining room. Rather, what had formerly been bedrooms, studies, sitting rooms, and whatever, had been remodeled into a confusion of small dining areas. This gave diners privacy and intimacy, and a chance to appreciate the interior of an old house that had been well preserved.

A uniformed waitress bearing menus showed up and led us through the maze of rooms, finally leading us into what had at one time been a large bedroom whose walls were covered with wallpaper in a flowered print. As I settled in to check out the menu, I happened to glance in at the room across the hall.

There sat Sylvia Bonner and a young woman. They were clearly looking, squarely into one another's eyes.

Softly I said to Annie, "Would you check out those two women across the way?"

Annie glanced across the hall.

I said, "Good friends or more than that?"

The waitress showed up with glasses of water, prepared to take our order. Annie said, "Much more than that."

I didn't want Sylvia to see me. Quickly I said to the waitress. "Do you mind if we change seats?" Without waiting for an answer, I switched tables, getting Annie and me out of the line of sight.

Annie, wondering what was going on, ordered a goat cheese omelet. I went for the biscuits and gravy—that is, buttermilk biscuits smothered with a gravy made from pork fat and containing chunks of "country" sausage. The country description simply meant that it was flavored with sage. It was a cholesterol cocktail, but delicious.

When the waitress left with our order, Annie nodded to the room across the hall. "What's up?"

I said, "The older one on the left is Sylvia Bonner."

Annie started to lean back to take another look.

"Ah, ah," I said.

Annie frowned. She was curious.

I said, "You said, 'much more' than friends. What do you think? Just met or friends for a while?"

"If you'd just let me take another look . . ."

I sighed. "Okay, but don't lean back again. Be cool. Go to the toilet and check them out on your way by."

"Got it," Annie said, and was away.

A few minutes later, she returned. She sat not saying anything, making me wait.

"Well," I said at last.

She grinned. "It's impossible to know for sure, but I'd bet they're new lovers, not old."

Sylvia was a survivor. Having lost Charlene, she had found herself somebody else. Good for her. "But Charlene and Willard are missing," I said. "Life goes on? Sylvia doesn't strike me as that coldhearted. Maybe she knows there's no reason for concern. Good idea coming to Tessie's."

Annie laughed. "You hate it. You're barely enduring it."

"I'm thankful for the luck-out encounter."

"See, good things happen to people who go sharesies. The fairness gods blessed you."

From my angle, I could see when Sylvia and her friend left,

which they did just as the waitress was bringing in our meal. But we saw them get into a large Chevrolet pickup. The friend drove. Annie jotted down the license number.

Later, in our bus, I waited patiently while Annie set about on her notebook computer to find out the owner of the pickup.

It didn't take long. Reading from the screen, Annie said, "Let's see here. I've got the good and the suggestive. The good is that her name is not any form of Mary. She's Suzanne Melinda Somerville, thirty-three years old, born in Newburg, Oregon."

"Suzanne is an okay name."

"The suggestive part is that she is the owner of Barb Ranches, Sheridan, Oregon. She raises mustangs."

I no sooner got the bus out of Tessie's parking lot than Wolfgang Strehmel called. "Mr. Denson, it's urgent that you and Ms. Dancer meet with Erika and me. The State of Oregon has audited Erika's financial records and the prosecuting attorneys are preparing to indict her on criminal charges."

I was dumbfounded. "Say again?"

"Please, if you value justice, listen to me. I told you Erika is the butt of a sick conspiracy by her mother. Well, it's now gotten out of hand. You said you like baseball. The Mariners are due to play the Yankees in a televised game this afternoon. Why don't we talk awhile here in my motel room and watch baseball? I have my own refrigerator. There are ice and Coke machines outside my door plus a convenience store just down the street where we can buy peanuts or snacks."

I glanced at Annie. "Will Ms. von Bayer be there?"

"Of course. Erika says she likes baseball too. And it's essential that you hear what she has to say."

37 · Hoyt Wilhelm's pitch

When Wolfgang Strehmel opened the door to his motel room, the Mariners–Yankees game was about to begin. Behind him, Erika von Bayer stood with red eyes and a handkerchief in hand. The lady had been crying.

"Ahh, Herr Denson, you made it," Wolfgang said. He tapped the mute button as the Mariners took the field in the top of the first.

I shook his hand. "Herr Strehmel."

Erika blew her nose. "Thank you for coming, Mr. Denson. I appreciate it."

Quickly Strehmel said, "I'll get us some beer. I like a beer called Full Sail Ale that you make out here."

Watching him retrieve the beer from his refrigerator, I said, "You want to tell me what the problem is?"

Sniffing again, Erika said, "Perhaps I should answer that, Wolfgang. The Oregon State police came to the suite in the Park Place Hotel where my grandmother and I have been staying. They had a warrant. They removed the laptop computer that I use to track my personal financial accounts. My lawyer says they found evidence that I had paid Sylvia Bonner to collect sperm, that I paid Willard Leopoldo ten thousand dollars each for killing the mustangs, and that I had recently banked a million and a half dollars traceable to my mother's accounts." Her face bunched up with grief, and she turned from me.

Glancing at Erika, Wolfgang gave me a cold bottle of Full Sail. "The lawyer says she can expect charges on killing the mustangs to be filed early next week."

Erika added, "That's if I'm not extradited for murdering Hans Juergen and my father."

In the dugout, the Mariner's manager looked grim. The Yankee manager, chewing gum, looked on impassively.

Doing his best to pretend that Erika wasn't crying, Wolfgang said, "Your Mariners leader . . . what is it they're called in baseball?"

"The manager."

"He has the look of an underdog."

"He has to be alert if the Mariners are to have a chance of winning. The Yankees have more sluggers and better pitchers than the Mariners. A baboon with boxing gloves could choose a winning lineup from the Yankee roster."

Strehmel said, "Ah, see, Herr Denson. Money takes all. Erika is rich, but Marya is even richer. She can buy better lawyers than Erika and more of them. She's set Erika up and is now ready to watch her go down. Her own daughter!"

I took a sip of ale.

Erika, who had recovered, said, "I am being framed, Mr. Denson. I swear it. I have no idea, none, how those numbers popped up in my computer."

Strehmel handed me a photograph. "Have you ever seen this man?"

I glanced at the picture. "That would be *Kriminalhauptkommissar* Rudi Fackler."

He shook his head. "Rudi Fackler is still in Germany. I talk to him regularly. This is a photograph of Heinz Steiner, the accountant helping Marya frame her daughter."

Dismayed, I studied the photograph of the man that Annie and I had entertained with an elk steak supper. He had been pleasant and admiring of my Oddball Ale and I had stupidly believed everything he said. "I take it Herr Steiner is skilled at moving money around electronically."

"If you're asking if he would know how to move money from Marya's accounts to Erika's so as not to leave an electronic trail? The answer is yes. But the data are like ghosts in the hands of a skilled tracker. It will be difficult if not impossible for Erika's lawyers to prove what Steiner did."

I said, "Why would Marya frame her own daughter? That I still don't understand."

Strehmel looked surprised. "Because Erika looks like her father. She is an international beauty with perfect conformation and natural grace. Marya is so bitter and resentful at Kurt von Bayer that she wants to eliminate everything having to do with him, including his daughter. That Erika is also her daughter is beside the point."

With that, Erika once again burst into tears, sobbing uncontrollably. "I still don't understand how she could do that to me. I'm not my father. What's wrong with her?"

A grievously wounded heart, I thought. I said, "If you're innocent, we'll find a way to prove it."

"It makes no difference if I'm innocent, Mr. Denson. All it takes for my mother to ruin my career as a television journalist is for me to be charged, just as the allegations of horse-killing destroyed my father's career as a rider. Whether or not I win or lose in court is irrelevant. Once the charges are made, I lose. My . . . my . . . my . . ." She couldn't finish.

"Erika will likely lose her job at Zone One. Her mother knows that," Strehmel said.

On the television screen, Ichiro Suzuki was on deck, taking practice swings. Watching him, I said, "A pitcher named Hoyt Wilhelm had this clever way of throwing the ball with his knuckles—" I did my best to demonstrate— "with no spin. The ball hopped and jumped this way and that. It was slow, but unpredictable. The batter would see it here—" I held my left hand up—"but by the time he swung, it leaped here." I moved my hand quickly. "Wilhelm's catchers had to use extra-large mitts."

I took a swig of ale. "On my way back from Reno, I called Marya. She said something that I might be able to use."

Strehmel looked interested. "And that would be?"

I said, "Your countryman, Friedrich Hegel, believed we all seek recognition. Marya von Bayer no less than you or me. She longs to be admired and prized, which is why she altered her appearance. And she wants a man. With a man, she thinks, she'll have peace at last."

On the television screen, Ichiro Suzuki reached out and scooped a pitch down the right field line, and he was off and running, head up, feet flying. It was a double for sure, may be even a triple. Ichiro had the amazing ability to hit a ball wherever it was pitched.

As a player in a lethal game, Marya von Bayer saw herself as a kind of Ichiro. No matter what the German authorities or Oregon State Police did to her, she got wood on the pitch.

Fun to imagine myself as Hoyt Wilhelm. I said, "Marya von Bayer is in her home here in Portland. After the game is over, I'll talk to her."

38 · *The riddle of Bitterroot Ralph*

After the Mariners edged out the Yankees, I drove to Marya von Bayer's jumble of copper and cubes with the rhomboid windows. I felt loosey-goosey and alert. If I was going to come away with something useful, I had to stay alert. I also had to follow Mademoiselle Marie's advice and be patient. A good studman, as I had concluded from watching Clint Eastwood in the movies, did not talk too much.

This time an elderly butler in a tuxedo met me at the door. Having a butler was a bit much for Portland, but never mind. "Mr. Denson? Mrs. von Bayer is expecting you. Won't you come in, please?" He was tall and slightly stooped with a long face and thin beak. He had a proper Southern English accent.

The polite gentleman ushered me into a sort of den or study, where Marya waited, wearing a black tube cocktail dress molded over her reconditioned body. As before, she was on her way to getting loaded, but seemed to be near the start of the journey. Evenly she said, "A Coors for the gentleman, please, Nigel."

Nigel disappeared. So did Marya.

While I waited for my beer and for Marya to return, I looked out over the city lights. Then Nigel was there with the beer. And

Marya too was back. She stood beside me at the window. "Are you wearing a wire?"

I shook my head.

She said, "It doesn't matter. What I have to show you I don't mind sharing with the FBI or the Oregon State Police. I told you I'm the butt of a conspiracy. Now I'll prove it. I'm told you grew up on a small farm. Your father had horses. Is that right?"

I said, "Yes, it is. He was what used to be called a 'horse trader.' The larger connotation of the term was somebody who lived by his wits." I took a sip of Coors.

"Then you might have gone with your father to check out a possible stud. He likely knew the owner of the stallion personally. He rode him to check out his gait. He watched him work with cattle, cutting and so on. Am I right?"

"Correct," I said. "Along with much palavering and maybe some whittling, storytelling, and beer drinking thrown in."

Marya took a sip of Scotch. She said, "We're now 'breeders,' not horse traders. We beam digital images of our horses back and forth on our computers. A Canadian breeder can send me a video showing what his stallion looks like in action and what his offspring looks like. If I want, the breeder can hire a veterinarian to collect and ship me the sperm."

"At this end, you hire a vet to impregnate your mare."

She said, "Correct. I tried to buy the sperm of the murdered stallions and wound up getting publicly ridiculed. I was perusing the Web sites of the horse breeders yesterday to see what was out there. I found a stud that I liked on a ranch outside of Phoenix, Arizona. This one."

She tapped the space bar of the computer and the screen lit up. "Honey Man." She tapped a key. The image enlarged. "Nice-looking horse, right?"

"Looks good to me," I said.

"I e-mailed the owner asking for a video of Honey Man. This

is what I got." She tapped another key, and a different stallion was running in a pasture. She said, "This is Bitterroot Ralph, one of the stallions that was killed."

"Oops," I said.

"Note the saguaro cactus in the background. Bitterroot Ralph was from Montana. No saguaro cacti in Montana." Watching me, she called up another horse. "I checked out a stallion on an Oklahoma Web site. I received a video of a horse killed in Northern California roaming around in a field that looks Oklahoma to me."

I blinked.

"I inquired about a stud in New Mexico." She called up another image.

"Good-looking horse. Looks New Mexico to me."

Marya's face turned hard. "The stallion was killed in Northern Idaho." She polished off her Scotch and refilled her glass. "Then I used a bogus name on a Web-based address and asked for Honey Man. They beamed me the real Honey Man. Everybody but Marya von Bayer gets to see a real horse. If I ask, I get a dead stallion." She scowled bitterly. "What's going on?"

I said, "Those are digital images. Easy enough to superimpose Bitterroot Ralph over an Arizona background. A talented high school kid could do it."

"I want to know who would go to that much effort to torment me. And why?"

I shrugged. "Don't have the foggiest idea."

She ground her teeth, the muscles of her jaw working rhythmically. "Nigel, another beer for the gentleman."

Furious, she looked me straight in the eye and said evenly, "Mr. Denson, I think that contrary to not having the 'foggiest' idea, as you so casually put it, you know *exactly* what is going on." She looked at me hard. "Tell me now, who's pulling this crap on me?"

I said, "I'll say it again, Mrs. von Bayer. I don't know."

Marya's face turned downright hateful. Her eyes narrowed to reptilian slits.

I said, "If you've got somebody out there tormenting you, Mrs. von Bayer, the best thing to do is show the bastards you don't give a damn." I scoped her butt, trying not to appear too obvious.

Her face softened. She looked down and back at herself. "You like that?" she asked.

I cleared my throat in the manner of Clint.

She studied me. A full minute passed, each second seemingly hours. Tick, tick, tick. Finally, she said, "You know, Mr. Denson, I believe you. I think you're telling the truth."

"I am. I told you I am, and it's true."

To herself she murmured, "John and Marya." She liked the sound of it. She tried it again. "John and Marya." She cocked her head and ran her hand over her rump.

39 · In pursuit of high romance

Marya said, "Let me tell you what I've got to offer to the right man, Mr. Denson. I got these." She wiggled her chest. "I got this." She waggled her behind. "And I have a bank account with so many zeros it's obscene. Bio-Source developed cancer drugs that actually work. People are willing to pay anything to gain a few more years."

"I bet they are," I said. I found myself lapsing into the pitch and timbre of Clint Eastwood's voice. Had to stop that crap.

"I was an only child. I inherited the whole BioSource wad. We're talking a genuine fortune, more than a hundred million dollars. I learned the hard way that I can't just go out and buy a fancy man and have it work. I want an honest man. Someone I can trust totally and without reservation."

"I don't know who is pulling these stunts, ma'am. Wolfgang Strehmel most likely, but I don't know that for a fact."

"For me the question remains, how do I know you're not w-working for *them*. What kind of toys do you like, Mr. Denson? I m-mean, things you might like, but never dreamed you'd have. Tell me. Go for it. Don't hold back."

"I don't know," I said. "An ultralight airplane sounds fun.

And one of those old Porches like your husband had. Throw in a sailboat capable of sailing around the Caribbean or whatever. Fishing trips. King salmon in Alaska. Snook in the Caribbean. Barramundi outside of Darwin. Is that what you have in mind?"

"All trifles. Earn my trust and they're yours and more."

Trying to sound as laconic as I could, I said, "Tough getting my mind off contents of your tube dress, I have to admit."

Marya liked that a bunch. "Oh, I know what you're thinking. You don't want to be t-tied d-down. I tell you what, I've learned something about m-men. Kurt was telling the truth about the strange. Earn my trust and you can even try out a little strange now and then as long as you deal me in on the a-action."

"You're talking threesomes?" I asked. Clint would be heading for the exit, but I had to stay put.

"I want loyalty. Total commitment. High romance. A threesome as a form of hobby or m-mutual entertainment seems the best way out. You get to have fun with some strange to break up the monotony. Sexy to watch as w-well as d-do."

"That's some proposal, but I don't believe in Santa Claus. Or Mrs. Claus, for that matter. What do I have to do to score all that?"

She pursed her lips. "The most romantic thing a man can do to prove his desire for his lady is to kill for her. I want you to kill a horse and a human for me. Prove you really want me."

"Kill a horse and a human?"

"A man killing for love is very, very romantic. Really juices a woman up. At least it does me." She grinned crookedly. "They give murderers a lethal injection in this state. Get caught and you get the needle. I can't imagine any gesture more grand than a man risking his life to prove his commitment to a woman. Everything else is nothing: stupid flowers, poetry, walks on the beach, and all that clichéd tripe."

"That's a pretty wild proposition, you have to admit."

"What do you say?"

I licked my lips nervously.

She brightened. "Ah, but I didn't hear you say n-no." Cocking her head, regarding me with a half smile, Marya moved closer. "Why, Mr. Denson, the truth is you're a bad boy, aren't you? A real s-sicko under that quiet exterior. Ambitious as a-anybody else."

I grinned. "Everybody wants a life with a little juice in it."

"You'd willing to risk your life for me if you can figure a way? Talk about a romantic!" She wiggled her sexual accoutrements with delight.

I stepped back, pretending to gape, out of control, at whatever it was she had become. "Hey, lady, wake up! A whole bunch of men would be willing to kill for equipment like you're packing." *A whole bunch of morons,* I thought.

Marya hadn't endured all that surgery for nothing. She *believed*. She was also a realist. "Not to m-mention my m-money," she added.

"I'd be lying if I said the money didn't figure into it. But there's no damn way in hell I'm going to risk the needle." I thought momentarily of asking her if somebody else had killed a horse and a man for her, but held my tongue. Instead, I said, "Just what horse and human are you talking about."

She shrugged. "Oh, I don't know, any old horse. Any human. You figure it out. The who is not important. I want a dead horse and a dead human to seal the deal between us."

"Any old horse or human."

"That's it," she said. She giggled. "Do you have the hair, Mr. Denson?"

I said, "Tell me, have you ever been to the Pendleton Round-Up?"

Shaking her head, Marya made a sour face. "Yuck! And sit out in that hot sun drinking draught beer out of a plastic cup? I'm not a hamburger-and-hot-dog kind of woman."

I said, "How about a date in Brahma Bill's tomorrow night? If I can't figure a way to give you what you want by then, well then, I just can't. No harm. No foul. We'll just dance and wish I could have come up with something."

She grinned broadly. "All right, Mr. Denson, you're on. This is the d-deal of a lifetime. I want you to think about it real, real h-hard."

40 · A rearin', tearin' cowpoke

Marya von Bayer's ostentatious digs on her spread north-east of Salem were a sprawling "ranch" house, meaning it was low and flat as opposed to something that poked up from the landscape like those hokey old houses in the Midwest. The roofs of its many wings were covered with shakes, ubiquitous in timber-rich Oregon. Its low facades were faced with rainbow stone, a marvelous sandstone quarried in Central Oregon, featuring wonderful hues of green, blue, and various oranges and reds. Originally said to have been inspired by houses designed by Frank Lloyd Wright, the style had, charitably, "evolved."

The house was surrounded by spiffy barns and white board fences, a spendy affectation out west where barbed wire normally did the trick. Spanish mustangs, pintos of one kind or another, buckskins, and sorrels roamed in pastures kept green by an expensive system of sprinklers and aluminum pipes that not a whole bunch of horse breeders could afford. No damn wonder Marya von Bayer was resented.

I parked Willie's Ford pickup. My mike was under my shirt. In the rear of the pickup, under the aluminum canopy, Wolfgang Strehmel and Annie Dancer would be maintaining contact with Willie and Bob Humping Buck.

Willie had a Model 94 Winchester 30-30 on a rack just above the back of the seat. On the off chance that Marya might be watching from one of the windows, I got my pint bottle of Jim Beam. It was actually filled with tea, although I had taken several swigs of the real McBeam to smell up my breath. I finished off the bottle. As I got out, I sent it sailing in proper country-drunk fashion.

Before I closed the door, I grabbed another Jim Beam bottle from the seat of the pickup, containing real whiskey, and stuck it in my hip pocket. As an added touch, I took a leak on the rear wheel.

I slipped the receiver into my left ear and thumped on the canopy. "Everything working back there?"

In the microphone in my ear, Annie said, "Seems to be."

Also in my ear, Wolfgang said, "Good luck, Herr Denson."

Annie said, "Test your beeper."

The beeper was in my pocket. One punch meant "yes." Two quick punches meant "no." Three quick punches said, "Not now, I'm busy." I punched once. I waited. Again, twice. I waited. Then three quick ones.

"Working just fine," Annie said. "Go."

I said, "I'm a hot damn cowhand. Ready to rip." I took another swig of real Jim Beam to freshen up my breath. Or rather smell it up. I adjusted my cowboy hat. With a rolling stride, grinning like a dog caught eating a turd, I walked with a bow-legged gait up the winding flagstone path to the front door. I removed the receiver from my ear. As I punched on the button of the doorbell—*ding-dong, ding-dong*—I flew.

———

I am in my human form, scrambling up a kind of rope ladder with hardwood rungs. The ladder spirals gently upward. Each rung has a tiny A, C, G, or T etched in the wood. I am facing another rope ladder spiraling upward, opposite mine. The ladders are separate, yet connected, making them one. On the opposite ladder, a woman with a monster face is matching my progress, run by rung. Koonran.

Is the beaver monster Marya or Erika? Could be either. Maybe even Gretchen.

The ladders swing with our exertions.

Koonran and I are in the dim light of a cavernous space. There is a hole high above us. A foul odor wafts up from the brownish murk below us. It is disgusting, but it is not excrement. It is more like rancid tobacco, and the female monster is slimy with it. It slides off her like loose dung. The bottoms of our connected ladders dangle in the slimy goo.

The smell is so vile I can hardly breathe. Gross! What is that stuff?

Koonran has feral eyes. Her mouth is gaudy with scarlet lipstick. Her beaver teeth sparkle in the dim light. Green slime trails from her mouth.

Koonran yells, "We're made for one another, my darling John. You're so cute. So earnest. Always asking questions. So many questions. You want to know who you are and what you're all about? Who is T? Where do you go when you fly? The answer is you're me, sweetie, part of a tournament."

Marya von Bayer opened the door wearing her crazed Mustang Marya outfit. The rattlesnake-skin cowboy boots with Chijuajua spurs. Blue silk tights masquerading as blue jeans. The buckle with the longhorn bull. The chaps with the bullwhip tassels. The sequined vest. The translucent red western shirt.

Reeling drunkenly, I grabbed my crotch. I said, "Marya, little darlin'! I been thinking about that see-through shirt ever since I first met you. That's one helluva outfit, if you don't mind my saying so. Very hip." I took a deep breath and exhaled, flapping my lips, making the sound of an outboard engine idling through the water. Leering at her boobs, I said, "Fun to make motorboat noises with numbers like those." I flapped my lips, moving my head from side to side.

Pleased, Marya said, "Why, aren't you the naughty one!"

I straightened. "You don't like to play motorboat? Left, right. Left, right."

Marya was amused. "I might be talked into playing a little motorboat if that's what gets you off. By the way, I have a toilet in here. You didn't have to pee on the wheel of your pickup."

"We cowboys pee on pickups on our way to go honky-tonkin'. Only yuppies got pickups that don't stink a little 'round the tires." I retrieved my bottle of Jim Beam from my hip pocket. "Here, take a hit of this. Gotta have some Old Crow or Uncle Jim for a proper night of honky-tonkin'."

She took a timid sip, making a face. "That ought to be enough for me to claim an authentic experience. I'll take along a bottle of Scotch if you don't mind. And I've got a flask covered with twenty-four-karat gold.'"

I said, "Whatever's your druthers. I know I've been drinking a tad and everything, but let me tell you, lady, you do look fetching in that outfit. Pokeable is the word. And I'm a hot damn cowpoke."

Marya arched an eyebrow. "Aren't you the sweet-talking man? My Mercedes or your pickup?"

I was shocked, shocked! "Why my pickup, what else? We're going to a country club. We pull up to Brahma Bill's in a fancy Mercedes and people'd giggle at us." With that I escorted Marya von Bayer out of the house and down the curving flagstone walkway to my pickup.

I helped the little lady into her seat. She took a swig from her fifth of Scotch and stashed the bottle in the glove compartment.

On the far side of the pickup, I quickly put the receiver back into my left ear. As I got into the driver's seat, I covertly switched my pint of Jim Beam for yet another Jim Beam bottle filled with tea. Eyeing Marya's preposterous body, I settled into the seat and held up the pint. "To our eyes and our thighs. Our eyes met. Here's hoping." I took a healthy swig of tea.

"To our eyes and our thighs," Marya said. Running her hand down the inside of a designer thigh, she wiggled happily and knocked off some Scotch from her fancy flask.

I cranked up the engine of Willie's pickup. I popped the clutch and spun gravel with my rear wheels. I was off with Annie and Wolfgang hanging on under the canopy over the bed of the pickup.

Watching me, Marya said, "Are you really going to do it?"

"I promised you that I'd put my mind to the proposition of shooting a horse and a human to win the Marya von Bayer jackpot. Well, let me tell you, ma'am, the way I see it there's only one proper way to do it."

Marya was giddy with the idea of such total commitment. I was going to kill for her. A man had to want a woman in the worst way to go that far. She had a glow in her eyes. "When? Now? Really?" She was excited. She ran her tongue over her Sophia Loren lips.

I took a swig of tea. I said, "Murderers with motive are murderers who get caught. The only perfect murder is one committed totally at random. No motive. I'll just take a swing out into the country and find myself a horse with nobody around and take it down."

"And the human?"

I shrugged. "I'll find myself a biker or a jogger or maybe a kid walking to the neighbor's house to play."

"A child?" Marya seemed mildly alarmed.

"You didn't specify age or sex. Only that it has to be human. My only requirement is that it be totally at random. Not good to think about it. Ruins the random. If I spot a little girl on the side of the road singing, 'Skip, skip, skip to my Lou,' I'll just splatter a few brains and fucking stomp on the gas."

In my ear Annie said, "Slow down there. Don't overdo it."

I said, "No motive. Nothing to trace. Our deal is sealed. We'll go honky-tonkin' and have a good time." I giggled happily.

Marya laughed. She was feeling good too and not a little turned on. "You're a baaaad, baaaad boy. That's very sexy. Did you know that? I'm hornier than all get-out."

41 · *To kill an Injun*

I drove too fast down a country road, knocking back the tea as I drove. I took a hard right down another country road. "A cow won't suffice? Gotta be a horse?"

"A horse." Marya said with finality. "A dead cow is nothing to these people. So what if a cow gets shot? They worship horses. Gotta be a horse and a human."

"Picky, picky."

"And I get your pistol for keepsies, prints and all."

I took another swig of tea. "You drive a hard bargain, lady, but I sure do fancy them tits of yours."

Marya wiggled her extraordinary mammaries for my benefit. "Motorboat for starters, then whatever turns you on."

"I like that fine, fine ass too. Pokes right out and goes this way and that when you walk. Very spankable."

She pursed her lips. "Oooh! Really? Naughty!" She squirmed on the seat. "Best butt money can buy. This is an Ipanema ass. Sexiest on the planet. And you forgot my bank account."

"No way I'm going to forget about your bank account. I didn't want to come off as crass. Motorboat. Poking that great butt for breakfast followed by T-bone steaks. And a threebie with a brace of big-titted ladies sounds good for lunch. Real men don't eat quiche." I leered happily. "Man's gotta have some strange now and then."

Up ahead I saw my marks. So far, so good.

From the canopy in the rear, Wolfgang said, "You should start slowing down."

I perked up. "Well, well, Marya darlin', would you look up ahead? We've got ourselves a man on a horse."

I looked right and left and checked my rearview mirror. "And not a soul in sight, can you imagine that? Time to splash a few brains. Yippee!"

As I drew near the man on the horse, Bob Humping Buck put Thunderballs into an easy gallop as he had many times as he attacked the cavalry on the big stage at Happy Canyon. I said, "Well, well, well, if it isn't a goddamn Indian. Let's play a little cowboys and Indians!"

"You're going to kill them?" Marya said drunkenly. "Oh, God yes, do it! Do it, do it, do it! Come to mama!"

Slowing the pickup, I reached under the seat and pulled out a .357 Colt magnum revolver with five big rounds in the cylinder. As I did, Marya retrieved a digital camera from her handbag.

"You don't mind, do you?" she asked.

I grinned. "You want insurance, you got it. We can watch the action in bed. Sexier than *Debbie Does Dallas.*"

With Marya's camera recording the action, I rolled down the window.

"Kill them. Kill them. Yes, yes, yes," Marya murmured, her voice alive with excitement.

Keeping pace with the galloping Thunderballs, I thumbed back the hammer and fired high over his head. *Blam!*

Thunderballs pitched over on his side, hooves flailing.

Bob Humping Buck tumbled ass over tea kettle.

Marya squealed with delight, then shouted, "Now the Indian. Shoot him! Shoot him!"

I shouted, in sort of a Dirty Harry parody, "Come on there, Cochise! Quit beatin' your tom-tom and get on your fuckin' moccasins!"

Bob struggled to get to his feet.

I thumbed back the hammer again and fired high over his head. Blam! Bob sailed off his feet like he'd been slammed point-blank by a howitzer round. I said, "There you go, lady."

"You killed for me," Marya cried." Oh yes, yes, yes! Now I have a real *man*. Very sexy!" She had her hand on her crotch and was breathing so hard she was almost hyperventilating.

As I floored the accelerator, I flew again.

"**You** all want to be happy," Koonran burbles. " 'We're not happy,' you wail. 'What is wrong? Boo hoo hoo.' Nothing is wrong, dearie. Happiness is not the point. Give it up," Green slime trails out of her evil mouth.

I climb as fast as I can, noting that in the dim light whatever it is we're trying to escape appears to be made of brass.

On the ladder opposite me, Koonran says, "I get orgasms thinking about those dead mustangs. Turns me on."

I concentrate on climbing.

Koonran shouts at me, her voice echoing in the chamber. "You're mine."

I refuse to reply.

She doesn't like being ignored. "You want me too, I know you do. You can't keep your eyes off these tits. Aren't they something? You've never seen anything like them. Never. Say I'm wrong."

"I'm outta here."

Grabbing one rung after the other, she shouts. "Fun being inside a hot female body showing off my equipment. Oh, I know we females are supposed to be nurturing and loving and all that. But you know something, darling, I adore *las desperadas*. Why should men have all the fun, leaving us on the sidelines wringing our hands or waving pom-poms or parading give-peace-a-chance placards? Murder is where the real juice is."

As we get higher, the dim light gets better and I can see that the exit of the container curves inward and then outward.

Looking back at Thunderballs and Bob Humping Buck lying still on the ground, Marya said, "Jesus Christ, but you're cold! My kind of man!"

I piloted the pickup down the country road at seventy-five miles an hour with fence posts whizzing by on either side. Up and over a hill I flew, which had been our plan in case Thunderballs got it in his head to get up before Bob gave him the go-ahead.

Marya needed to know that I was firing live rounds. As I drew near a crossroads with a stop sign, I slowed and stuck the pistol out of the window. I put three slugs into the stop sign, *blam, blam, blam.* The sign turned left. The sign turned right. I knocked it flat.

I gave the revolver to Marya. "There you go, pardner. Your insurance along with your video. No motive. No witnesses. Now let's go dancing. I want to see you shake that Ipanema ass of yours and give 'em all boners."

Using a handkerchief so as not to smudge the prints, Marya put the revolver in her handbag along with her camera with its incriminating digital images. "Whew! That was exciting."

"Good as hiding the sausage?" I asked.

She rubbed herself between the legs. "Got me juiced. You killed for me. Risked your life for me. That's my idea of romance."

"Blood on both our hands. Bonded forevermore," I said.

"I never dreamed anything like this would ever happen to me. We're gonna be good together, John, I can see that." She leaned against me and ran her hand up and down my thigh.

I said, "Oooh, lady."

Marya said, "I want to tell you what happened in Europe."

"Go for it if you want," I said as if I really didn't give a damn. I took a nip of bogus Jim.

"*Ja!*" Wolfgang cried in my ear.

"My mother-in-law figured that I'd hired Juergen to kill those horses to set up Kurt. She was furious. On the night he got killed, Kurt was going into town to drink with his friends, actually to screw a Kraut blonde, but he had some kind of problem with his Porsche."

"The bathtub Porsche," I said, sailing Willie's pickup nearly sideways around a curve. I almost overdid it. My stomach twisted.

"Right," she said. "The thermostat needed replacing or some damned thing. It was my usual night for a facial and massage by this Kraut with great hands. I'd had a fever all afternoon, so I told Kurt to go ahead and take my Jaguar. A few minutes before he was set to leave, a man called saying there was a bomb planted under my Jag's gas tank. The bomb was set to explode twenty minutes after the engine started. He said the person who hired it put there had had a change of heart. The bomb was clearly visible under the car. All I had to do to disarm it was to flip a toggle switch on the side. A red light above the toggle switch would go off."

"Wow! So what did you do?"

She wiggled against me. "I wondered if the caller was for real or some jerk playing a sick prank? I went outside and took a look under the Jag. There it was. Easy to reach the toggle switch. I even touched it."

"Whoa," I said. Holding the steering wheel tightly, I deliberately strayed off the side of the road, sending gravel flying.

"If anybody wanted to kill me, I knew it was most likely my mother-in-law. All I had to do to save Kurt's life was flip the switch, but I thought, 'Why the hell should I? You want to blow people up, try this, lady.' I went back inside. When Kurt was getting ready to go, I drew myself a hot bath. Felt good. I was still soaking when Kurt went up." Marya smiled at the memory. "The odd part is that Fackler spent as much time asking me about the dead horses and the murder of Hans Juergen as he did the details about Kurt being detonated."

"He needed to establish motive," I said. "Who killed the horses? Who murdered Hans Juergen? He knew it all had to be linked."

"That's what I figured. So, you see, I didn't murder Kurt. His mother did. At the same time I suppose you could argue that I did kill him."

In my ear, Wolfgang said, "You nailed her for Kurt's murder. We've got the horse killing and Hans Juergen to go."

He was talking about the jumpers. I wanted to nail her for the dead mustangs also. I took a hit of tea, grimacing at the taste of pretend Jim Beam. I looped the empty bottle over the cab of the truck and grabbed another one from under the seat. I opened it and took another swig.

I went off the side of the road again, slamming Wolfgang or Annie against the canopy. I heard a loud thump in the rear of the pickup.

Marya turned quickly in her seat. "What's that?"

"Willie's stuff sliding around," I said.

In my ear, Annie said, "Wolfgang lost his balance. Stall her when you park. We'll bail out of the back with our gear."

42 · *An achy, breaky heart*

I damned near slid Willie's pickup backward into the gravel parking lot at Brahma Bill's. On the off chance that the paranoid Marya had second thoughts about the honesty of her inebriated escort, I quickly exchanged the pint bottle of tea for a hip flask of genuine Jim Beam. Good thing.

Marya said, "You mind if I have a little sample of your firewater?"

"Go for it, lady. Uncle Jim will put hair on your chest." I handed her the flask.

She took a tentative sip, making a face. "Yuck! I thought I could get used to it, but no way."

I grinned broadly. "It's an acquired taste of us connoisseurs of cheap whiskey and wild women. Damn that outfit of yours is getting me all hot and bothered." I grabbed a silicon boob, giving it a vigorous squeeze.

She squealed happily. "You want wild, bub, you got wild."

I squeezed her again.

She slapped at my hand, pretending to be angry. "You've got six weeks to stop that!"

Without warning she clapped her mouth to mine like an obscene leech and rammed her tongue halfway down my throat. Yuck!

"We're going to have a good time tonight." I broke off and took another swig.

"We're clear," Annie said in my ear as I returned to whatever was going on in the dark chamber or container.

A familiar voice, a dim echo, T calls down at me, "You can do it, Denson. You're my main man. You've got grit. Climb!"

"You're mine forevermore!" Koonran cries.

I ignore them both. I am wet with sweat. My muscles burn.

Koonran yells, "I am you and in all living things. I am in the trees and seas and forests. I fly. I swim. I run. I pop up out of cracks in the sidewalks. You like sexy pony girls? I am them. I show them how to ride. How to turn this way and that. How much skin to show and when. How to use their great big eyes. I am Annie Dancer too."

Above me T shouts, "I didn't create any goddam quitter. Never give up, Denson. Never. Fight on. Climb!"

As I get closer to the top of the basin, I see that the sloping entrance is stained with gross brown crap. The two ladders are flattened against the disgusting crud, attached to the top edge of the basin by hooks.

Trembling with exhaustion, I continue up the rungs.

"I even teach my lovelies how to have sex. They learn everything from me. Even your precious Annie, little bitch."

At the top I find T straddling the lip, looking down at me. He's wearing his stupid bucket helmet and brandishing his broomstick sword, the same Don Quixote getup he had worn on our ride with the pony girls.

I grab the lip of the basin with both hands. "Drop her ladder," I yell.

"Can't!" T shouts. "It's connected to yours."

Brahma Bill's offered its customers real western swing bands, no jukebox or pimple-faced kid with a drum singing to recorded background music. In Bill's the folks still mixed romping swing music with drawly, bluesy songs of heartbreak and love gone wrong, sung in a country twang. The song that sealed the country image in my mind was about a poor bastard, who, having six kids to feed and the crops still in the field, found that his lady, a no-account named Lucille, had left him.

Well, it's a fine time to leave me, Lucille.

Indeed. And then there was the poor fellow named Sue, given that sissy name by his parents to guarantee that he'd be tough. And so he was, getting down there in the mud and the blood and the spit to defend his manhood.

My name is Sue, how do you do?

Such were the vicissitudes of life in the country. An achy, breaky heart plumb summed it up.

There were some differences to be sure. Now there was a big-screen projection television for college football on Saturday afternoons and NFL football on Sunday afternoons and Sunday and Monday nights. The food had changed. Thirty years earlier, nobody would have had any idea what the hell a buffalo wing was or a plate of nachos might be. And, although Bud Lite or Coors were nearly mandatory, a cowpoke could, if he was man enough to endure the smiles, order a foo-foo designer beer made in a regional brewery.

In setting up the evening, Wolfgang, Annie, and I had sat down with the manager; he had riding horses for his two daughters and didn't like horse killers any more than we did.

When he said that a country band called Horse Dumplings played the bar circuit, we all said yes, that was the group we wanted.

When we got out of the pickup, Marya, curious, peered in the back of Willie's pickup. Satisfied that there was nothing there, she took my arm, and we walked from the pickup with Marya twitching along in her bizarre outfit, silicon boobs bouncing, Ipanema ass jumping this way and that.

43 · Beautiful Betty

I could hear the band before I opened the front door. The Horse Dumplings were playing a romping swing song.

> *Beautiful Betty, won't you bump up to me,*
> *Bump up to me, bump up to me.*
> *Undo those buttons, I'm sure you'll agree*
> *Let me see, let me see, let me see.*

The house was packed. Wearing cowboy hats and western shirts covered with red sequins, the three Dumplings—a drummer, a bass player, and a lead guitarist—held forth on a diminutive bandstand.

> *Beautiful Betty, won't you bump up to me.*
> *Bump up to me, bump up to me.*
> *Comes now the snap that'll send 'em both free*
> *Let me see, let me see, let me see.*

I looked around and spotted the table being held open for me. The lead guitarist, who had a long neck, huge Adam's apple, and a deep voice finished his urging of Betty.

Beautiful Betty, won't you bump up to me,
Bump up to me, bump up to me.
Slip off the bottoms, I'll like it, you'll see . . .

The lead guitarist paused. He sucked in his breath.

Oh, Betty, that's groooooovy!

Grinning at the applause, he said, "All we boys love them cute little grooves, don't we? That little number was 'Bump Up Betty' by Bobby Clanahan."

I pointed at the table that was being held open for us. "Hey, there's a good table. Let's grab it while we have a chance." I steered Marya to a round table maybe a foot and a half in diameter. Knowing everybody was watching her, she walked with one foot in front of the other in the manner of a fashion model so as to swing her hips, sending her amazing rump hopping to and fro.

The management had mashed the maximum number of diminutive tables into the smallest available space. All that was required of a table was that it was able to hold the profitable drinks. We sat. If Marya wondered how it was that a table remained open in an otherwise packed house, she gave no sign of it.

A harried waitress arrived almost instantly.

I said, "We'll both be having a Seven and Seven. Also a plate of buffalo wings. You like nachos, Marya?"

The daughter of Thompson Sturgis and the former wife of Kurt Herzog von Bayer had no idea what buffalo wings and nachos were. Too much quiche and shrimp cocktails for her. Or so she wanted everybody to think.

In my ear, Annie said, "We're picking you up well. Good picture. Good sound."

"And a plate of nachos," I added.

Marya said, "Seven and Seven being?"

"Seagram's Seven and Seven-Up," I said. "Country nectar. A woman who owns a spread as big as yours has gotta know what a Seven and Seven is."

The bandleader, having taken his cue from Annie and Wolfgang, called for a break. "Got to air out shorts and water the plants out back."

Koonran grabs my ankle. Her grip is so strong I can hardly believe it. She jerks. "Join me, lover!"

T deals Koonran three vicious blows on the hand with this broomstick sword. "Bitch!" he cries.

Crying out at the pain, Koonran tumbles backward off her ladder, eyes wide. She plunges downward, screaming, "I'll be baaaaaaaack!"

Unfortunately, she takes me with her.

We both land, *plop*, in the disgusting goo of the primordial soup.

Koonran, floating on her back, says, "You think you can get rid of me. Good luck."

I start the climb all over again.

Koonran, climbing onto the ladder opposite mine, says, "If I fail, you all fail. You go out of business like the dodo, the Tasmanian devil, and the Tyrannosaurus rex. That's what the tournament is all about."

Climbing hard, vile crap sliding off my body, I pause on a G rung.

"You're asking yourself what tournament? The tournament of the conforming and the nonconforming, silly. The winners and the losers. A kind of wild horse and burro show. Oh, yes, yes, the competition causes a lot of hard feelings, I know. All the frustration and bitterness. It's the price of the juice and the passion, sweetie. Can't be helped."

"Stuff it," I yell at her.

"Would you rather be part of an anthill or beehive or school of fish? Oh, please!"

"This is the great test of existence," T shouts. "One way or another we all fight it. Never mind that few of us understand or accept Koonran. Nobody is spared. Just keep climbing."

44 · I was dancin' with my darlin'

The waitress arrived with our Seven and Sevens, buffalo wings, and nachos. I truly did love buffalo wings, and Brahma Bill's made 'em good and hot. Chewing on a savory chicken leg, I said, "You know this all seems hardly fair to me, Marya. You recorded me blasting a horse off its hooves and popping the skull of an Indian out minding his own business, and yet you're all coy with me. Your mother-in-law 'figured' that you had the jumping horses killed. You murdered that husband of yours, yet you didn't. That's no fun."

Marya frowned.

I said. "If you don't mind my asking, if not you, who did kill the jumpers and the former stable hand? That's not to mention the mustang stallions."

She made a face. "The horses. The horses. The horses. Who cares about the damn horses?"

"I don't know. The people who owned the horses, I suppose."

"If you've just gotta know the story, oh, hell yes, I hired Hans Juergen to kill those precious horses. Then I shot the stupid bastard myself. Splattered his brains against flowered wallpaper. Juergen was a stable hand. He shoveled horse manure for a living.

Who *really* cared whether somebody shot him in the face? I mean, get real." She giggled at my stupidity.

I found myself saying, "You got a point."

In my ear, Annie said, "A sick point!"

But Marya was tired of keeping her triumph to herself. *Finally* she was getting to brag a little. "Of course, everybody thought Kurt hired Juergen to kill the horses and then murdered him to shut him up." She grinned broadly. "Everybody wanted it to be that the fancy duke who killed other riders' mounts so he could win an extra trophy. It fit into a popular prejudice that ordinary people are morally superior to the asshole royals." She savored the memory. "Easy frame. Kurt richly deserved it."

"And the mustang stallions?"

"That little jockey and his slut of a girlfriend took 'em down for me at ten grand a head. Worth it until I found out that witch of a veterinarian switched semen on me. She's supposed to be a professional. Can you imagine a professional pulling a stunt like that? Makes a person wonder what this country is coming to."

Koonran bears her feral teeth. "You want me, Denson. I know you do. Deny it all you want, but I bet you're getting hard. Can't help yourself."

I pause for breath on an A rung. My eyes are burning from sweat, which I swab from my brows with my forearm.

Koonran too needs to catch her breath. "My men prefer perfect pony girls. Pretty ones with bodies and skin and hair just so. And those eyes and lips! I set the standards of desire to which the pony girls must conform. Older women too. I am the sole, undisputed judge of the standards."

I glare at her.

"You think about conformation and strange all the time. I know you do because I am you."

"Shut up."

"Look at this body of mine. Check out these tits. Look at this ass. This is what you men want. A teenager's body, never mind anything else. A hard body is all it takes to stiffen your cock. See here! I've got it all. Everything. A regular pony girl. I conform to every man's dream! Conformation!"

I gain on the vile bitch, gaining an advantage of several rungs. A load of crud bounces off my shoulder. I gag at the stench.

Marya sampled a nacho. "Kurt thought it was funny when I got slapped in the face with that girl's tit. Well, it was my turn to laugh at *his* torment. Such shame the fancy sportsman endured. As for those horses, do you know why they were preened and fussed over and given expensive rations of grain?"

I shrugged. "I dunno. Because they were good at jumping?"

Marya rolled her eyes. "Oh, come on."

I said, "Colts don't know anything about jumping barriers. They have to be trained."

"The reason they're chosen for training is because they're beautiful. They have white stocking feet or perfect little white blazes on their foreheads. They're all neat and trim and athletic. They conform. Do you think those uppity riders in their ta-ta little outfits want to ride an 'ordinary' horse? There isn't an ordinary horse among them, not one."

"They're all fancy stuff."

"Fancy? They're *perfect*. The same for the mustang stallions. They all had perfect conformation. The buckskins had those neat little hooked ears and those black stripes up their backs. Why do you think their owners were able to use the Internet to sell their semen? So, please, don't cry for the mustangs either. Until they were forced to stop, people ground up ordinary wild horses and fed them to minks. But not the good-looking ones, no, no, no. The conforming mustangs got green pastures and rations of oats."

"And you sent the handsome Kurt to his grave with everybody thinking he was a dishonorable son of a bitch, a horse killer and a murderer. Well done!"

"No, no, no! His own mother killed him for me. Tried to murder me, and it backfired. Never mind that she had second thoughts." Chewing thoughtfully on a nacho, she looked momentarily dispirited. "Unfortunately, there was a problem."

"A problem?"

Marya looked bitter. "I spent months planting all kinds of evidence that the police eventually would have found. I wanted to put that fancy ladies' man in prison with all those horny males. Turks and the rest of them. Sodomites with giant cocks. And then, at the very last second, when I had a chance to disarm the bomb, I got excited. I didn't think."

"Bummer," I said.

"You got that right." Marya clenched her jaw. "No fun burying Kurt in the ground with nothing but worms to enjoy what was left of his corpse. I was so crestfallen and disappointed that I'd gotten screwed out of watching my frame unfold that I bawled like a baby at his funeral. Everybody thought I was grief-stricken. Isn't that a kick in the ass? Morons."

"**Las** *desperadas* who fail to conform owe their resentment to me. Amusing to observe their fury and rage. I love it when they turn lethal. Nothing more fascinating than a female murderer. We all pretend to be shocked. A woman committing murder? How can that be?" Koonran laughs, green slime flowing out of her mouth, over her awful teeth.

I ignore her.

"I light the erotic fire with pony girls and the strange then smother it slowly with the increasingly familiar."

I'm at the top of the ladder again.

T unloads a wicked swing, smashing Koonran's hand with the walking stick. Screaming in pain with each blow, she continues yanking at my ankle. Her strength and power are incredible.

"Let me be honest with you, honey, if you cower timidly before all that desire bumping around in your noggin, you die a little each day. Come to me, sweetie. Don't be afraid. I'll show you some strange that would shock your sweet little Annie. Sleeping Bag Monica! Mademoiselle Marie! She thinks those are turn-ons? Yawn."

T rips the bucket helmet from his head. Holding it by the handle, he swings it as hard as he can, unloading a horrific blow flush in Koonran's face, surely enough to take out her teeth and break the jaw of any mortal.

The bitch pitches backward off the ladder.

Below me, her eyes blazing with hatred and determination, snuffling slime, Koonran begins the long climb back. "You can't escape. I am unstoppable. Invincible."

Marya said, "For the life of me, I still can't understand the fuss over all those horses. They're animals, not people. Who gives a damn about stupid horses? Their owners have got more euros than they know what to do with. They'll just buy themselves some more fancy jumpers." She finished off her Seven and Seven. "Hey, these are good!"

"Another round," I called to the waitress.

The waitress arrived with another round of drinks, and Marya fell silent.

When the waitress left, Marya raised her highball glass. "Here's to Kurt Herzog von Bayer, dishonored horse killer."

"I'll drink to Kurt, sure," I said. "You remember when I asked you if you had ever been to the Pendleton Round-Up? You said no, you don't like to sit in the hot sun drinking beer out of a plastic cup. You're not a hamburger-and-hot-dog kind of woman, you said. The reason I asked that question is that I was wondering if you had ever been to Happy Canyon. You want to check it out."

The large projection screen that ordinarily featured the Seattle Seahawks losing as usual, or the Portland Trail Blazers or the Seattle Mariners sometimes winning, now showed Bob Humping Buck on Thunderballs being chased across a huge stage by cavalry soldiers with guns blazing.

Watching Thunderballs go down, sending Bob flying, Marya said, "What the hell is this?"

"That's a video clip from Happy Canyon, a big attraction at the Round-Up. That's my friend Bob Humping Buck on Thunderballs. He goes down here, but in the next scene, he comes back as Crazy Horse and gets a little revenge."

Her mouth dropped. "He—"

"He's the Indian I 'killed' back there. Realistic dive, huh? Fooled you big-time!"

Wondering what I was up to, her face turned hard.

I said, "If you'd like to meet Bob, I can introduce you. He's in here someplace to watch the big show."

The singer with the long neck and big Adam's apple said, "And now, by request, a slow one so you sweatier folks can have a chance to grope one another. Release a little of that frustration. Hey, we're all adults here. You gentlemen better mind you don't get too tanked now." He waited for the laughter to die down. "Here we go."

Well, now my lover . . .

Nobody rose save for two couples. With the rider silently jumping barriers on the big screen above them, Erika von Bayer and Wolfgang Strehmel started waltzing around the tiny floor in our direction. They were followed by Annie and a tall blonde man.

Sends me spinning . . .

A bucketful of the brownish crap splashes against the slope of the container a couple of yards to my right. Trying to dodge the splatter, I almost fall off the ladder. I start to climb out, but T whacks me on the hand too. Hurts like hell. He begins poking me with the broomstick, nearly gouging me in the eye.

He says, "Now just where the hell do you think you're going, pal?"

Again, I try to climb out.

T gives me another whack with his broomstick sword. He pokes me again. "No! I told you no, Denson."

An incoming load of yuck. I lean to one side, barely getting out of the way.

Koonran yells up at me. "We'll kiss and make up, my darling. I'll show you an extra good time. I promise."

I take a loathsome load straight on, followed by thunderous laughter from Willie and Bob, who are apparently above the container. I vomit. Can't help it.

Willie and Bob laugh even louder. *Har, har, har!*

I scream, "Knock it off up there, you stupid bastards. Give me a break!"

T says, "To get out of there, you have to figure out who Koonran is and what these spiraling ladders are all about. If Koonran climbs back before you figure it out, she can have you. You're too dumb for me and not good enough for Annie."

"What?"

T looks depressed. "I'll be forced, however reluctantly, to write a scene where Annie, all depressed and downhearted over your death, meets a new detective with half a brain."

Erika and Wolfgang waltzed past us, seeming oblivious to our presence.

Marya's eyes widened on seeing Annie and her partner. "What is this?" she demanded.

"My girlfriend dancing with a good-looking German."

Around that big, old empty floor . . .

Annie and Kurt von Bayer reached us. They stopped dancing. Kurt bowed low. "My sincere thanks, Herr Denson. That was very well done."

I said, "No problem. But I couldn't have pulled it off without Bob and Thunderballs, that's a fact."

Kurt said, "Sexy outfit, Marya. Revealing." He and Annie continued dancing around the floor as though nothing unusual had happened, much less his resurrection from the dead.

This is the first time . . .

Marya was dumbfounded. "He's alive? What the hell is this?"

On their second turn around the floor Erika and Wolfgang stopped at our table. Erika said, "Sorry, Mama. We couldn't let you get away with framing Daddy. Couldn't."

Wolfgang said, "Kurt's bogus murder was my idea, Frau von Bayer. Your husband wanted to be sure of your complicity, which is why I gave you an opportunity to disarm the bomb. Better that Kurt should lay low for a few months than to go to prison for a crime he didn't commit." With that, Wolfgang continued guiding Annie around the floor.

I stood. "I think I'll go take a leak. Too much tea for me. Begging your pardon, Mrs. von Bayer."

He's sent me spinning . . .

Marya's face, a pastiche of famous actresses, a nose from one, lips from another, chin from still a third, turned hideous in defeat. Her hateful eyes bore in on me.

Since I sent him packing from my door . . .

Marya hissed, "Hear this, John Denson. Before the night is up, I'll have the last laugh, guaranteed. I've got plenty of time to arrange it before I start the drill with the lawyers and all that crap. You're history! A dead man."

45 • *Rendezvous at Timber Jim's*

We decided to celebrate our conning of Marya von Bayer in Timber Jim's. Annie and I led the way for the ninety-minute drive from Brahma Bill's. Behind us, Wolfgang Strehmel brought Erika von Bayer and her father in his rented car. Willie and Bob Humping Buck brought up the rear in Willie's pickup in case Wolfgang took a wrong turn.

At length, we arrived at Jim's and the fun began.

While Annie and Jim entertained our German guests, telling them about the history of Timber Jim's, I nudged the filthy spittoon and told Willie and Bob about the repeated, disconcerting flights to the spittoon during my date with Marya. As near as I could figure, T was writing a parallel struggle: Denson versus Marya; Denson versus Koonran.

"I was smaller than a cockroach," I said. "The interior of the spittoon was cavernous. It's awful inside. The stench! Koonran is down there floating on her back in tobacco juice and spit. I'm still down there too. Can you imagine? Dante couldn't dream up anything worse."

Willie looked disbelieving. "T just left you down there? Threatened to create a new detective for Annie if you don't figure out what Koonran and the spittoon are all about?"

Bob burst out laughing. He leaned over and spit a great, disgusting wad of tobacco into the spittoon.

I winced. "Hey, hey, easy, Bob. Give me a break. Knock off the spitting until I can figure this out."

Annie and the Germans were curious to know why we were standing around the foul-looking basin engaged in such passionate conversation.

Willie outlined the situation. "If you peer inside you won't see anything because you're not an animal spirit. But Denson and Koonran are in there for a fact. Fun spitting on Koonran. Good for what ails the vile bitch. The problem is Denson's still down there too."

I said, "They're giving me a time-out until I can figure out whatever it is that T is trying to tell me."

Annie looked amused. "Ah, then you do believe you've been flying out of your skin!"

I gave her a look. "Please, Annie, this is hard enough."

"I'll shut up," she said.

Willie said, "Go for it, Dumsht!"

"We know you can do it," Bob said.

"You say you're down there too?" Wolfgang asked.

"T won't let me out until I figure out who Koonran is and the mystery of the twin spiraling ladders."

T had tucked mysteries within mysteries like little Russian dolls that fit inside each other, each one smaller than the one before.

The spiraling ladders in the spittoon were linked to the mystery of the horse killer. That and the strange, a term Kurt von Bayer had used to explain his infidelities.

I thought of the mustang branch of the great flow of DNA and the dominant and recessive horse genes.

Marya felt no remorse about hiring the stable hand to kill the

European horses because only the most beautiful, conforming horses were trained to be jumpers, just as her husband had bedded down only the most beautiful, conforming women.

The ladder I had climbed had the letters A, C, G, or T etched on the rungs.

Koonran was in me and in all living things. He was in the trees and seas and forests. Annie too. I could never get rid of him.

In the Old Testament, Jacob reported a dream of a ladder from earth to heaven. Upon that ladder, angels ascended and descended.

To Kurt, I said, "Two opposing, connected, spiraling ladders with the letters A, C, G, or T etched on the rungs. What does that say to you, Kurt?"

"It says DNA," he said simply.

"She told me she flies. She swims. She runs. She pops up out of cracks in sidewalks.

"DNA," he said again.

I thought, *Is that it, T? Is that what you have in mind?*

46 · For Marya

The door to Timber Jim's opened.

I turned.

Heinz Steiner, standing in the open door, looked dapper with a neat olive green jacket and orange ascot with black polka dots. He said, "Mr. Denson!"

"I take it you're not *Kriminalhauptkommissar* Fackler this time."

He sighed. "No, no. This time I am plain old Heinz Steiner, the accountant who loves Marya von Bayer."

"I'm truly sorry about what happened to Marya."

Steiner drew an automatic pistol and aimed it at me. "No, you're not. You deliberately set her up. You think she is a drunken freak, some kind of plastic surgeon's joke. You're wrong. Blind, just like the rest. I know the real Marya."

"Easy, easy," I said, eyeing the pistol.

"I have something important to say and I will say it. I want everybody except you, Denson, to lie flat on the floor. Do that, listen, and nobody will get hurt."

Annie, Willie, Wolfgang, Erika, and Kurt all did as they were

told. Unfortunately for Heinz, Timber Jim had ducked behind
the bar, and Heinz didn't know he was back there.

To Erika, Heinz said, "You think you're 'beautiful,' Erika.
You're a bitch, bad as your philandering father. You all think
you've pinned Marya for murder? Wrong."

I said, "Marya told me she hired Juergen to kill the horses
then she murdered him herself. We taped it."

"You can't get anything straight, can you, Herr Denson?
Marya didn't murder anybody. She is protecting me. She loves
me, you idiot. It was me all along."

"You?" I said, sounding stupid.

"Me. My idea from the start. I hated Kurt. I couldn't stand what
he was doing to her. So I decided to get rid of him. I hired Juergen
to kill those jumping horses then I murdered him. Do you know
what she said when she found out?"

"Tell me," I said.

"She said the most romantic thing a man can do to prove his
love for a woman is to commit murder for her. For me, bringing
down Kurt for Marya was an honor. A privilege. What were some
stupid horses and a stable hand compared to her broken heart?
After she bought her stable here in Oregon, I secretly bought the
mustang semen for her. And I arranged for the stallions to be
killed. It was my gift to Marya, so she could achieve her dream of
being the most famous breeder of Spanish mustangs in North
America. Better known than Kurt and her bitch of a mother-in-
law. Do you know what Marya's shortcoming is?"

I shook my head.

"She is a romantic who cannot abide an unromantic world. I
loved her from the moment I set eyes on her. Before all her sur-
geries. I told her I loved her just the way she was, but she
wouldn't believe me. For all her torments, she is gorgeous inside. I wrote beautiful poetry for her. I sent her a dozen roses

once a week. Kurt thought the idea of her receiving roses from a secret admirer was amusing. What idiot would do that? Once, he accused her of sending the flowers to herself. Didn't you, Kurt? Didn't you think that, you bastard!"

Sensibly, Kurt said nothing.

"You sent her a dozen roses once a week?" I asked.

"I cannot stand the idea of her in prison. I cannot. With me, it makes no difference. But not her. Not my sweet, sweet Marya. By 'confessing' to you, she tried to sacrifice herself to save me. Can you imagine? Was there any love greater than that?"

Watching his eyes, my gut twisted. I dove . . .

As he fired.

Above my head, a glass jar of pickled Polish sausage exploded.

"I love you, Marya!"

He fired at me again . . .

As I tumbled across the floor.

"For you, Marya."

He fired wildly at me and at Kurt, then dove outside as Timber Jim fired a round at him with a 30-30 caliber Model 94 Winchester. The lever-action Model 94 that Jim kept behind the bar was the rifle that he used for hunting deer.

Willie shouted, "Somebody douse the lights!"

"Got it," Jim replied. He plunged Timber Jim's into darkness.

On the floor, Strehmel said, "The loyal accountant. All these years Steiner was in love with her. How he must have hated you, Kurt."

"The handsome, titled philanderer," Kurt added dryly.

Annie said, "Somebody needs to call nine-one-one."

"Doing it," Jim called back.

We could hear Jim describe the situation to the 911 operator.

I got up, crouching against the wall. When Jim finished with his call, I said, "Jim, do you have a computer in here?"

"A computer? We've got a love-struck idiot on our hands, and you want a computer?"

"The guy's an accountant," I said. "He can't hit the broad side of a barn. I love you, Annie!" I sprinted out the open door, zigzagging as Steiner fired wildly at me from behind one of the cars in the lot. I skidded to a stop beside my bus.

As Steiner fired at me again, I threw open the door and snatched Annie's notebook computer.

I shouted back at Timber Jim's. "Cover me, Willie."

"Damned fool!" Willie shouted back. Using Jim's Winchester, Willie laid down a horrific barrage in Steiner's direction.

Under cover of his fire, I sprinted back inside Timber Jim's.

47 · *The author G*

Annie was furious. "What on earth is wrong with you, risking your life like that? Moron!"

"That damned T sent this jerk after me," I hissed between my teeth.

"I thought T is supposed to be a figment of your imagination. Leave that Koonran stuff to Willie."

"Tell that to Blaise Pascal," I said. I was referring to Pascal's gamble. The faithful loses nothing by accepting the Christian notion of heaven or hell; the skeptic risks everything.

Jim said, "The cops are on their way, Denson. They say hang tough."

I said, "I have to figure the link among conforming and non-conforming horses and women, murder, Koonran, and the spittoon. Kurt has helped me with the spiraling ladders, but there has to be more to it than that. Annie, Jim has a laptop in back, will you please find me an on-line Biblical reference site and look up the part where Jacob has a vision of a ladder."

We joined the others behind the bar.

Willie cranked a round into the chamber of Jim's Winchester.

Annie found the reference to Jacob's ladder in seconds. "Here it is in Genesis," she said, stepping aside so I could see.

Reading about Jacob telling us his vision, I grinned broadly. I thought, *T, you bastard!*

Annie blinked. "Genesis?"

" 'Finding the earthly realm full of travail, the dispirited Jacob discovered a ladder upon which angels ascended and descended. He climbed the ladder. On reaching the top, he discovered the Lord. Jacob said . . . ' " I read from Genesis 28:17, which was on the screen. " 'How awesome is this place! This is none other than the house of God; this is the gate of heaven.' " I thought a moment. "When I got to the top of the spittoon, I found T, my creator. Tell me more about DNA, Kurt."

Annie was disbelieving. "We've got a fool out there with a gun!"

I said, "The police are on their way. Willie's got Jim's Winchester. Talk, Kurt."

Kurt said, "DNA, deoxyribonucleic acid, carries coded instructions for passing on the inherited characteristics of all plants and animals on the planet. Found in all cells of every living thing, it's made up of complex molecules of nucleic acids containing deoxyribose, a kind of sugar. It's shaped like gently spiraling, opposing, connected ladders, the so-called double helix.

"A helix being?"

"A three-dimensional curve lying in a cylinder or cone, cutting the elements at a constant angle. The rails of the DNA ladders alternate between phosphate and deoxyribose. The paired rungs of nucleotides contain nitrogen."

I said, "And the letters A, G, C, and T? What do they mean?"

"Those are the four nucleotides. A is adenine. G is guanine. C is cytosine. T is thymine. Only A and T or G and C form pairs, so we can deduce the identity of one 'rung' from its opposite."

"Jacob's ladder," I said.

"Say again, Herr Denson?"

I said, "The Bible is said to be the word of God, making Him an author. He could be any kind of author He wanted. Would He choose to be a plodding literalist? I don't think so. We remember a 'good book' because it resonates with meaning and takes us in unexpected places."

The author G, I thought. *Both G and T are mystery writers, lovers of riddles.*

I said, "Suppose God wrote Jacob's vision of the ladder to describe the DNA of evolution. He knew we wouldn't understand the parable for centuries, but we'd eventually figure it out. All living things on the planet, the blessed and the damned, ascend and descend the rungs of the biological double helix. You know T's challenge, assemble the analogy for me, Annie."

Annie thought a moment and said, "The double helix of DNA, two opposing, spiraling ladders, is the lair of Koonran, the gene monster. Koonran pursues us up the rungs of nucleotides."

"Our genes sometimes produce monsters, that's so," Kurt said.

"Those of us that Koonran yanks back are descending angels. Upon reaching the top, the ascending angels discover that the heavenly gate is the acceptance of the human condition—the way we are. Lovers. Murderers sometimes. Horse killers. The works. All competing in Koonran's tournament."

I said, "The gene monster douses passion with the increasingly familiar, but she also promised me 'strange.'"

"An adjective used as a noun. I'll check the definition." Annie found an on-line dictionary in seconds and read the entry. "Not previously known. Alien. Unfamiliar. Differing from the usual. The unaccustomed. Striking. Odd. Uncomfortable or peculiar. Not of one's own or particular locality or kind." She burst out laughing. "Your T! Some kind of author he is."

Joining Annie in laughter, I looped my arm around her shoulders. "T concedes that maintaining the juice is likely a quixotic ambition. Romantic. Impossible to achieve. That's why the bucket helmet and the broomstick lance."

Annie grinned mischievously. "Hey, I'm game! No embarrassment at my end."

48 • *Mirror, mirror on the wall*

Heinz Steiner, still determined to avenge my conning of his true love, burst into Timber Jim's in a suicidal rush, firing wildly into the darkness. Willie eased the barrel of Jim's Winchester over the bar and laid a 30-30 round inches from that disconsolate lover's already broken heart, knocking him backward off his feet. It looked like T was going to let me live to see another day.

Steiner was still alive when I got to him. Telltale rivulets of blood flowed from the corners of his mouth. He was bleeding internally. Looking up at me with hollow eyes, he said, "Your partner is a terrible shot. Why didn't he shoot me in the heart? That's where the ache and the pain and the awful suffering is."

I said, "Tell me what happened after you killed the jumping horses and Juergen."

"Marya said . . ." He stopped.

"She said what?"

"She said we were soul mates. Our love was eternal and beautiful. We would never be separated."

"Why didn't the two of you get married or whatever?"

"Marya said if we became carnal lovers, it would ruin everything. We would become just like everybody else, coarse and quarreling, bored with one another, each day a predictable routine of the banal and pedestrian. She didn't want the crass and the mundane to ruin our spiritual bond."

"Do you think she meant that?"

Steiner looked me straight on with sad eyes. He looked like he was about to weep. "Once, when she was angry at me, she called me an ugly troll with a big nose. She said she could not imagine herself being intimate with someone like that. Imagine waking up in bed with me. Yuck! I should take a good look at myself in the mirror and grow up."

"Oh boy!" I took a deep breath.

"I'm sure she regretted saying it. We went on as before as though nothing had happened. But she had let the truth slip out, and there was no taking it back. That's the way she sees me. An ugly troll with a big nose." He looked up at me with sad eyes.

"Go ahead and finish it, Heinz."

He said, "What she said hurt, yes. But it didn't change the fact that I loved her. I couldn't help myself. I would have done anything for her and pretty much did. Here in the Pacific Northwest, I secretly hired Sylvia Bonner to collect semen for my darling's mares. I hired Willard Leopoldo and Charlene ReMillard to kill the mustang stallions."

"I have to tell you the truth, Heinz. It's hard to forget that Marya confessed to hiring Juergen to kill the horses then murdering him herself."

Struggling to breathe, Steiner said, "I tell you Marya's lying. She's trying to protect me. She loves me. Is that so impossible to believe? You want so badly for her to be the murderer that you can't believe anything else. Isn't Marya sweet? I told you she is sweet."

I said, "Did Marya send you over here with a cock and bull story to save her bacon?"

"I, Heinz Steiner, killed Hans Juergen. I—"

I interrupted him. "As for murder being a grand romantic gesture, Marya used that same crappola on me, do you know that?"

Steiner's mouth opened slightly, disappointment and despair in his eyes.

"I don't think she used that horseshit line after you killed the jumpers and Juergen. She called you after she screwed up in Brahma Bill's, didn't she? 'Oh, I love you, Heinz, if you care for me, please, please help me.' "

"I repeat. You must believe me. Marya is an innocent. It was me all along. I was love-struck."

"I ask you again: whose idea was it to kill the jumping horses and murder Juergen, yours or Marya's? And whose idea was it to buy the semen and hire Willard Leopoldo to kill the mustang stallions, yours or Marya's?"

"As I lie dying, I'm telling you that I framed Kurt von Bayer for killing the horses. The idea was mine and mine alone. I was jealous of Kurt. I hated the way he treated Marya. I hired Juergen to kill the jumpers. I murdered Juergen myself. I bought the mustang sperm. I paid for the stallions to be killed so nobody's mares would bear foals with such conformation as Marya's. It was a kind of gift to go with my weekly roses. I accept full responsibility. You'll find my full confession on tape in my jacket pocket. I recorded it in case something happened to me."

"Please, I have to know the truth here."

"Tell my precious Marya she is loved. Tell her she's—"

"Beautiful. I know. I know," I said quickly. "About Juergen's murder—"

"Thank you, Mr. Denson." He rested momentarily, making a gurgling sound as he breathed.

I screamed, "I want to know the truth!" Heinz Steiner was dead. No way he could hear me. "Tell me, you fucking moron!" I shouted and banged his corpse's head on the floor for emphasis.

Steiner had been neither rich nor a hunk. Men too paid the price of nonconformity in Koonran's barbarous tournament.

As I stood up, looking down at his body, I knew that shouting at Heinz Steiner had likely been unnecessary with regard to the mustang stallions. I had a gut feeling that the fate of the horses was likely far different than either Marya von Bayer or Heinz Steiner imagined.

49 · *Hopelessly in love*

The Oregon State Police arrived a few minutes later and took our statements regarding the suicidal charge of the love-struck Heinz Steiner, and took away his body. I was obliged to tell them Heinz Steiner's dying admission of guilt and give them the tape I found in his jacket pocket, although I had my doubts that it was anything close to the whole truth.

Wolfgang Strehmel and I then stepped out onto the porch for some fresh air.

I said, "You got the idea for the Mustang Mary drawings after I told you about her Wild West getup, didn't you, Wolfgang? I remember telling you she had called herself Mustang Marya. Out with it. What happened? Or what do you think happened?"

"An hour after Marya discovered Willard and Charlene together in the Motherlode, somebody delivered a note to their hotel offering to pay them ten thousand dollars a head for killing mustang stallions, payable after each death was confirmed. If they refused, their affair would be exposed. Willard and Charlene knew about the horse killings in Europe, and they knew Erika was going to shoot a piece on the casino later that day, so they went back and told her about meeting Marya and receiving the note."

I said, "And Erika told her grandmother. The stallions are still alive, aren't they?"

Strehmel grinned broadly. "Their owners helped me fake their deaths, and we moved them to safe havens. The FBI helped with the exhumation ruse. I got Erika to cultivate you as a source. And yes, I commissioned the Mustang Mary drawings. I also set up Sylvia Bonner's press conference and talked the breeders into sending Marya videos of the 'dead' horses."

"Marya thought they were faked digitally. Clever. But after all of that, she didn't give a hint of cracking."

Strehmel sighed. "The German police think Steiner moved incriminating payments through Kurt's accounts on their way to Juergen. Until I saw Annie's printout, I didn't know horse-killing payments had been routed through Erika's accounts. When the Oregon State Police were preparing to arrest Erika, we knew we had to do something dramatic."

I said, "When we first talked here in Timber Jim's, you said it was possible that Heinz Steiner was in love with Marya. Were you serious or was that just a hunch?"

"Just a hunch," Strehmel said. "Marya took advantage of Steiner, as Kurt had taken advantage of her. She's a quick thinker, give her that. The old soul mate, pure love gambit. Poor credulous Steiner."

I said, "What if it's true? What if she loved Steiner but just couldn't accept the way he looked or the fact that he wasn't a rich man? In the end, she decided to lie for him."

Strehmel gave me a wry look. "Do you really believe that? Never mind that she was an ugly, scorned little gnome herself, Marya von Bayer wanted nothing short of a fancy man. A handsome German duke was perfect. Even a flaky American private detective. But a large-nosed accountant hardly larger than herself? No, no, no."

"Stranger things have happened in the name of love."

Strehmel laughed. "Steiner put his 'confession' on tape. Now who do you think would have thought of taping that nonsense before he barged into Timber Jim's, a conniving murderer or a distraught lover?" Strehmel looked disgusted. "And the poor sap did exactly as he was told."

"So you think."

"So I know," Strehmel said. "Steiner 'admitted' to murdering Hans Juergen. That was impossible because the real *Kriminal-hauptkommissar* Fackler told me the German police placed him in New York at the time Juergen was murdered. He was there talking to money managers for Marya. What happened tonight is vintage Marya. The instant she understood that she had been conned into confessing to murder, she shifted into her 'hope-lessly in love' alibi, hustling the poor sap who really was hope-lessly in love."

I sighed. "Once again Koonran did his damnedest to wiggle free of justice. He did it in drag this time."

Wolfgang arched an eyebrow. "Koonran? I thought you and Kurt pegged the Evil One as the gene monster. Wasn't that the answer to T's riddle?"

I corrected myself. "You're right, sorry. The gene monster. A fast thinker."

50 · John Flies at Dusk

As Wolfgang and I step back into Timber Jim's, I am again in the parallel reality. The clever Wolfgang takes on the head of Wolf. He grins a canine grin, his tongue flopping happily over his outsized white teeth. Willie has a coyote's head poking out of his shirt. Bob is a four-point mule deer, chewing tobacco judging from the bulge in his cheek. Jim has the head of a black bear. T is there too, looking mischievous. He is naked save for a pair of white boxer shorts covered with little red hearts. His bucket helmet is on the bar and his broomstick lance is leaning against it.

Annie sees our human heads, not the heads of a European wolf, a mule deer, a coyote, a short-eared owl, and a black bear. T is invisible to her.

Grinning broadly, T grabs my hand and shakes it gravely. "Congratulations, Denson, you worked your way through a mountain of riddles. You've passed your initiation as a logical warrior. Close call, but you pulled it off. Not bad for a blockhead. No offense."

"Right," I say.

"I did my Ahab number because of the whales and Koonran. Quixote is the real me. Hip helmet, don't you think?" T lowers his voice to a barely audible whisper, his blue eyes boring in on me. "Good job, hustling Marya von Bayer like that. The gene monster was telling the truth about one thing. If you and Annie don't do your best to create your own strange, Koonran will kill your passion a little each day. Are you tracking, Denson? Do you understand what I'm saying?"

"I think so," I said.

"This broomstick's just a prop, a diversion. I pack my real lance under my boxers. Such a weapon it is. Upon beholding its magnificence, the ladies get goose bumps. You should hear the squealing and swooning and carrying on. It's amazing." He grins broadly.

"I bet it's a real scene," I say.

"Romance, Denson! Passion! Never quit. Never give up. Go ahead now, get acquainted with your fellow animal spirits. They've got a ritual to complete." T's mug is empty. He holds it up for another refill.

I shake Wolf's hand. "Wolf? Herr Strehmel? I'd forgotten there were wolves in Europe and Siberia."

Wolf says, "Don't tell me you believe a human would have thought of faking the murder of a German duke and the killing of twenty-two Spanish mustangs? I was up against Koonran. I gave it everything I had."

I laugh. Wolf has me there.

Coyote sticks out his hand for a shake. "Congratulations, Owl. Welcome to the club. A dubious honor perhaps, but there you have it."

I glance at the mirror behind the bar. I have the head of an owl. I blurt out, "*Voo-hoo-hoo-hoo! Voo-hoo-hoo-hoo!*"

I say, "Nice rack, Deer!"

Deer runs his left hand up his antlers. "It's getting there. Every year a little bigger. I got a kick out of listening to your conversation in the pickup. Cochise? Quit beatin' my tom-tom and get on my fuckin' moccasins?" He bursts out laughing.

A dim, barely discernible scream echoes up from the spittoon.

"Hear that?" Deer says happily. "The little lady hates it down there being spit on."

"'Baccas on the house." Bear reaches up and sweeps all the plugs of chewing tobacco off a shelf. He walks up and down the bar handing them to all his animal spirit customers.

I unwrap my plug and take a big bite. It has a pungent, slightly sweet taste that immediately starts the saliva flowing. Relieved that I had found a way to escape, I spit with gusto into the spittoon and listen with satisfaction at Koonran's howls of enraged protest.

Looking at me, tongue still flopping, Wolf murmurs softly so Annie can't hear, "You know, Owl, I'm thinking about taking a little trip to Alaska before I go back to Germany. They say the bitch wolves up there have got white patches on their asses that are sexier than all get-out."

Coyote says, "Can't get your mind off a piece of tail, can you, Wolf?" As Annie heads for the john to relieve herself, Coyote looks me up and down. "Isn't it time for the naming of our fine feathered friend here?"

"*Voo-hoo-hoo-hoo! Voo-hoo-hoo-hoo!*" I reply.

Deer sails a wad into the spittoon. "I say we make John Cooks Good permanent. As Denson squats by the campfire peeling an onion with a Swiss army knife, no apparent threat, he eyes his adversary's throat. He simmers the facts, reducing them to the flavorful truth. He seasons with wit. His adversary thinks he's getting tasty vittles, but Cooks Good serves him crow in disguise."

"John Cooks 'Well,'" I say. "'Good' is an adjective, not an adverb."

Coyote spits. "I think it should be John 'Flies at Dusk,' hunting time for the short-eared owl. Is dusk still daylight, all clarity and science and logic? Or is it night, the unknown and unseen, with Wolf and me out and about on four legs howling at the moon and twinkling stars? What do you think, Dumsht?"

I shrug. "It's true that I've learned to fly in the dusk. Daylight. Darkness. Dusk is a little bit of both. And it's a whole lot better name than John Prick with Ears." I glance at T. The decision is his.

T straightens. The romantic knight spits into the container with gusto. "I agree with Willie. John Flies at Dusk it is." Saying thus, he puts on his bucket helmet, picks up his lance, and departs Timber Jim's, digging at his behind as he does.

51 · *An awesome place*

After we said good-bye to our friends in Timber Jim's, Annie and I stepped outside to a clear, starry night, a relative rarity in western Oregon. Since I was the proverbial three sheets to the wind, well beyond Oregon's legal definition of sobriety, Annie agreed to drive.

She slipped behind the wheel and cranked up the engine. I hopped up onto the seat beside her. As she pulled onto the highway, Annie said, "Okay, tell me, I want to know what you think happened."

I said, "What with all the talk about horse breeders, frozen sperm, and a murdered geneticist, the double helix of DNA was subconsciously on my mind the get-go. The imaginative *thymos* inside me came up with the Jacob's ladder parallel as an entertaining possibility. I have no idea why I am having these hallucinations. One thing is certain, no such author as T exists outside of my skin, much less Ahab or Don Quixote. T is me, John Denson."

She rolled her eyes, pretending to be disgusted. "Ah, I see. A logical explanation for everything. No real change for John Flies at Dusk."

As we turned onto the highway that led to Jump-Off Joe

Creek, I thought about my evolving relationship with Annie, which was rewarding for us both in all kinds of ways. With each passing year we would, by Koonran's standards, become less conforming, but when I looked at Annie, I still liked what I saw. When Annie looked at me, so did she.

I said, "You know what, Annie, I have this terrific urge to jump your bones once we get back to the cabin. Much sweating and rolling about. We can make all the noise we want, nobody to hear us on Whorehouse Meadow."

She geared the bus down for a curve. Eyeing me, she said, "You're on, big boy."

Later, as we walked together to our cabin, I started singing the song the Horse Dumplings had played at Brahma Bill's.

> *Beauitful Betty, won't you bump up to me,*
> *Bump up to me, bump up to me.*
> *Undo those buttons, I'm sure you'll agree*
> *Let me see, let me see, let me see.*

Annie unlocked the door. She threw it open with her left hand, unbuttoning her blouse with her right. Grinning, she said, "You want Betty? Betty I can be."

I laughed, leaning back to enjoy the seductive parting of the buttons. "Oooh, let me see, let me see, let me see."

"No turning the tables on Mademoiselle Marie tonight?"

"We should save that for tomorrow when we're both rested. I want to do it right. Sundown to sunup until you're exhausted. You've got it coming, Ms. Hot Stuff."

"All right," Annie said, her eyes teasing. "I can't wait!" She reached behind her back.

"Let me see, let me see, let me see." I started stripping off my shirt.

Annie's bra fell.

Watching me, enjoying my reaction, she brushed up against me, an exquisite softness.

I groaned.

"Patience," she said, hooking her thumbs on her underpants. She skinned them quickly off her hips.

Off came my jeans. I almost fell down getting out of my shorts, white boxers with little red hearts.

Annie bumped provocatively up against me, her body moving. "Your mighty lance is ready for action. What do you think, Quixote? Want it crazed?" she asked.

I said, "Give me your best shot, lady."

Annie sprang into the air in a single, catlike motion, wrapping her legs around my hips and her arms around my neck. She clomped onto my shoulder with her jaws and began chewing with feral abandon.

I cupped my hands under her butt and slipped quickly into the groove. She was hot inside. Exciting. Wild woman.

She bore down, squeezing me, a trick she had. "Like that?" she asked. She knew I did.

Wrapping her up, thighs and all, jousting furiously with my mighty lance, I slammed her hips hard against the wall. She was double-jointed and so able to hook her ankles over my shoulders. The thumping of Annie's rump knocked my autographed photograph of Bill Walton to the floor, shattering the glass. She was growing slippery in my hands.

I didn't want to drop her. I slowed to get a better grip. Her slender torso heaved as I adjusted my grip.

Struggling to catch her breath, she said, "Is this great strange or what?"

Still joined, we tumbled to the floor. Crying out, Annie arched her spine, nearly looping back on herself.

Feeling my pony girl shudder beneath me like she'd been electrocuted, I said, "Jacob had it right. We've come into an awesome place."